THEY'RE
GOING
TO
LOVE YOU

THEY'RE GOING TO LOVE YOU

A Novel

Meg Howrey

DOUBLEDAY NEW YORK

Copyright © 2022 by Meg Howrey

All rights reserved. Published in the United States by Doubleday, a division of Penguin Random House LLC, New York, and distributed in Canada by Penguin Random House Canada Limited, Toronto.

www.doubleday.com

DOUBLEDAY and the portrayal of an anchor with a dolphin are registered trademarks of Penguin Random House LLC.

Book design by Anna B. Knighton
Front-of-jacket painting: Sketch of Ballerina by Boris
 Uspensky © The Gamborg Collection/Bridgeman Images
Jacket design by Emily Mahon

Library of Congress Cataloging-in-Publication Data
Names: Howrey, Meg, author.
Title: They're going to love you : a novel / Meg Howrey.
Other titles: They are going to love you
Description: First Edition. | New York : Doubleday, [2022] |
Identifiers: LCCN 2021050862 (print) | LCCN 2021050863 (ebook) |
    ISBN 9780385548779 (hardcover) | ISBN 9780385548786 (ebook)
Classification: LCC PS3608.O9573 T48 2022 (print) |
    LCC PS3608.O9573 (ebook) | DDC 813/.6—dc23
LC record available at https://lccn.loc.gov/2021050862
LC ebook record available at https://lccn.loc.gov/2021050863

MANUFACTURED IN THE UNITED STATES OF AMERICA
1 3 5 7 9 10 8 6 4 2

First Edition

"Oh Ralph, I am very happy now," she cried through her tears.

"And remember this," he continued, "that if you have been hated, you have also been loved."

—HENRY JAMES, *The Portrait of a Lady*

THEY'RE
GOING
TO
LOVE YOU

Gods

Feel what I feel.

Stand with your legs together, toes pointing forward. Open your hips so the backs of your knees are touching. Slide the heel of one foot in front of the other until it meets the toes. This is fifth position.

Under certain conditions (flexibility, training) your two feet will be firmly locked together: heel to toe and toe to heel. Your knees will be straight, your pelvis will sit squarely above your knees. It's not natural but it *is* elegant. Da Vinci's *Vitruvian Man* but pulled together and not human spreading all over the place.

Contained.

Fifth is a position to begin things from. Fifth is a frequent point of return. It's also itself. Movement. Dance, even if it is still.

See what I see.

James is teaching class. He wears a soft T-shirt and a pair of loose sweatpants. The soles of his dance sneakers are split like ballet slippers so he can demonstrate a pointed toe more easily. He's a little vain about his feet, their high arches.

". . . And contain," James says, as the dancers close their legs to fifth position. ". . . And contain."

The class—at an Upper West Side New York City studio—is by invitation or introduction only and filled with professionals. I picture the dancers, spaced out along the barres lining three sides of the room. I see the additional freestanding barres in the center, a spot where I might have stood. I'm not there. This is part of a story that was told to me.

James is prowling the studio in his soft clothes, his soft shoes. Not prowling. Gliding. He doesn't appear to scrutinize the dancers, but they're aware of his gaze, mild but penetrating.

". . . And contain," he says.

The dancers think they know what he means by *containment*. He's asking them to keep their upper bodies still and placed, to not let the motions of the legs disturb the carriage of the torso. To come firmly to fifth position and not rush through or blur the moment. James means a little more than that. He *always* means a little more. He raises his hand and says, "Thank you, Masha," which is Masha's cue to stop playing the Chopin mazurka she's been plunking out with heavy-handed precision. Masha lifts her hands from the keyboard and picks up the *New York Post*.

James walks slowly to one of the center barres, where everyone in the room can see him.

"Containment," says James, "is one of the things ballet gives us." He takes fifth position on demi-pointe: heels raised, balancing. He's not demonstrating technical perfection; he is middle-aged and wearing sneakers. He's demonstrating intention.

James steps out of fifth position, impatient with his body. "Music tells us to move, to dance," he says. "But when we are still *within* music, we absorb all of its power. We are its container. Not every movement needs to go out into the world. We can keep some for ourselves. Contained. Powerful."

James smiles.

"Restraint," he says. His voice confers full sensuality to the word. "Restraint."

Such a subtle thing to describe. "Other side," he says, with a nod to Masha, who rustles her paper down. The dancers turn and place their right hands on the barre. It's still morning, still barre, but the dancers feel James has said something beautiful, or true, or deep. It's why they're here. Even when his words don't make perfect sense, they create an atmosphere that is pleasurable. It's nice to be reminded one is an artist, especially on a Monday, with a full week of rehearsals ahead and a weird pain in your hip.

James looks across the studio, scanning the dancers. To teach is to hope.

His gaze falls on Alex, although he doesn't remember his name. The boy had been brought along by one of James's regular students and introduced as "My friend visiting from Atlanta Ballet."

James has been observing dancers, teaching dancers, a long time. His assessments are swift. He looks at Alex and thinks, *Nice but stiff, maybe a late starter, the body is good but—*

James stops. It's been so long since he's been surprised.

Imagine what I imagine.

Alex has been listening hard.

"Contained."

"Being still *within* music."

"Restraint."

Something turns over in Alex's mind, like a combination lock sliding into its last number.

He raises his heels, shifts his weight to the balls of his feet, recrosses his legs. He lifts his arms. He is still.

James watches.

The music plays. Masha vamps, giving the dancers time to find their balance, "find their center," as they say.

What Alex finds is that his body has changed. Somehow, James's words are within him. He understands he is a container. For music, for movement. These are things he can hold and control. It's a small click of rightness that opens everything. He's never felt like this without drugs.

This boy, this young man, did, in fact, come to ballet late and his love for it still embarrasses him. The culture, the music, the costumes, none of it is "for" him. He's a straight man, a mixed-race American kid, a lower middle-class boy. He should be putting his coordination, his strength and flexibility, to use in some other field. Why should he prance around stage in makeup and tights, pretending to be a prince?

In his teens, he justified his obsession by calling it an escape, an opportunity, a place to meet hot girls. He could jump and he could turn. He was a boy; he got scholarships. Now, his career has started and he's ambitious. He doesn't understand why he's also a little depressed. He doesn't like the way he dances.

He wants it all to mean something. Ballet. His life, maybe.

Now, in James's class, for the first time, he sees how he might *make* something. In stillness. With his body, which is not perfect, and his mind, which is a total shitshow. He's twenty-two.

He's beautiful. He's making beauty.

He doesn't feel like a man or a kid or a boy.

He feels like a god. "But not in an asshole way." (This is what Alex tells me, when I hear his side of the story. Except for style and point of view, it's the same as James's version. If they were unreliable narrators, they were—in this—a perfect pair.)

James watches Alex feel like a god.

Perhaps a bar of light penetrates the speckled grime of a nearby window and goldens Alex's cheek, his clavicle, a sinew of his raised arm. The features of his face are too harsh for conventional beauty, but everyone looks noble in chiaroscuro.

"Yes," says James, nodding at the young man and raising a finger. "That's exactly what I mean. Beautiful."

Alex looks at James. Confirmation. He's not crazy. What he feels is real and someone sees it. James.

James finds himself shaping the class around the young man, testing strengths and probing weaknesses. He watches his words take shape in the boy's body. It's one kind of power to understand, and another to *bestow* understanding. James feels something in his chest and notices that he's happy. When class ends, he sits on a little chair in the corner for a few minutes, approachable. He accepts gratitude and exchanges gossip. Alex hangs back, wanting a little privacy. Later, he will tell James he was afraid he might embarrass himself, say something stupid. Words aren't his thing. But when it's just the two of them and James is looking at him with kindness and interest, he does his best.

"I learned more in the past ninety minutes than I've learned in my whole fucking life," Alex says. "I'm going to be in New York for the summer. I want to, I mean, is there a way I can study with you? Is there a way, even, I don't know if you coach privately or, maybe we could, I don't know."

What he wants to say is "I feel as if I've only now been born."

"Yes," says James, in just the right way. With gravity, with depth. "Let's work together. All right."

"I need—" Alex says, and then stops. He needs a lot. "I need someone to—" He can't finish the sentence. It's not that he needs help, although he does need that. But help has been given to him. He's a man who wants to dance ballet, he's had no trouble being seen. What he needs is for someone to help him see himself. He needs love. He needs a friend. He needs beauty. He needs someone to talk to him about art. He needs—

"I understand," says James.

This is what I remember.

James is telling me about meeting Alex. We're in our usual positions at Bank Street, where my father and James live. (I don't live there, I visit.) Bank Street is what everyone calls the apartment, as if it were the only one on the block. It's the parlor floor of a four-story brownstone, the apartment purchased in 1975 by my father with money from an inheritance. James sits at the piano in the large front room, and I'm perched nearby, on the rolling library steps that serve the tall bookcases by the windows. The steps don't roll very well and have been much clawed by the cats.

I don't live at Bank Street, have never done so, but in my heart, this is my home.

James and I are family and not. Teacher-student, and not.

Confidants, and not.

I could be his daughter, but I'm not.

My father and James have recently started using the word *partner* for each other. James used to say *companion.* I've never heard either one use *boyfriend* or *lover.* They've been together for twenty-three years.

I love James very much. I love my father too.

Or: my father, I love, and James I sort of want to *be.* Maybe I mean: *have?* I'm twenty-four.

I haven't met Alex yet. I will soon.

"I'm not a young person anymore," James says. He folds his arms and frowns at the keyboard. "At a certain point—and I've reached it—you realize your moment has passed. You won't achieve those dreams of youth. You have to make new dreams. But I don't *have* any new dreams."

He plays a single note on the piano.

"It's not about me," he says. "It's wanting the things I care about to continue. To give that to someone else. Otherwise, everything I care about dies with me."

He plays a few chords. The piano needs tuning.

"That's not quite true," he says. "One wants another *chance* at things."

I think I understand about wanting another chance at things, and I'm only twenty-four.

"Oh, Carlisle." He almost smiles. "You know what's more terrible than giving up a dream? To discover you *haven't*."

He might be crying.

"It's not about this boy," he says. "You do see that?"

And then—

"Is it worth it? All this—" He shuts his eyes. "All this *wreckage*."

I'm not sure what he means by *wreckage*. Himself? His career? His relationship with my father?

Perhaps he only means *life*.

Summons

It's a shocking phone call. Not because it's a surprise but because it's so close to what I expected. Things never happen exactly the way you envision, but this really *is* James, saying that Robert's health has been increasingly bad and now they're nearing the end. It's mostly a matter of making Robert as comfortable as possible. They are thinking in terms of weeks, not months.

Robert. My father.

Nearing the end. As comfortable as possible. Even the sound of James's voice saying *Oh, Carlisle.* I had them all right. Perhaps not so remarkable. These are the things one says.

James apologizes for calling so early. It's nine in the morning in New York, only six here in Los Angeles. I hadn't imagined that part. Time. The body understands whether it's morning or evening, but it doesn't always recognize the past from the present. I've had feelings about this phone call, for years. My body has already had this conversation.

I ask if Robert wants to see me.

"He's always wanted that," says James, on a sigh. "Only he painted himself into a corner. But what does that matter now?"

When did it ever matter? Still, I think I understand. Robert wants me to forgive him, but also to have it understood our estrangement is all my fault. He wishes none of it had happened but wants to keep all the emotions he got to have. He wants—

"You know Robert," James says.

It's hard to tell if I understand my father's nature or am projecting my own. I might know Robert because I've essentially become him. What's bred in the bone.

James continues, thinking out plans. Robert's still in the hospital. It will be better if I wait until he's home and settled at Bank Street. Of course it will. Hospitals are infantilizing—the gowns, the pans. Robert would be at a disadvantage. Bank Street is the seat of their power. Which leaves me as a petitioner. One hopes to get *into* an enchanted kingdom, or to get *out* of it, if things go badly. You don't visit an enchanted kingdom to forgive the sorcerers.

"I want it to go well," James says. "Your meeting. There's a sweet spot, with the medications. When he's lucid but also sort of beatific. It's the release from the pain."

I think a deathbed reconciliation is probably a good arrangement for the dying, who are soon to be free of all burdens whether you assist them or not. It's the living who need to stumble on, heaving from arm to arm the weight of all those wasted years and now grief too.

"Carlisle." There's a pause and for a moment I think I see James very clearly, standing by the small table at Bank Street, holding the phone. "I don't know what happened," James says. "I mean, he's never told me exactly what went on between you. But I know whatever caused the break is *not* what kept it going. It's him, it's how he is. I don't know if you can forgive him. I don't know if you *should*. I'll understand if you don't want to come."

I try to picture Robert, find his body in space and time. I feel a burning in my own chest, not in the heart but in the lungs, the ribs, spongy cartilage, bones. Bred in the bone. *What's bred in the bone will come out in the flesh.* That's from the Bible? Shakespeare?

Blood of my blood. Flesh of my flesh. I'm his daughter. He is my father.

I close my eyes.

"Of course, I will come," I say. "Of course."

Poulenc for Beginners

Bank Street. New York. Going to see my father and James. It's 1983. I'm ten, and on a plane.

I'd fallen asleep shortly before landing and wake to find my row companion looking at me. We'd not spoken during the flight and I had only a vague impression of a "businessman," because he had a briefcase and looked at papers during the flight instead of reading a book or a magazine. "I must say you look very innocent when you sleep," he says. *Must* he say that? His comment makes no sense, but this is the year people will start to get my age wrong in ways that are uncomfortable. It's because I'm so tall.

As it happens, I'll never fall asleep on a plane again.

I'm wearing white linen pants and a tangerine linen top with fluted cap sleeves. This ensemble had been chosen by me, over my mother's objection that white pants are not practical for New York City and linen always wrinkles. She taught me to iron, although ironing is something my father enjoys. I think she's forgotten what he's like.

My father is waiting for me at LaGuardia Airport, a *New York Times* tucked under his arm. He likes the crosswords but always saves one easy clue for me. He compliments my outfit right away. "Don't you look terrific." He remarks on my new hairstyle, my additional inch and a half since the last visit, and that I'm wearing the bracelet he sent for Christmas. He's a great noticer of these kinds of details. He likes seeing effort.

My father does have a car—a Cadillac Eldorado with pillowy white seats and a red steering wheel; he claims this is the last comfortable car ever made—but he never brings it to the airport. I'll get to ride in it if we go to someone's house outside the city on the weekend, if there's an invitation that is not, as James puts it, "too *too*." (Without understanding the distinctions, I've gleaned Fire Island is too *too*, but the Hamptons are usually not.)

We always take a cab to Bank Street.

It's the end of August. Everyone says August is a terrible time to be in the city, but for most of the summer my father is running the Boxhill Dance Festival in upstate New York. He's the managing director, not the artistic director, which means he's the one to solve problems. My trip (I also come for a week at either Easter or Thanksgiving) is timed for when the festival has concluded, and my father is back in the city. James sometimes goes to Boxhill to teach, and sometimes not.

This visit, when I am ten, my father tells me James is not well. He says this while we're in the queue for cabs at the airport.

I ask what's wrong.

"Feelings," he says. He puts his arm around me. He wears a heavy gold watch. His Izod shirt carries the scent of the laundry detergent they use, different from the one my mother buys. My father's body is very solid except for his midsection, which is soft. You might not guess he was once a dancer. My mother, you can tell instantly even though now she just works in an office. Her posture is performatively straight and she walks splay-footed. She can get her long hair up in seconds, and needs only one or two pins to secure a perfect bun. I have bushy hair and need more pins.

My father did dance professionally, for a few years. He's older than my mother and has bad knees, which cause him to move stiffly. He also has bushy hair, if you see it in the morning before he's smoothed it down with Vitalis hair tonic.

"The thing is," he says, "some of our friends are getting sick. It's been happening for a while and James is upset about it. I'm sad too, very sad, but James isn't always able to put his feelings to one side. He's not," my father says, "like us."

I'm not sure about this alliance. I want to be like James, who is so brilliant. After every visit I return to my mother with extracts from his vocabulary, complete with mid-Atlantic accent.

My father says he and James are okay. They're fine, very healthy. They're worried about *other* people. "You may have heard of things," he says, "from your mother."

I have not. Just now, my mother has a man in her life. I've never seen her do dating before because she's so particular about everything. I've caught Ben looking at her boobs. Realizing my mother has boobs a man wants to look at makes me anxious. I feel, obscurely, it's a bad portent. *A bad portent* is a James phrase.

My father tells me not to worry. It's only that James is blue, and we need to be gentle with him. We all need to be gentle with each other, he says. I add this quality to the list of how I will behave during my visit. In the cab, I practice being gentle. I look out the window in a tranquil way and answer my father's questions in a soft voice. It feels nice to be like this. He hands me the newspaper and a pen so I can fill in—with a little help—the last clue of the crossword.

We take the Williamsburg Bridge. The city skyline is too important to need to be welcoming. It tells you to get with the program or go home. I love it. Once in Manhattan, my father gives the driver instructions because Greenwich Village is so twisty. We're almost there. The cab turns and the pavement changes to something that looks like cobblestones, but I know is correctly called "Belgian blocks." We're here.

Stepping through the front door of Bank Street is my favorite entrance to perform. The sitting room and dining room are one grand space with thirteen-foot ceilings. When the curtains are drawn on the tall street-facing windows, it's like being inside the set of a play. In fact, you can sometimes catch even locals pausing on the sidewalk, arrested by a glimpse of the William Morris Strawberry Thief wallpaper, or the crystal-and-bronze Beaux Arts chandelier. Everything at Bank Street is either a reproduction or a flea market find—except the wallpaper—but you can't tell that from the street.

In Ohio, I have a friend who lives in a big house with stairs and a giant lawn in front *and* back. Her parents have a water bed. These are what I take to be the markers of rich people. (I have no understanding of Manhattan real estate.) I've been told by my mother that Bank Street is valuable. "Just, you can have a valuable thing and not be wealthy," she's said. I know money is a thing to be careful about and most things are too expensive to have.

Bank Street is precious. It doesn't matter if the things inside it are real or not, because they are beautiful.

James is not waiting in the central room when we arrive. I'm greeted by Olga and Maria, muscular white cats of indeterminate breed. (All their cats are named after the murdered Romanov children; my father is good at naming things.)

I look around for my favorite objects. Everything is always the same because everything is *supposed* to be old. I'm mildly allergic to the cats and the prewar-building mold.

Beyond the front room is a large and meticulously organized kitchen. (Things do change here; my father has a weakness for culinary gadgets.) Continuing on, there's a tiny bedroom, a bathroom, and a medium-size bedroom. These all have small windows looking into an alley. A hall with closets runs the length of the apartment. If someone asks for "the tour" they're not shown past the kitchen.

I hear James coming down the hallway from the bedroom. My father puts down my bag, straightens, smiles. I try to make my eyes gentle and kind.

James appears. He's not as tall as my father, who is extremely tall. Unlike my father, James is quite thin. He laughs and says my name and crosses his arms and smiles. We don't hug. At the end of my visit, he'll kiss my cheek. For greetings he crosses his arms and smiles. (I have seen him hug adults.)

James says I am going to be a Gloria Govrin. I don't know who this is but don't ask because sometimes when I don't know things James will raise his eyebrows and sigh and say, "Well, I suppose soon *no one* will know these things."

James is only forty-one, this summer. He seems the same age to me as my father, who is fifty-two.

My father explains that Gloria Govrin was a very tall and glamorous dancer with the New York City Ballet. He tells James he's going to get me settled in and James says wonderful, and the weather is *beastly*, but he's made a cold soup. "Then we will want to hear all your news," he says, as if I am a regular grown-up guest.

My father and I go to the tiny bedroom I've been told was probably a maid's room when a single family occupied the entire building. Now it's referred to as "Carlisle's Room" even when I'm not there, which makes me happy. For most of the year, it functions as a catch-all storage space and den, undergoing a transformation just before my arrival. "Carlisle's sheets"—purchased at intervals by my father according to his notions of my maturity—are washed and pressed—by my father—and dressed on the single bed. The small bookcase is emptied of old *New Yorker*s and paperback mysteries and restocked with things my father and James have chosen. (I'm an early and good reader and their choices flatter me.) The everyday rug is replaced with a fluffy one thought to be more girlish.

I'm here for only seven days but my father doesn't like "living out of a suitcase" and drawers in the bureau have been cleared for my use.

My father and I are quiet because he's not a big talker and I'm saving conversation for James. I move around the room, touching things. The window just misses facing a frosted-glass one across the alley. You can make out the shadow silhouettes of shampoo and conditioner bottles lining the inside of that window's sill, and occasionally hear the toilet flushing. I've never seen the people. Instead of curtains, my window has shutters, which open like doors. I think this is magical, and "like Europe," where my father and James sometimes go. The closet has four empty hangers for me and is otherwise jammed with all the things that have been in the room before my arrival. Everything smells strongly of rose. I'll learn later that James hates my father smoking inside, but since it's my father's apartment, James sometimes compromises by allowing him to smoke out the window of this room. While my father is at Boxhill, James sprays it daily with a rose-scented spray he says reminds him "favorably" of his mother. You can just detect the cigarettes underneath it.

There are five teddy bears lined up on a shelf too high for me to reach. A nighttime ritual is for me to select one for my father to bring down. This summer, the summer I'm almost eleven, we realize I can reach the shelf if I stand on demi-pointe.

"Just when you're too old for teddy bears, you can reach the teddy bears," says my father, and looks sad. I'm surprised to learn I'm too old for teddy bears and remember again the plane and the way the man looked at me. There's an additional worry here. My mother thinks I'm going to be too tall for ballet.

Later that week I will learn my father is a gay man.

They all thought I knew. I'm a good reader. I can carry on adult-sounding conversations on a number of topics. No one has ever tried to hide anything, it's simply I've never been told, explicitly, that my father is a gay man, or that James is a gay man, or that they are lovers. My curiosity is for the imaginative, not the actual, and I sometimes don't notice real things. Perhaps all children are like this.

What *did* I think? James is James. I've heard my father refer to him—to a waiter or perhaps an usher at the theater?—as his friend: "We're waiting for a friend." They're not physically demonstrative, and I've never seen them kiss or hold hands. The bedroom they share has only one bed, but it isn't a room I'm ever really in. James stays up late, and my father gets up early.

My mother never talks to me much about my father, or James. It isn't a *forbidden* topic. I've been told my parents like and respect each other, and they both love me. None of my friends have divorced parents, but fathers aren't usually visible, so I think mine being absent isn't so noticeable. I'm aware—always—of tension or stress, a possible fracture, in the lines connecting the adults of my life. Silence is a kind of suture over this potential problem, which does have something to do with James, who needs to be sheltered or protected or preserved. I'm happy to help. James is the most wonderful person I know. My hope is that if I behave well, the lines will hold, and I'll be able to keep coming to Bank Street.

Coming to Bank Street is my ambition, even above ballet. Coming to Bank Street *is* a ballet. The version of myself I present here takes effort and I'm sometimes uncomfortable and don't know what's happening and it's absorbing, and I like to be absorbed.

I'm not *perfectly* clear about the word *gay*. At school, in Ohio, people say it when they mean someone, or something, is cheesy or uncool. Like a spaz. *Don't be gay.* I've heard my mother use the word *homosexual*, without emphasis or judgment, and my maternal grandmother with audible italics. I think *homosexual* means unmarried or possibly theatrical, like many of the people I see in New York.

I understand that my father is a gay man in the same conversation I learn about a disease killing gay men.

"You've been told about it, yes? AIDS?" James asks. We are several days into my visit. My father is out—maybe at the store, or the small Midtown office he and his Boxhill staff share with a theater company—and James and I are having one of our talks. He sits at the grand piano and I've rolled the library steps near one of the street-facing windows. These are our places. I'm often among adults, but James is the only one who tells me about people, about himself, without trying to make it a lesson. The talks are moments of confidence, gossip, explanation. They're dioramas of adult life.

James has been explaining about depression. He tells me he's been quite seriously ill at different times in his life with this sickness, and he always tries to hide the worst of it from Robert. I'm proud he's not trying to hide it from me. I tuck away the phrase *quite seriously ill*, for use later. It sounds serious and brave.

When James asks me if I know about AIDS, I say I know a little. (I know nothing, but with James if you say you know a little, he will keep talking; if you say you know nothing he will sigh.)

"They called it the 'gay cancer' at first," he tells me. "A plague. Like a judgment on the seventies. Because for a few minutes we all stood around in the sunshine."

Neither James nor my father has it. He says this several times, although it's 1983 and they can't know. There are no tests. It's because the government doesn't care about gay men, he says, and starts to speak of gay men's lives.

After a while, I realize he's talking about my father's life, and his life. I keep still, and nod, so that James will go on talking.

He says something about how my father "passes."

"Well obviously Robert passes," James says, waving at me. "Though his brothers go on pretending like they don't know. Maybe they don't. One assumes their wives do."

I understand now about gay—with some hazy spots on the mechanics—but don't understand about passing. I think it means Robert has passed from being someone who could be my father into being a gay man. I keep repeating *gay man* in my head over and over. Does my mother know? My grandmother? I'm passed too, as in I have passed the point where I can ask.

"He's always been private," James says. "That's just who he is. We don't all have to be the same kind of gay man. But people will go on thinking it's about shame or calling him a Republican. And, of course, there's you."

I agree there is me although I'm beginning to wonder *how* there is me. James sees I'm distressed and calls me over to the piano to turn pages for him. "Poulenc is good for restless souls," he says. "If you don't like one part, just wait. Every eight bars he becomes a completely different composer."

My father returns and I feel intensely shy of him, for about an hour. Everything he does and says now feels mysterious. *I* feel mysterious, with this new understanding. Important. We get dressed up and go to a musical that turns out to be, of all things, *La Cage aux Folles*. The show is about a son who is bringing his fiancée and her goofy religious parents home to meet his family and he wants *his* parents—both men—to pretend not to be gay and running a nightclub of drag queens. It's the first cultural representation of gay parenting I've seen—or will see for over two more decades—but I mostly notice the differences from our own arrangements. (For them, the mother is absent, the child is a boy and already grown up, everyone sings.)

The show is wonderfully funny but also there is crying in the audience when the man who has always been a mother to the son sings "I Am What I Am." I cry a little too, impressed and wanting to join in the feeling of the men onstage, in the rows around me, my father and James.

A few days later I watch my father, standing in the Bank Street living room, listening to someone on the telephone. He looks up at James and covers the mouthpiece of the phone and says, softly, "Danny." His face looks like a little boy's when he says it. James crosses his arms and goes to the window and looks out.

I don't know if Danny is the same person, but the previous summer I'd spent a wonderful afternoon with a Danny in the pool of someone's house in Montauk. When the rest of the adults gathered for cocktail hour, Danny stayed with me, practicing dance lifts. "Arabesque," he'd say, and he'd sink down in the water and I'd stand there on one leg, giggling, until strong hands were on my waist and leg and Danny was hoisting me high up in the air. We'd pose, the people on the patio would applaud, and then Danny would pop me up out of the lift and I'd dive back into the water. He had curly hair, and it was so hot it would almost instantly start to dry when his head came out of the water. Dark curls springing up around his face. He had brown eyes and told me he missed his sister. Is this the Danny they're talking about? Does he have the sickness?

It is. He does. He'll be dead in eight months.

My father's face, outrage and grief. James crossing his arms and standing by the window, looking out. There'll be so many phone calls, so many men and stories and images, but whenever someone says "AIDS" or "the AIDS crisis," it's that moment I see. A vision of a young man in a pool, his strong hands. My father, looking at James, and saying, "Danny."

At the end of every visit, my father takes me out for a fancy afternoon tea at a hotel. Neither of us likes tea but we both love the little sandwiches and scones and cookies and pastries. We have a sweet tooth. My father always wants to hear about my favorite things from the week. I want, very much, to ask him about being a gay man and if he's worried about the gay cancer, but I can't think of a way to put it. He suggests we go to FAO Schwarz. At the store, so lavish and hectic, I become shy. I'm embarrassed to look at toys in front of my father. My mother doesn't like shopping and always seems irritated by what she supposes are my tastes. "So, I guess you want a *cute* one," she might say, grimly surveying a kitten-themed selection of notebooks for school supplies, causing me to hastily grab something plain. Also, I'm not supposed to ask my father for things. But my father enjoys the toy store and is in no rush. When I pick up a small, cinnamon-colored teddy bear he says, "Well, I think we better take him home with us." I suggest that maybe this bear can sometimes sleep on *his* bed. "With you and James," I say. He puts his hand on my shoulder and I know *for certain* we've made each other happy.

Oh, the way things combine: those white linen pants my mother thought were a mistake, the expression on a man's face as he tells me I look innocent while I sleep, the secret sorrow of James, the curse that had struck the lives of gay men, the tune "I Am What I Am," from *La Cage Aux Folles*, and the young man who missed his sister, his dark curls springing up around his face, gone forever from this world.

I feel the cat-mauled nap of the fabric covering the library steps scratching my bare thighs, smell the cigarettes just under the roses in Carlisle's Room, hear the out-of-tune creak of the floorboard as I rise on the balls of my feet and just touch the corduroy paw of a teddy bear.

I blink. Sit up straight. I'm forty-three and living in Los Angeles. The last time I stood in Carlisle's Room, I was twenty-four. I haven't seen my father in nineteen years.

Containment

Morning in Los Angeles. I make coffee and return to bed with it. I'm shaking, a little. There's prickly heat inside my chest and face, that internal sunburn of guilt.

"What if you weren't always so hard on yourself?" a boyfriend once asked me. I agreed my being self-critical had not made me a better person, which was a clever way of being hard on myself about being hard on myself. He said—we were stoned—that we had to "put forgiveness into the universe."

"It's because I think I might lack moral fiber," I tried to explain. "I'm afraid I'm capable of great betrayal."

He forgot about the universe and I could see a speck of fear in his eyes.

I start to type a message to my best friend, to tell her my father is dying and I'm going to New York to see him, but don't complete it. Freya, my best friend, is absolutely on my side. She would say things to salve this burn in my chest. I picture her in London, squeezing in another fifteen minutes of work before going to pick up her kids at school.

No.

I don't want words. I don't want to hear them or say them. I lie very still. After you injure your body, the biggest temptation is to constantly test yourself for pain. Does *this* hurt? Does *this*? Does it hurt *now*? You want to poke and provoke.

Okay, lying still isn't the right move. No, the thing is to get up and get moving. Today is my teaching day. An acquaintance is coming over for dinner tonight. I go to the gym and then to Hollywood, where my Contemporary Ballet class is gratifyingly packed. I chat a little with dancers I know. People ask me, "What are you up to lately?" and "Are you working on anything?" I see it's possible for me to talk about jobs when my estranged father lies dying in another city. The sensation of shame grows in my chest.

I drive to Thousand Oaks, where I'm giving a series of what are still called "master classes." The students are charming and work hard. A few times I catch my own eyes in the mirror and think, *What are you doing?*

My breathing is not great.

In the car, I try listening to a mystery audiobook: Agatha Christie, lots of dialogue, no surprises that matter. "This is bad," I say out loud. If I were to turn off Christie and listen to the news, every story would be worse. This is only a man in his eighties dying at home, and a woman—a daughter—what? Doing what?

I run the calculations of my life—what money I have, what money I need. My schedule. I suppose I can afford to stay a couple of nights at a hotel in New York—there's that pod one in Midtown—but maybe I should email some friends and ask to crash? Death on a Budget.

I imagine calling Freya or other friends and saying, *Robert is dying. My father. My father is dying.*

Oh no, this new friend I'm seeing tonight might say. *I'm so sorry.*

Thank you, it's okay. We aren't close. He and his husband are complicated people and I had to make some boundaries. I'm going to say goodbye. Get some closure.

I try another version of this narrative.

We all had a part to play in what went wrong between us, but they put me in a bad position and then punished me for it. I'm no longer angry but I have to take care of myself.

I think about seeing Robert's body and my own begins to fill with anticipation and dread, as if I were staring down a first performance. It's possible that by *not* telling people he's dying, I'm hoarding the words. Emotion on a budget.

At home, I listen to a Maki Namekawa recording of Philip Glass's Études. I love her musicianship. With the études, she's not trying to tell me how to think about anything. She's not playing on my feelings, she's playing her piano, she's *working*. If she—and Philip Glass—is telling me anything right now it's *Look at what this goddamn instrument can do if you get good at touching it.*

"It's nice to have an instrument that isn't one's own body," James told me once, before attempting a Scriabin étude. "Pianos don't have pain. Of course, there's still the player. Études are for improving technique, so I recommend them for a crisis. One can plonk away at an étude and look like one's *practicing* and not having, as Mother used to say, 'a come apart.'"

Containment.

Zoe, my guest for the evening, arrives. She works at the Los Angeles Opera, in the hair and makeup department. We got chatting during a dress rehearsal of the *Don Giovanni* I choreographed last season. She'd made some fabulous wigs for the "Descent to Hell" section, but the wire components kept getting tangled on the way to Hell and the girls were latching on to each other like paper clips. We solved it quickly, then sat together in the audience, making friends. She had me to dinner at her place a few months ago and I wanted to return the hospitality. We've been exchanging what's-your-week-like? texts for months.

"This fabric," she says, going straight to my gray-blue velvet curtains. "So dreamy. I'm a textiles girl."

Zoe used to be a theater actress and still moves like a person who knows she is watchable. I'm glad I didn't cancel. Her confidence will carry us through this evening. I make Negronis. Zoe tells me about the current production of *Medea* at the opera. (I'm not involved; it's hard to shoehorn dancing into *Medea*.) I describe a crazy project I have on right now with a conceptual artist. Zoe sails around my apartment, picking things up, asking questions. She wants to know if it's always this clean. It is. I'm fussy. Also, my design aesthetic is at odds with other parts of my nature; I like to collect things and mix colors and patterns but am afraid of clutter. Because of my peripatetic job, I don't have animals or plants, but my apartment doesn't feel lifeless to me. It's a still life.

Still life.

The containment of dread and excitement is pressing against my eyes. If I burst into tears, I know Zoe will be kind. It will certainly move us past the transition from funny texts to sustained conversation. But I can't do it.

Zoe goes to the bathroom and pauses in the hallway to ask about the photos there.

Isabel, in the late sixties and early seventies, when she was in New York City Ballet.

"That's my mother," I say. "She's actually pregnant with me here."

The first one is a rehearsal shot, in black-and-white. The cut of Isabel's leotard shows off the delicate bones of her chest; she has a short chiffon skirt tied around her waist. Next to her: the great genius of twentieth-century ballet, George Balanchine. He wears a western shirt and jazz shoes. His face is alight, his arms raised. He's demonstrating a step and Isabel is giving it everything she has. "Mr. B" is not quite looking at her.

"She's pregnant?" Zoe points at my mother's reed-thin frame. "Come on."

"*Just* pregnant. But she ended up performing into her second trimester."

"Ballet dancers." Zoe shakes her head. "You're all so fucking tough."

"I wasn't ever a *real* ballet dancer," I explain. "But yeah. I'm in awe of the real ones."

Zoe smiles at the photo and then admires the next one, a more formal composition, in color. Isabel in her *Stars and Stripes* costume: blue tutu, crimson bodice with an American flag panel, gold majorette-style embellishments, little white gloves, and a regimental cap with feathered plume.

"Oh, okay, you get your height from her," Zoe says.

"She's only five-seven. But that *is* on the tall side for ballet. On pointe she was almost six feet."

I don't consider my height as coming from Isabel since I top her by six inches. In the fairy-tale world of ballet, I'm less sylph and more ogre. Not a princess. A yeti.

"She's beautiful," Zoe says. "I can tell you're close. You're lucky."

Zoe's mother died a few years ago, a thing I already know.

Women talk about mothers; it's practically the way we greet each other. I wouldn't say Isabel and I are "close" exactly, but you don't complain about living mothers to daughters of dead ones.

"She was sixteen when she got into the company," I tell Zoe. "She had a little apartment on West Eightieth that she shared with my grandmother. Robert—my father—lived upstairs. That's how they met. He helped her pick out her stage name."

"People meeting each other in hallways." Zoe sighs. "The old days. Was she famous? What's her name?"

"Isabel Osmond. Her real name was Eleanor Turnball, but only her sister kept using that. Even I mostly call her Isabel. It suits her."

Zoe laughs. "Eleanor Turnball. I love it. Like if my name was Zoe Haircurl. Was your dad in the arts too?"

"Yeah, he danced for a few years and managed LaGrange Ballet. Then he ran a dance festival in upstate New York."

It comes naturally, the past tense.

"Wow, you were totally born into it," she says. "You're a legacy kid."

You can have a legacy but not be an heiress. I feel the compression in my chest, against my eyelids.

"Let me get my vol-au-vents in the oven," I say.

We chat and drink and eat. Zoe tells funny stories about opera things going wrong and this is a much more entertaining topic than "My father is dying, and we fucked up our relationship nineteen years ago and I feel like a monster."

Zoe is thirty-eight and wants children. I say I don't. She says she used to be like me, and not want them, but now she does. I don't argue but carry out a testy argument in my head. I'm not a stage, I'm a person who has never wanted children and never had them. That is its own separate sort of person. It requires an act of self-relevance that should not be confused with selfishness. I realize I'm a little drunk.

The mood for confidences comes, like dessert. Zoe talks about a problem she's having with her sister. She apologizes for "dumping," and I tell her—sincerely—she didn't and I'm glad and it's good to talk. We hug. She takes a Lyft home. I clean the kitchen.

I've refused an opportunity of intimacy with a sympathetic person by not sharing this sad thing *that is happening* and feel vaguely as if I've won something. What a silly game. If I prove my loneliness, I might earn the right to be sad?

Robert wants to see me and doesn't want to see me. Perhaps neither one of us can imagine this long performance coming to a close. I don't mean his life.

I will see my father. We will forgive each other. He will die.

Curtain. And then?

I go commune with Isabel's photographs. Zoe had called her "beautiful," but Isabel always says, "I was the talented one, Pat was the beauty." (Aunt Pat never really loved this summation.) The sisters were both taken to ballet school by my grandmother, who'd been refused dancing lessons by *her* mother, and lived ever after in a state of thwarted curtain calls.

Isabel wasn't famous, but she danced for Balanchine. It's an identity. For her, for everyone who worked with him. Like having been an actor in Shakespeare's company or laboratory assistant to Thomas Edison at the invention of lightbulbs. More, like having been the actual lightbulbs.

Isabel's *Stars and Stripes* costume always makes me smile. It's so fun and cute and tacky. America! Balanchine choreographed the ballet to John Philip Sousa music in 1958. He genuinely loved his adopted country, felt himself to be more American than most Americans. Sousa's marches amused him, they were so fast, "like how French people walk. Americans walk like this too." I don't think there's an ounce of irony in the work, though plenty of good-natured winks. It's always been a real crowd-pleaser. A giant flag unfurls at the end. When you put patriotism into tutus and tights, it doesn't look jingoistic, it looks zippy.

Isabel is balanced on pointe, saluting the camera. Her American story is not one of systemic oppression, nor does it beat to the quick march of capitalism. Not quite zippy either. She rose to the—almost—height of what was possible for a ballet dancer. Is it harder to outlive your greatness or to come short of it? She did get a second act.

The history of ballet in America isn't long. Three generations of my family covers a lot of it.

In 1940, my grandmother attends a performance of the Ballet Russe de Monte Carlo, on tour in St. Louis, and applauds so hard her hands are sore for days. She has her program signed by the ballerina Alexandra Danilova, who appears at the stage door in a fur coat. My grandmother races home to show her mother an advertisement in the program for a local ballet school. It offers a Complete Course in Classical Ballet Dancing, plus Special Courses in Toe, by a real Russian teacher. Special Courses in Toe! "Ballet is just for little girls," her mother says. My grandmother is already sixteen. "Too late," her mother says. Besides, ballet constitutes a trifecta of evils to the midwestern sensibility, incorporating as it does "dreaminess," "fanciful notions," and "getting above yourself." My grandmother is told she'd be better off with a Special Course in Cooking or Typing. So my grandmother frames her program, eventually marries a man called Stuart Turnball, moves to Cincinnati, and takes her daughters Patricia and Eleanor to ballet school.

Patricia loathes ballet and leaves it for the more temporal

rewards of cheerleading. For Eleanor, a better school is found, extra lessons provided, a ballet barre installed in her room for home practice. My grandmother doesn't have to urge Eleanor to work hard, indeed, my mother's self-absorption and flesh mortification skills fill her with awe. (My grandmother has let her Catholicism lapse.)

The center of American ballet is New York, and the center of New York ballet is George Balanchine, a Russian who has created a world-class ballet company and a school to train his dancers. My mother is taken to an audition and invited to attend Balanchine's school, prompting a family crisis. Eleanor can't go to New York by herself, obviously, she's fifteen. My grandmother is not inclined to trust her daughter with the chaperonage of another Mother, who will not promote Eleanor's interests with the same zeal. But what about—admittedly neglected—Patricia, still in high school herself? And the girls' father, Stuart Turnball? He's the manager of a lumberyard and has tolerated his wife and daughter's ambitions but is not accustomed to fixing his own dinner.

My grandmother arranges a series of surrogates for herself in Cincinnati and moves with my mother to New York. "Just to see her through the first year or so." They take a basement studio on West Eightieth. The apartment has one small window, set too high to see out of unless you stand on a chair. They each have a single bed and share a dresser. My mother fits in schoolwork between classes and rehearsals and performances. My grandmother babysits a neighbor child during the day. It works, it all works. (It doesn't all work. My grandparents' marriage won't survive the separation and Patricia will resent her sister until the day Patricia dies—too soon—of breast cancer.)

Robert Martin introduces himself to Eleanor Turnball over the mailboxes. At this time, he is thirty-four. He had begun as a dancer with LaGrange Ballet but moved quickly into management. LaGrange Ballet may not be a rival to New York City Ballet in terms of prestige or size, but it's popular, hip, an exciting place to be. Eleanor has no interest in LaGrange Ballet—she's utterly devoted to Balanchine—and is shy and awkward, but Robert draws her out. He invites her and my grandmother to his top-floor apartment for tea. My grandmother assesses his interest in her daughter as avuncular—Robert is much closer in age to herself than her daughter—and assumes his art and furnishings were picked out for him; she has never met a man with taste. Eleanor is too lonely to question his attachment, knows only that he understands everything about ballet. (Unlike her mother, who is always hovering but never gives good advice.) When she's asked to join New York City Ballet a year later, Eleanor consults with Robert about her name.

There are the glory years. The newly christened Isabel lives for her art, and as far as she's concerned, what makes an artist is what makes a woman: suffering, devotion, endurance. It's more fun than it sounds. It's *safer* than it sounds. Her world has rules and codes and structure. It has rewards. There are costumes and flowers. There's a god, George Balanchine, who loves them all and gives them miraculous ballets to dance.

But Isabel joins the company when Balanchine is at the height of his obsession with a particular dancer. He's in his sixties, his muse is just out of her teens. He creates masterpieces for her, leaves his fifth wife in the hope they might marry. The muse gives her prodigious talent and utter devotion but chooses to marry a man her own age, another dancer in the company. Balanchine is heartbroken, and possibly vengeful. Soon, muse and husband are both gone—forced out or fled depending on who you ask. All of this causes strife within the company: jealousy, speculation. (Not exactly condemnation. Balanchine is a genius; the muse was considered blessed, not harassed.)

"Will my daughter become a great ballerina?" an anxious mother is supposed to have once asked Balanchine, who reportedly answered with a shrug and, "La danse. C'est une question morale."

To be a great dancer is a question of morals. He didn't name which ones.

Who will be the next muse? When Balanchine is teaching or running a rehearsal the air is so thick with perfume the company manager complains. Isabel has copied the departed muse's hairstyles and makeup. She is tall like the muse, devoted and pious like the muse. She's not as pretty, not as mysterious, but she works and works. She believes she has the right morals.

She doesn't advance. She remains in the corps de ballet, her name always one of a group on the casting sheets. The company is large, over eighty dancers. Of course, Mr. B loves all of them, especially his girls; he has devoted his genius to their glorification. But sometimes, when she sees him in the hallway or the elevator and he says, "Hello, dear," she wonders if he's forgotten her name. Mr. B says they can sleep five together on the floor, it will make them better dancers. Mr. B says all they need is their work and the theater and maybe at night they can sip a little red wine before going to bed. Isabel is now sharing the basement apartment with another dancer in the company. She's happy to live this way—it's a proof of her constancy—but hates setting mousetraps.

My grandmother has gone back to Ohio; has troubles of her own. ("I didn't blame Dad," said Aunt Pat. "And I certainly learned my lesson. I always put my marriage first, ahead of my children. That sounds harsh, but a man marries a woman, not a mother.")

Isabel has been in the company for only five years, but already seen new girls come in and be given roles above her. All of the women in Balanchine ballets are unattainable goddesses, but in life it's hard to act unattainable when no one is trying to attain you.

Except, possibly, Robert Martin? He likes Isabel, believes in her, is impressed by her. She's a Balanchine ballerina but she needs him. She needs his eye, his help with her hair and her clothes and her conversation and her confidence. He sees what she could become and it's what she wants to become too. He attends as many of Isabel's performances as he can and is always willing to talk about everything.

He would like to be married.

He is her best friend.

Aunt Pat believed Isabel "took a look around and realized you can't dance forever. Of course, he was a lot older than she was, but Mother always said an older man was right for Eleanor. Excuse me, *Isabel.* Goodness knows, my sister was sheltered. She lived in New York City and I lived in the sticks and I knew a lot more about life."

"Mr. B never encouraged marriage," my grandmother told me. "But LaGrange Ballet was real popular and Robert knew lots of people. There's more than one way to fleece a lamb."

"One week they were engaged and the next month they're getting married at a courthouse," said Aunt Pat. "Because of their touring schedule, was the story. I guess she married Robert because she couldn't marry Balanchine. Don't get me wrong. We *liked* Robert. He seemed totally normal to us. You wouldn't necessarily even know he was an artistic person, let alone *one of those.* I mean, he could talk about regular things and play bridge. He and your uncle Joe could go on about sports. I always wondered if it was being around dancers all day that got to him."

Isabel marries at twenty-one. Is pregnant at twenty-two.

"Which just goes to show you," said Aunt Pat. "You can lead a horse to water *and* make him drink. As long as it's a male horse."

"Your father was over the moon about it" was my grandmother's assessment. "And he promised to get Isabel help after you were born, so she could go on with her career."

Isabel dances well into her second trimester, in order to perform in the company's first Stravinsky Festival. She's told no one about the baby except Robert. Perhaps she thinks the issue will resolve itself in a tumult of pointe work and dodecaphony. It does not. Robert installs a barre in their bedroom, and Isabel takes a leave of absence, giving herself class up until water breakage.

The birth itself is traumatic. Isabel doesn't want a cesarean; it will make her return to dancing that much harder. She prides herself on her ability to withstand pain. After thirty-one hours, I am born. I'm not small.

Aunt Pat thinks Isabel will decide she's had enough of dancing. My grandmother—still in thrall to the ballerina in her daughter—says Isabel will bounce right back. Isabel's postpartum depression goes, for a while, unnoticed. She's taciturn by nature, has perhaps overworked herself during the pregnancy; the birth itself was exhausting. None of her friends who visit are mothers. They bring tiny dresses, coo, and go back to rehearsal. Isabel tells Robert she can manage on her own, there's no need of a nanny until she rejoins the company. Suffering, devotion, and endurance make the artist, make the woman, make the mother?

I'm fussy, colicky, a bad sleeper. My grandmother comes to help and is the first to identify my mother's lethargy, her flat affect, her unease with me. There are consultations with doctors, more doctors. A course of electric shock therapy is recommended.

"It wasn't as bad as it sounds," Aunt Pat assured me. "She just needed a kind of jump start, I guess, to get her back on track. Her memory went kerflooey for a little bit but then she seemed just fine. Robert was wonderful about the whole thing. Best doctors, best everything. I don't think you noticed at all. You fussed but you figured out how to self-soothe quick enough."

Isabel returns from the hospital. The medication she's given makes her puffy and stiff, so she discards it. Psychotherapy is suggested, but she's allowed to abandon this too. She begins taking class again, focuses on getting in shape. Everyone agrees this will be the best medicine.

Then a blow. Isabel was young for marriage, for motherhood. If there's a right age for a woman to learn her husband is in love with a man, she is also not that.

"All of a sudden your mother says she's leaving Robert." Aunt Pat was critical. "None of us could understand why she was doing what she was doing. Robert treated her like a queen. She had whatever she wanted. He was even going to let her go back to dancing full-time. She didn't want to talk about it. But I guess we weren't being *supportive* or what have you, because she ended up telling me and Mother about the whole business with the James person. Well, we didn't need to know all that. I told her, 'If you make a fuss over it, you'll make it real.' Like with toddlers when they bang themselves up a little. They'll cry unless you ignore it. That's how you have to treat men sometimes when they have their feelings. Because Robert swore he hadn't been unfaithful; it was *just feelings.* He could have sued for partial custody, but he was classy about it. He said he'd do whatever she wanted and he let her burn her boats."

Isabel leaves New York with her young child. (Me.) My grandmother—now divorced—is living just outside Cincinnati. Isabel will be able to dance with Cincinnati Ballet and my grandmother will help take care of the child. (Me.) It will be a fresh start.

My first memory: being led down the aisle of a theater by my grandmother. I'm five. My grandmother and I are going to see *The Nutcracker.* I have on red tights, which are too small.

I know about *The Nutcracker.* I've started ballet classes at the company's school and seen the older girls rehearsing. I've been told that I may one day be one of those girls. A mouse, or a soldier, or a party child. I want to be a mouse or a party child. I don't like the soldier costumes.

My mother is the Sugar Plum Fairy, the most important role.

I watch the ballet carefully, conscious of being better-behaved than other children in my row, who have to be held or shushed periodically. "Disruptive," says my grandmother, and we scowl at them. The Music Hall is very grand. It all feels important, but I would like to take off my too-small red tights.

I'm disappointed the mice lose the battle with the soldiers. When the Mouse King is killed, he's carried off by his remaining minions, who beat their chests in mourning. The audience laughs, but in between the divertissements of the second act, I worry about the king-less mice. They'd been so sad. They had cried.

After the performance, I'm allowed to go backstage to visit my mother. In a hallway, I see the head of the Mouse King. It's on a prop table, eye sockets empty. A door swings open and my mother is there, wrapped in a peach silk robe, her hair still slicked into a tight bun. Her face is bright and shiny and large-featured, like a doll version of herself. She is strange, bony, glamorous. There are flowers and makeup spread out on her dressing table, rows of shoes lined up against a wall, a pink tutu hung upside down on a rack. There's the scent of Shalimar and baby powder. I realize the person I just saw onstage was this person, my mother. "That's Mommy," I'd been told in a whisper by my grandmother when she first appeared, but it hadn't seemed plausible. The ballerina was someone else's mommy.

In the dressing room, I'm afraid of her. She looks at me and says, "There's my little girl!"

I hide my confusion and present the flowers I've brought.

A few months later, Isabel's chronic lower back pain spreads to her hip and she must take a few months off to rest. A spiritual crisis collides with her physical one. It's been four years since she left New York City Ballet. Leaving, she sees now, was a mistake. Mr. B would have taken her back after her pregnancy, if she'd proved her commitment. He'd taken others back. (Including his departed muse, although not the muse's husband.) Why did she flee New York in shame? How could she have left working with the greatest dance genius of the twentieth century?

She blames the "baby blues." They'd made her resentful to the point of madness. Probably they'd also caused the break with her husband. Yes, he had fallen in love with a man, but he hadn't wanted to get divorced. He was loyal. They could have made it work; *he* had wanted to make it work. He'd wanted to be a father; had agreed to not be a part of her daughter's life—except for financial assistance—only because that's what *she* had insisted on.

There's still a chance. To heal her body, heal her marriage. Isabel and I travel to New York. Isabel is going to see a specialist who works with dancers, and we will both visit Robert, who is now living in an apartment on Bank Street.

At the doctor's, Isabel is told her hip pain is the symptom of a more serious back injury. She needs surgery. It's unlikely she will be able to dance at a professional level once this is done. At Bank

Street, Robert is kind, Robert is supportive. Robert is living with James.

I'm given a teddy bear and lifted into my father's arms.

Isabel feels that her life is over.

She's twenty-eight.

I open my eyes, realize my forehead is almost touching the glass of Isabel's portrait.

I need to let her know Robert is dying. This is all part of her story too.

It's funny that tonight, I want her. I mean, it's a funny feeling for me. To want my mother.

I haven't called her Mother in a long time.

I was a disloyal daughter to her too. I allied myself with men who let me into their lives for two weeks a year. I pushed her away and she let me do it too easily, which I resented.

I take a step back from Isabel's picture, consider her brave smile.

Maybe no fight is a fair fight.

Baptism

Bank Street. Easter 1985.

The sickness killing gay men is attached to more names and acronyms now. It's not a cancer, it's a virus. You get it from blood and fluids, but not everyone agrees on which fluids and how. Before I came to Bank Street last summer, my grandmother told me I shouldn't go in swimming pools while I was in New York and to line the toilet with paper at Bank Street when I had to sit down. Isabel got pretty angry about this, and told my grandmother that AIDS wasn't *polio.* "It doesn't hurt to be careful," my grandmother said, and the subject was dropped. I don't consider her or my mother qualified to speak about the lives of gay men. I know they once both lived in New York, but we're all in a suburb of Dayton now and I've never seen anyone with Kaposi's sarcoma here. I've also never seen men in Ohio holding hands or calling each other "honey" or "sweetheart" in public.

My mother asks me if I have concerns and I say no. I can't lose Bank Street.

This year, I think she's nearly as eager for me to go to New York as I am. She and Ben are married now. Their son, Yuto, was born in January. For months there was talk of me having a baby brother, and now he is here, but he doesn't feel mine. Yuto is *their* baby and I feel he has made *them* a family. I don't know how to be a sister.

I'm twelve, and the same height as my mother. The tallest girl in my class, taller than most boys, taller than some teachers. Every day I hope that I've finished growing, but my body shows signs of not being done with me. My feet are so big. My arms are so long. "Where's the rest of you?" I am teased. I'm flat-chested. If I get boobs on top of everything else, I think, I will kill myself. I don't hunch because I'm a dancer and I don't starve myself because it's not my temperament, but my happiest moments take place in the dark, where I'm invisible. I listen to music on my headphones and disappear into possible dance. With my eyes closed, or the lights out, I can imagine ballet on other bodies, wonderfully not mine, free.

I arrive in New York and in the cab from the airport my father outlines plans. The Ukrainian Museum is having an Easter egg exhibit. We've got tickets for a musical. There will be Bach at the Cathedral of St. John the Divine. "And we're going to have people over, for a dinner party," he says. "We'd like you to be a hostess."

A hostess! At Bank Street, my father says there's a present waiting for me in Carlisle's Room. It's a dress to wear to the party. "I called your mother for your measurements," he says. "And consulted with a gal at Lord & Taylor." When I see it, my heart sinks. He's gotten me so wrong. There's a clique of popular girls at my public school who wear preppy clothes: bright colors and jewelry that looks like candy, jelly shoes. I wear plain button-downs and jeans, which never fit, because there is both too much and not enough of me for regular sizes. The dress my father has chosen isn't preppy, but it's a pattern of bright stripes and is silky and has a belt. I'm not the girl who would wear that, look good in that. I put it on and immediately feel fantastic. Whatever girl this dress is right for, I want to be her.

"Doesn't Carlisle look terrific?" my father says to James, when I show myself.

"Robert knows what he's doing," James tells me. "He knows how to bring out the best in women."

My father is pleased about the party, particularly since it was James's idea. "Oh, these days we have to celebrate everything," James tells me. "Especially the resurrection." (He is not religious except, as he says, aesthetically. We'll go to St. John's for the Bach.)

I love meeting my father and James's friends, who are all funny or interesting and who give me extravagant compliments. The party does feel like a celebration, although it has a brittle, crackling edge. "Joy is political now," someone says. "It's defiance." I hover with a tray of deviled eggs around a group talking about a new HIV test and how it's meant to screen for people donating blood. "Protecting the innocent," a man says, twisting his mouth. "Because Americans could give a fuck if fags die, or junkies, or Haitians." Another man puts his hand on the speaker's arm, notices me, and says, "Look at this angel and her *eggs.*"

That fall a boy, almost the same age as me, is barred from his middle school. He's a hemophiliac who got AIDS from a blood transfusion. His case will become famous. I'll feel sorry for the boy, but every time I hear his name, I'll remember the words *pro-*

tecting the innocent, and think of the nice young man who practiced ballet lifts with me in a pool. Danny.

There are only two other women at the dinner party: one is my father's college girlfriend Betsy, who my father refers to sometimes as my "honorary aunt." She's a quick-moving, wiry person, sarcastic and a little scary. She calls my father Bobby. There's also a glamorous young woman who used to be called by a man's name and is now called Shayna. She has a fan and teaches me how to snap it open and shut, like a flamenco dancer.

Sometimes the talk sounds like insults, but then everyone laughs. James puts on an apron and brings the ham out for my father to carve at the head of the table. "Oh wonderful," my father's friend Allen calls out. "Look at June Cleaver over there in her apron." I don't know who June Cleaver is, but I can tell there's something wrong with the way Allen has made the joke. People aren't really laughing. Allen spills a little of his wine on the tablecloth. "I'm sorry, am I not supposed to notice this is a farce?" he asks. He doesn't look sorry, he looks furious. "We're all going to be just as boring as the straights? These are our choices? Boring or dead?"

The noise of the room collapses in a whoosh of silence.

"God, James, take off the fucking apron," Allen says. "You used to be an artist. What the fuck happened? You should be making ballets, not hams."

I look to my father, who is looking at James. I've never seen James blush. He stammers a few words—I've also never heard James stammer—and then my father is on his feet, telling Allen to come into the hall. He speaks with such flatness I can't tell if he's angry. Everyone looks at their plates. Allen knocks his chair over getting out of it. Shayna rights it.

"Oh well," James says. I can see him swallow. "I expect Robert is going to help Allen get a cab."

There's a murmur of assent. Allen had too much to drink. He didn't know what he was saying.

Of course he didn't. Anyway, I almost say, it was my father who was in charge of the ham.

"Holidays are hard at the best of times." James's voice is unnaturally light and his face is still pink. There are nods. "Holidays are hard for Robert too," James adds, more confidently. I twist a napkin around in my lap. Are they? I thought my father was happy. I know some of the men at this party can't see their families, but James and I are right here.

The man sitting next to me nudges my elbow. He'd arrived wearing a headband with Easter Bunny ears and produces it now, putting it on and giving me a wink.

James goes to the kitchen. There's the sound of the front door closing. Betsy's neighbor says something to her in a low voice. Betsy says, "Nope. He insulted James. Bobby will *never* speak to him again."

"Don't cross Robert," another guest comments.

"Part of his strength," Betsy says, and makes a slicing movement with her hand. "Take it or leave it."

I remember a story James told me: how during a midwestern tour of LaGrange Ballet, my father had arranged tickets for his parents and planned a dinner in a nice restaurant to introduce them to Leonard LaGrange. "Well, his father begged off at the last minute," James said. "With a casual excuse and a joke about ballet dancing. So, the next day, Robert extricated himself totally from his father's business. Not that he'd been directly involved, but he had shares or stock or whatever, and I believe he *gave* all that to his brothers. His father tried to mend things when Robert married your mother, but there were no more invitations. And the same thing happened when your father broke with LaGrange.

Leonard tried to apologize. But when Robert draws a line in the sand, it runs to the center of the earth."

This had seemed impressive, even thrilling. My father is not afraid to fight, or hold a grudge. He is someone to be reckoned with.

When he returns to the table now, though, his neck is red, and his expression is like Yuto's when he's stopped crying but is still angry. James emerges from the kitchen with another dish, which my father takes from him. They don't quite look at each other. Everyone starts talking at once. The laughter and chatter return, in a determined key. After a bit, James and my father seem, if anything, happier. I watch James rub my father's shoulder, and my father—quickly—kiss his hand. After dinner there's singing, and Easter egg dyeing, and people taking turns at the piano. Someone says, "Oh God, let's *not* talk about *The Normal Heart*," and everyone starts talking about *The Normal Heart*, which is a play about AIDS. My father and James have both seen it already. They're not taking me. We've got tickets for *Sunday in the Park with George*.

I show off by being helpful about dishes. I feel womanly doing this, in my pretty dress. Betsy observes my movements with a raised eyebrow; she's always on to me. My father and some friends come back to the dining table for a card game. From the kitchen I hear my name and return to listen to my father describing my mother, her talent and strength and excellence as a parent. (This praise grows more fulsome every year, as it can with people you never see whom you've outshone.)

My father starts telling the story of giving my mother her name. He's not someone who tries to get the attention of the room, but once he has it, he's a good storyteller. He takes his time, setting the scene, evoking 1960s Manhattan, their apartment building, Eleanor Turnball and her mother, living in the basement.

When my father gets to the part where he christens my mother Isabel Osmond, there's applause but also laughter. It occurs to me, for the first time, that there might be something silly about that name. Or my mother.

"It just came to me," Robert says, about the name. "Out of the blue."

My father gave me my name too. Some people think it's for the fancy New York hotel, but he got it out of a novel. "There was a gal named Carlisle in it, and I thought, *If I ever have a daughter, I'll name her Carlisle.* He forgot the name of the book though, only that it was a detective novel.

There's a sudden thump from the other end of the table.

"My God." James is smiling. "I can't believe I missed it until now." He rises from his chair and moves to the bookcases, saying, "Robert, it *didn't* come to you out of the blue."

He returns to the table waving a battered Penguin Classics copy of Henry James's *Portrait of a Lady.*

"*Isabel* Archer," James says, flipping through the pages. "Who ends up marrying, yes, Gilbert *Osmond.* Isabel Osmond. I can't believe it's taken me so long to put it together, but it's been ages since I've looked at Henry James. Robert, were you really not referencing this?"

My father shakes his head, looking bemused.

"Then how Freudian," says my neighbor with the bunny ears. "Isabel has all these men after her and realizes too late she should've gone with the one who wants to fuck her." Someone shushes him and points to me. "Oh my God!" he cries. "I forgot about the daughter. Gilbert Osmond has a daughter who's called— wait for it—*Pansy.* Robert, this story needs its own therapist."

People laugh a little at this, although James doesn't. I know *pansy* is a slur these men have taken ownership of, and trade for comic effect. Not my father. He isn't someone you call "sweetheart," much less "pansy."

"It wasn't psychological," my father protests. "I liked the name. I knew it would suit her and look good in the program. Don't make a goddamn opera out of it."

The air goes out of the room, as before with Allen. My father rolls his eyes and sniffs.

"Freudian, give me a break," he says. "Sometimes a pansy is just a pansy."

The room is released. Everyone laughs. James looks relieved and sets the book down on the table. I take it and put it in my lap. Conversation continues to the usual topics. Mutual friends, shows, dance. Jokes about Nancy Reagan.

"Carlisle, come help me with the coffee," my father says, and I trail him to the kitchen, carrying *The Portrait of a Lady.*

"One day," he tells me, "I'll find the book with *your* name."

My father always says this, and in the past, I've loved the idea of my name being out there, to find. We both like puzzles and mysteries and crosswords and things with clues.

"You're a little young for Henry James." He gently encourages Olga the cat off the counter, where she's been hunting broccoli, her archnemesis, off someone's plate. "The language is dense," he says. "Although that one isn't so bad. And you're a good reader."

What I want to say is "Please tell me *I* am not a joke."

My father maneuvers a coffee urn out from a lower cabinet. "It *wasn't* Freudian, if you understand what that means." He kneels to lift the urn, huffs, and then gets to his feet with grace. He produces these remnants of his ballet training like a magic trick. "Edward's always wanting everything to be complicated," he says. "It makes him feel like there's meaning. Anyway, Isabel is a great character in that book, and your mother is a wonderful lady. I admired her from the moment I met her and never stopped. I think it's terrific she found someone to make her happy. And now a new baby."

I don't want my mother to be an object of ridicule, but I also don't want to hear about how wonderful she is.

"You can wear an apron and be an artist," my father adds quietly, almost to himself. He rubs the worse of his two bad knees. "Anyway, *housewife* isn't a—a slur."

Of course James is an artist. If not him then who? Or is he talking about my mother? I don't think of her as either an artist or a housewife. Does he mean *me*?

"Got your socks pulled up?" He asks this once a visit. It means, *Are you okay?* I always say yes. I know my father likes strong women. I bring a pitcher of cream and a sugar bowl out to the table and set it next to James, who doesn't like sweets except for very sweet coffee. I still have the book tucked under my arm.

"The thing is, it's a *fabulous* name," James whispers, and repeats what he said when I put on the new dress: "Robert knows how to bring out the best in women."

I return to feeling pleased and important, but don't relax until the guests start to leave. *I* don't have to leave. I belong here.

In bed, I flip through *The Portrait of a Lady*. The language does look hard, but I do my best and stay up late for the rest of my visit making my way through it. An American girl (Isabel Archer) comes to England and inherits a fortune. Many people are in love with her: an American businessman, a nice English lord, her interesting but quite seriously ill cousin. Isabel befriends a glamorous widow (Madame Merle), who introduces her to an impoverished aristocrat (Gilbert Osmond). Osmond has a young daughter (Pansy) and a house full of art. Everything is gloomy but impressive. Isabel marries Osmond. He treats her horribly and Isabel learns that he and Madame Merle were once lovers and Pansy is *their* daughter, not his dead wife's. The whole marriage has been a setup. Osmond wanted Isabel's money for himself and his gloomy art, and Madame Merle wanted to secure her secret daughter's fortune. Isabel has messed up. She's trapped.

It's the first book I'll read that doesn't have a happy ending. I hadn't known you were allowed to do that, with stories.

I return to Ohio. My mother listens to the tales of my week and says, "Neat," or "That sounds fun." She looks at her baby with possession and greed, like she wants to eat him and get him back in her body.

She has—without my charting it—become a different person. For so long she was a former something, without a new title. A former ballerina, who'd needed back surgery and had to stop. Then she was getting a job as a receptionist at the place where she had physical therapy. She was going to night school for college, then more school for being a physical therapist assistant. But every inch of her body—even her damage, especially the damage—proclaimed her past. As did her friends. If you had asked anyone to describe her, it would've been the first thing: *She used to be a ballerina.*

I realize the framed photographs I'd grown up with—her with Balanchine, and the one where she's wearing her *Stars and Stripes* costume—have disappeared. They've not been hung in this new house, with the husband and the baby. Her family.

I watch her handle Yuto's body. He has a bluish splotch on his back, a "Mongolian spot." It will fade in time. I never had one.

She puts Yuto on her chest and holds the back of his head the way I have seen her hold Ben's head when they're kissing. This is what she looks like when she's in love. This is what she looks like when she's happy.

I would not fit on her chest. I may not fit anywhere.

I begin to tell her in a loud voice about the Easter dinner party. How it was filled with all of my father and James's friends, who are so awesome and funny and fabulous, and how my father told the story about her name. I explain to her the plot of *The Portrait of a Lady*. I say everyone at the table got the joke, and thought it was funny.

She rubs her hand in circles across her son's back. When I'm done, she regards me over his rather frightening head.

"I think you've grown even *more* in a week," she says.

We are silent. I've tried to hurt her, by making it seem as if my father and his friends were laughing at her, and she has hurt me back. She knows how worried I am about getting too tall for ballet. How is my father able to fight and *win*?

"Anyway, I knew about that book," she says. "I didn't care. I liked the name."

"Yes," I say. "My father knows how to bring out the best in women."

Yuto makes a little coo. He's an exceptionally sweet baby.

My mother will start saying to people, "I'm a mother and a physical therapist. But a mother first."

I will start calling her Isabel.

Shifty

Morning in Los Angeles.

The drinking last night brought no relief and so the punishment today feels unnecessarily cruel. I bump around the kitchen, trying to drown my headache in water. I need to make decisions about going to New York, set plans. Normally I love how quiet and calm my apartment is, but this morning there's an oppressive quality to the stillness. Like I'm cowering here, shut up with my precious objects, entombed, and now I see how small they are, how little solace they provide.

It's not me who is dying.

I put on Purcell and send Isabel a text.

Have some news about Robert. James got in touch.

She calls me right away. As soon as I hear her voice I think, *That was a mistake.*

My head is all disorganized longing. Isabel isn't the right person. The woman never met a nuance she couldn't ignore. She's like those warnings for trekking in the forest: if you stick to the trail, you'll be fine. Only somehow, we so rarely seem to find each other.

I haven't thought through the sentences and make a mess of telling her the news.

"Yeah, so he's not doing so well," I say. "James says—they—Robert—is getting near the end. So, yeah, I guess I'm going to New York. To see him. Them."

"Robert is dying," says Isabel, checking her facts.

"Yes. James called me."

"I'm very sorry, Carlisle," she says, in a formal way. And then, "Are you"—it takes her a few seconds to locate the word—"okay?"

"I'm okay. I'm going. To see Robert before he dies."

Now I sound puffed up. The ghoulish self-importance I've seen in other people, at hospitals or even funerals, where there's always one person who has appointed themselves *Chief Handler of Crisis* or *Most Important Mourner*. I haven't earned this. I wait for Isabel to prove herself an antidote for death's pomposity. She can make her face impressively blank, totally expressionless, but in such a way it's clear she's gone into some other mental room to have opinions. The phone version is silence.

"Do you want me to come with you?" she asks.

It's a saying, a rhetorical question: *Are you sitting down?* I don't think I've ever had to sit down because of what someone said.

I sit down.

"Thank you for offering," I say. "Thanks, Mom. That's incredibly nice of you."

"Of course," she says, but I can tell she's impressed herself too. To the point where she goes even further. "I'm here," she says, with wonder, "if you need me."

We are maybe both realizing I called her "mom." I put my hand on my dining table. Too much salt last night, my rings are tight. I feel it in my calves too.

I tell her I'll be fine.

I can't see it: Isabel and me on either side of Robert's deathbed. James hovering in the background? We were all together only once, at my college graduation. I'd been braced for something awkward to be managed, but everyone was charming. James asking Isabel about her physical therapist training, Ben and Robert talking tennis and cars. Yuto in a bow tie.

I hadn't thought, *Oh my family, all together.* More that I was hosting two separate families.

"When was the last time you spoke to him?" Isabel asks.

"James? We don't usually do the phone. Emails and texts a few times a year. Sometimes he sends me a book or forwards an article."

"I meant your father."

If we're talking meaningful exchange, then nineteen years. Since then, interaction peaked at bare civility. No emails or texts. We exchange holiday cards. Well, James writes them, but they're signed by them both.

"A while," I say.

Isabel doesn't know what happened, between me and Robert. Her understanding is only that we had a fight after James was going through his troubles and have steadily grown apart. She never asks for details, about anything. It's because her own mother had been so nosy, she explained once. She doesn't want me to feel like I'm being watched.

"I guess Robert *has* lived a long and full life," she says now. "And he's not young."

"Eighty-five."

"But with the smoking and the heart issues he has in his family. Or is it something else?"

"Complications from heart disease, I think. James said something about how he needed a surgery, but they thought he wouldn't survive it."

"It's his time, I guess."

"Yes."

Silence.

"I think we're meant to forgive each other and say goodbye," I suggest. "Me and Robert, I mean."

"Right."

I stand to retrieve my coffee mug from the counter. *Right* is an extreme placeholder in my mother's vocabulary. What she means is *I hear that* you *believe whatever you're saying. I acknowledge it's been said. I reserve my own opinion.*

"James didn't try to lay a last-request-from-a-dying-man trip on me," I tell her. "It's about closure, as they say."

"Right."

I realize I'm doing that thing where I shift my weight from side to side, a sort of compulsive lateral rocking. It was Tanya, my friend who does somatic healing, who pointed out I do this whenever I talk about my family. Literally not standing firm, vacillating. She suggested that thoughts of my family provoked feelings of ambivalence. "I don't know," I told her. "It might just suggest I'm really fucking shifty."

"I'm not envisioning a Prodigal Daughter returns moment." I put my foot on the counter and stretch my hip. "No crawling on my knees and up into his arms." (I'm not being imaginative; this is how Balanchine's ballet *Prodigal Son* ends. The father stands still, not helping his son until the very last moment, when he pulls his cloak around their bodies. Incredibly moving.)

"Well, no." Isabel's dryness is as much of an opinion as she'll offer. Whatever contract she signed with herself over never saying anything disparaging about Robert remained even when I told her we'd basically stopped communicating. She had the biggest *I (didn't) tell you so* available to her and declined to use it. The impressiveness of her self-discipline. The woman deserves a statue by Rodin.

"I'd like to say goodbye to him," she says. As far as I know, they haven't spoken since my graduation. I realize I've not been particularly gentle in relaying this news. Isabel was once *married* to Robert. He's a part of her past. There will be things to process, even for her.

"I can ask James," I offer. "I can put you in touch with him."

"*I* know how to get in touch with James." She's crisp, I've offended her. "We've spoken, over the years."

I hadn't known that.

"I tried to help." I can hear her swallowing. "I did *try* to get through to Robert, to remind him he only has one daughter. He's the parent. He doesn't get to hold a grudge."

Freya used to say that to me too. A parent doesn't get to hold a grudge, a parent's job is to be forgiving, et cetera. It's not an argument that satisfies me, perhaps because I'm not a parent and don't understand unconditional love. My view is Robert should have forgiven me not because I'm his daughter and he has to, but because what I did was *forgivable.*

"Do you *want* to come with me?" I ask. "We could see him together." Who I'm thinking about now is James. As a buffer between myself and James, Isabel might be perfect.

"I can talk to Robert on the phone," she says. "I don't think I need to see him in person."

"Right." It's a useful deflect; I should have started employing it earlier.

"What on earth is that music?" she asks.

"Purcell. Um, 'Now Does the Glorious Day Appear.' I have a film job coming up where I need to provide some Baroque dances."

"That's nice. Work is good?"

"Work is good. You know. Lots of little things right now, to pay the bills."

Another silence.

"I'm sure James will want to talk to you about everything," she says. "And there will be Robert's affairs to sort out."

Robert's affairs? It takes me a minute.

"Do you mean money?" I ask. "Because there won't be any for me."

Another silence. Purcell's "Now Does the Glorious Day Appear" ends and we move on to "O God, Thou Art My God."

My expectations about money—from any source—are modest. Not that I don't dream about things being easier, but I don't see how financial security will ever be a reality for someone like me. It's best to keep overhead low and hustle enough union work for decent health care. I'm making dances in America. Nobody is going to fight to protect *my* American job.

"I don't mean Robert will have cut me out," I say. "Just, you know, unless things have changed, he's never had as much money as people thought. Well, *you* know that. The one big thing is Bank Street, and that will go to James."

"Carlisle?" Isabel clears her throat. "This isn't my place. But I don't want you going in there unprepared. I think I should tell you that Bank Street was part of a trust."

"I know that."

Robert's father established a trust for his money, with a number of conditions of where and how everything should go. Robert, the son who'd made such a point of separating himself from the family business, came in for the smallest portion, with the most stipulations. Robert never talked about money—or his family, or much of his past for that matter—to me, so James (as always) had been my source of information. The lump sum Robert got had to be used for residential real estate. "You see," James explained, "LaGrange Ballet was always on the brink of financial disaster. I think the trust was drawn the way it was to keep Robert from sinking his nest egg into LaGrange. Which he absolutely would have done.

"It might also," he added, "have been about punishment. For the divorce. For me."

"Bank Street will go to James," I say to Isabel. "That would have happened even if Robert and I hadn't, you know, gone our separate ways. They're married. It's their home. Or I suppose James can sell it and retire. It has to be worth a lot."

"It can't go to James. He can't sell it." I listen to Isabel's hesitation. "Your grandfather put conditions in the conditions," she says. "I don't understand it all, but Robert had to establish a living trust and name who the property would pass to. At the time all that was done, we weren't officially divorced. Your grandfather was *very* nice to me, the one time we met. Just after you were born."

"Bank Street goes to you?" For a moment, I'm appalled. *Poor James*, I think.

"No, no," she says. "To you."

Oh.

I'm an heiress.

Like Pansy, after all.

"Huh," I say to Isabel.

"Right," she says. "Right."

I grip the counter, distinctly nauseated. Bank Street. So, this is why James has summoned me. Why I'm meant to see Robert. They will want me to sign over Bank Street to James. This is the price of forgiveness. Fuck this. Fuck *them*. I won't take their forgiveness, or Bank Street.

"Does the trust bind me?" I ask. "I mean, once it's mine I could do what I want, right? Give it to James."

"I'm so glad you said that." Isabel's voice is filled with relief, more emotion than she's expressed so far.

"You're glad I said that." I echo her words because it now seems like lunacy. *Give my inheritance back? After all they took?*

"Well, because it's James's home. It's not—" She's caught, too late, my change of tone.

It was such a mistake to pick up the phone. I need to get out of here. I have work to do.

"Right. Right. Right." I take my foot off the counter. "Because of course I should have nothing."

This was a mistake.

"I didn't mean that at all," she says, quickly. "Of course I didn't."

"Because I'm not really a part of their family, so anyway." I sound like a child. It's a humiliation.

"You are his daughter," Isabel says. "I only thought—"

I pour a glass of water and drink it through her broken-off sentence.

"You said yourself." Her voice is small. "You weren't expecting anything."

When that trust was established, Robert and James couldn't be married. The law—and my grandfather—favored me. So many rights and protections denied to them for so long. Can I swoop in and say, "No, this is *mine.*" I didn't earn it. The opposite.

"I shouldn't have told you." Again, Isabel's small voice.

No, no, I tell her, and manage a few formal things about how it *is* better to know, and I appreciate it.

"Carlisle," she says. "I'll support you whatever you do."

Oh will you, I think. *And what will that look like?*

Not fair. My fight isn't with her.

"Gotta go to work," I say. She can hear this conversation has gone badly for me, for us, but she doesn't press to correct it. She never presses. We say goodbye.

Bank Street.

It's almost like panic, what I'm feeling.

No. This is what I'm going to do today. I'm going to think of the life *I* have and my work. This is where I am, and what I have. This is what belongs to me.

I drive downtown, where I have a session with Luis and the team who are building the installation art piece for Xavier Larks. In the car I play Fauré's Requiem, like a test. It's a piece that reliably wrecks me at some point in every listening. I'm not sure why. As a send-off for the dead, it's so gentle, even cheering. No fear or judgment. I guess what kills me is the compassion.

Am I going to come apart? My body refuses to succumb to the requiem, even the "Pie Jesu."

I'm fine.

I can work. I *need* to work.

At the studio, I tell Luis I might be in New York for a few days next week, and he says that's cool, we're at a good stopping point anyway. I warm up and his words become a rhythm in my head. Good stopping point. Good stopping point. Good stopping point. I put on kneepads and tell Luis where to position the crash mats. "Is there any kind of ballet move where you do sort of a belly flop?" he asks. "Xavier texted me this morning and said he wants a belly flop."

I'm making a ballet for an animatronic puppet. Well, it can't all be making ballets for prestigious companies. (For me, it's *mostly* not.) If asked, I'd say choreographing for a visual artist, or a TV show or opera, is a fascinating process, and I learn so much from dealing with different constraints. That's true, but so is the fact I do these things for the money. This particular job also has its unpalatable aspects, which I find interesting.

Assigned Seating is the piece the artist Xavier Larks is most famous for. Visitors queued in a line marked "Consumers." When it was your turn, you entered a sort of polling booth and were given an opportunity to select from a list of identifiers. The usual race, gender, religion, sexual prefixes, et cetera. But also things like being left-handed or lactose intolerant. There was a check-list for trauma and aggressions micro and macro. After completing your survey, the computer performed an algorithm and you received a printout, like a receipt. This told you your Level of Oppression. There were many think pieces on who or what was the target of the work.

Xavier himself is disinclined to investigate his art past the Idea. The Idea, he feels, is all. The Idea is also nearly all he contributes to his own work, Construction and Execution being almost entirely put into the hands of others, and Meaning being left to the gallery who represents him and writes exegeses on his behalf. (That part I get; I'm crap about explaining my own work.)

Xavier is generally loathed, but somehow not dismissed. People pay attention to him and he receives insane amounts of money for his projects, which all get installed in major museums. I find this fascinating. Xavier is a white male, but is there another factor that explains his success? Or is it one of those attributes, like arrogance or sense of entitlement or emotional volatility, that only work in your favor if you're a white man?

I expect if I dug around a little, I'd find that Xavier started out with serious connections, or money, or both. I had serious connections too, and lost them—forfeited them?—nineteen years ago. It's probably nonsense to take pride in making this career on my own. Having to struggle doesn't necessarily make you interesting, it might just make you tired.

I want my work to be seen, to be part of the conversation of my art form, to collaborate with people I admire and respect. But these things are only important. They aren't sacred. The sacred thing is to feel—if only for a moment—that I am not consuming or forgetting or losing the things of this world but adding to them. That I have made something true or beautiful or both. That I might do it again.

This moment will not happen today. Today is about getting paid.

The team that constructs Xavier's ideas includes my friend Luis, who once did carpentry and rigging for Rose et Noir, a weekly cabaret/burlesque show I performed with in my twenties. We've kept in odd touch over twenty years, the way one sometimes does, and he put my name forward for this job. Eventually a puppet—still being built—will perform this balletic solo I'm choreographing to an audio loop of 1960s radio and television advertisements. My work—along with that of Luis and his team of engineers—will be uncredited, which I prefer, considering the absurdity of it all. The pay is fabulous.

I met with Xavier only once. He's younger than I am, mid-thirties, thin and large-headed and bandy-legged. With his loose, unorganized limbs and pristine white sneakers, he looked like a puppet himself.

"I want the ballet to be pretty sometimes and sometimes not. And sort of, like, suicidal," he said. "But it should look like real ballet." I asked him what he saw in his head when he thought of "real ballet." He made, with a seriousness unexpectedly sweet, an approximation of a jewel box ballerina: putting his arms above his head and teetering on his gleaming sneakers. I asked—carefully—if he'd ever been to a ballet performance. He said yes but that he hadn't noticed what he called "the details." He wanted the figure to be on pointe. "Those shoes make your toes bleed, right?" (Everyone wants ballet to be so gory.)

His instructions ended there.

Luis said it would be helpful to film a dancer doing things, so they could work out the body mechanics and re-create the moves for the puppet. They would bring mats and pads and things, for any "flinging" I might do. I decided to choreograph it on myself, rather than hiring a dancer. It was a weird job, and I didn't want to injure anyone. Also, I could keep all the money and think about getting a new car.

Today, I wrap the tips of my toes in gel pads and slide them into the shoes. Back in the day, I loved pointe shoes, and not because they were pretty objects and a sign of maturity, though they were. Girls start pointe work around eleven or twelve, an introduction to controlling and overcoming pain at just the right time. It's not torture. The pain gives a return that I can't imagine torture does. Dancing on pointe weaponizes ballet for girls. We get taller, and our turns gain speed. Everything becomes more dangerous and more direct, literally more pointed. Our legs become swords. We even become louder; the shoes make a heavier tapping noise than ballet slippers. The technique involved accentuates our femininity at the same time it produces larger, stronger muscles. The sense of our power, our primacy, grows. It's as if you said to boys: "Okay, you can catch the ball and throw the ball, but only the girls get the *bat*."

I had a problem though. Standing on my toes made me several inches taller. I was already taking up a lot of space.

Now, I can barely dance on pointe. My ankles aren't as strong, and my feet are more tender. Pointe shoes are not forgiving objects. And yet, when I put them on, the sensation of power returns, slightly twisted. A perimenopausal Cinderella pulling the glass slippers out of the closet to dance for herself, not for a prince. Well, not quite herself.

I try an off-balance arabesque that ends with me face-planting onto the fluffiest of the mats. The first fall is always the trickiest, calculating how much of yourself needs to be protected.

"Cool," says Luis.

After some various pirouetting into wreckage, Luis turns on the loop of ads and jingles serving as our score. I dance—as best I can—snippets of solos from the Great Ballets. These are things I was taught as a student, but never performed. True ballerina roles. Giselle's Act One entrance. The Lilac Fairy variation from *Sleeping Beauty*. *Swan Lake*, of course. I dance them to advertisements for Dream Whip, for Pontiac Grand Prix, for Cameo copper cleaner. I invent ways to break the formal beauty down, fall, crash. I can feel the risk of moving like this, summoning up anger I've been trying to ignore. Emotions have a way of collecting and hardening inside us, like neglected grease. We are all smoking stoves.

I don't want to be dancing. Or doing these weird gigs, no matter how lucrative. It's been too long since I've worked with a proper ballet company. I love rehearsal rooms. Watching the dancers come in, drop their bags along the walls, sprawl beside them. Pull out shoes, snacks, sweatshirts. Redo their hair, roll a sore spot on a tennis ball, tape up a toe. Chat to each other about a movie, a pet, a weird dream they had the night before. I love the way they get to their feet and come forward, eager, haughty, open, nervous, hopeful, canny, detached. How they watch me and watch themselves in the mirror. The flares and dips of their egos and insecurities. How carefully I have to love them because if you don't remain critical, they'll distrust it. That moment—sometimes just a glimmer—when the ordinary and extraordinary parts of themselves are fully visible together. "There," I will say. "That's exactly what I mean. Beautiful." I suppose rehearsal rooms are the least lonely spaces I have ever occupied.

Now, for a moment, as I'm waltzing in circles, I see Bank Street, the way it felt to step through the front door. And I'm a child again.

It's easy to tell people I grew too tall for a career in ballet. I mean, look at me.

It's not all of the truth. I didn't have what it takes. The heart. The fire.

C'est une question morale.

My dancing is terrible today. I feel old and clumsy.

It's okay, it's okay. I have the life I'm meant to have. This is what belongs to me, what I earned for myself.

Bank Street was never mine. I couldn't possibly take it.

I hear my father's voice, devastated, devastating. *What have we ever done to you that you would betray us both like that?*

C'est une question morale.

What am I doing?

"Carlisle?"

Luis calls for a break. Everybody checks their phones. I press my fingertips into my chest, hard, digging into the spaces between my ribs. Trying to find pain or trying to make it?

It could happen that in a few days my father might tell me he forgives me, and I will reject his forgiveness like it's an organ my body doesn't recognize.

Will I be allowed, then, to come apart? Will I have earned it?

All pain is equal at the moment of suffering, but after that, suffering gets Assigned Seating. Just because Xavier's a shitty artist doesn't mean he's wrong. (If that's what he meant.)

I take off my pointe shoes, unforgiving objects that need, and bestow, such strength. The worst my body ever felt was when I totally stopped dancing for a while. All my joints and tendons are organized for ballet, for its unnatural and unforgiving postures. I need them to be strong. I need my fucked-up things that work so beautifully together.

Luis says he thinks they have everything they need. The engineers come over to say goodbye. One of them tries a pirouette, and soon they are all attempting dance moves, laughing, but with the hunt for glory in their eyes. Ballet makes fools of us all.

I call my sometime-assistant Ian on the way home and ask if he can cover my classes when I'm in New York. "Are you on a panel?" he asks. This is a joke between us. In recent years, company directors realized they were going whole seasons, whole years, without presenting a single work choreographed by a woman or person of color. Well, they didn't realize it so much as they started having it shamed into them, as did organizers of public lectures and such. I'm asked to be on more panels to represent being a female choreographer than I'm given chances to *be* a female choreographer.

It's almost always men who give me work. It's even mostly men who put me on a panel to speak for women. In both cases, these are usually gay men. Xavier Larks just paid me to pretend to kill myself with ballet.

I come home and run a bath. I put on the Glass études again. As long as there is music, I can sort of always be working.

A message from my occasional lover Milo arrives. *Will be in LA for three weeks in May. Don't have any stupid boyfriends around.* Ah. Three weeks of Milo. Dinners and rolling around. Well, two weeks of that and a third week of last-minute cancellations and charming apologies. It usually suits me very well. Oh, it's not that I don't imagine arms around me, from time to time. Something a little more than Milo's light offering of low-expectation intimacy.

I look at photos on social media of the last guy I officially dated, a smart fellow whose too-recent divorce had him erupting in unpredictable spells of bitterness and depression but who still follows me on Instagram. He wasn't a stupid boyfriend. They've none of them—the handful—been stupid or abusive or anything like that. But hasn't there always been something dutiful—on my part—with these attempts at a "real" relationship? As if I were proving myself capable of something more than a gorgeous pas de deux in good lighting. The unrepeatable dream. The memory of lightning.

I tend to my social media sites, posting photos from yesterday's master class with appropriately gracious and boosting hashtags. I don't message Milo back. Who will I be in May? *They are thinking in terms of weeks,* James had said. My father will not be alive in May. My life going on. His, ending. Ended.

In the bath I try, a little, to cry. It doesn't happen.

Where is my assigned seating for this grief? Orchestra? Balcony? A private box with an obstructed view? Over the past nineteen years I've told myself the story of how it all happened, my banishment. I've thought about Robert and James and their roles in my life. And not thought about it. There *have* been other things. But the past gets caught in the lungs, the joints, the interstitial tissues of our bodies. It was part of the dance I was making today. A waltz with time, with oneself. With anger. With shame. With love?

Balanchine famously said there are no mothers-in-law in ballet. Meaning, it's not an art form suited for portraying complicated family relationships, or psychological subtleties. It's a place to get away from them, into a purer realm.

Dance *is* very good on romantic love. Love is one of its best, easiest, most beautiful and wonderful expressions. The dive, the swoop, the swoon. (Dance is also excellent for anger, pride, and sorrow.)

I love better in my work than I do anywhere else.

I'm not stony. I'm not. I experience love for people. My friends, my family. I just *do* love better in my work.

I get out of the bath and put dinner together. I compose a list of things I need to get done before this trip.

I would be a fool to give up Bank Street. A fool for what? Not for love.

But in giving it away, I lose nothing I haven't already lost.

And gain what? My dying father's gratitude? His love? James's love?

I can't even seem to book this ticket. Well, it's tough to reserve a seat for your day of reckoning. And going to New York always riles me up. This was true even before the break with Robert and James. It touches on a source of shame, a distinctly New York kind of shame: *If you can make it here, you'll make it anywhere, but if you don't make it here, making it anywhere else is unconvincing.*

There was a time when all I wanted in the world was Bank Street. I didn't call it that, I called it wanting to be a ballet dancer. I failed at both. But I'm not that girl anymore, and her dreams are no longer my dreams. Why should I feel like I failed her?

I'm not that girl anymore.

Oh, she's still there.

Like a Cat

Nobody wants me to become a dancer.

From around the ages of five to eleven, I'm allowed to want to become a ballerina without opposition. That is, my mother makes noises about my "outgrowing it"—literally—but once we move from Cincinnati to a suburb outside Dayton, I suppose she thinks the local dance studio is harmless enough. A nice woman with some solid ballet training runs it. Sometimes I try to show Isabel steps at home. This doesn't go well. She overcorrects me, and when I complain, she switches to nodding in a polite way I find even more deflating. We withdraw to our corners.

My father says I should do what makes me happy. James says happiness isn't what people think it is. James understands, but he isn't my parent and doesn't want to be. "If you were any other child, Carlisle, this would all be a bit sticky. Fortunately, you're wonderful at looking after yourself. Like a cat. Who reads." He adores cats and books. The comparison makes me proud.

My grandmother continues to look after me quite a bit during these years, while Isabel works, and gets a college degree, then puts herself through school for physical therapy. My grandmother's ambitions for her daughter do not replant themselves in me. Neither she nor my mother is up for "going through all that again." If I want to take class, fine. It's good discipline and exercise and will help me manage my long limbs.

My father and James, especially James, take far more interest in my progress. On the visits to New York, we always go to the ballet, or watch videos. James will tell me which dancer to watch, and why. "Pay attention to the way Alessandra Ferri runs across the stage. You won't see finer." Standing in the kitchen at Bank Street, he might demonstrate a step, a position of the arm. My father likes to watch us. "That looks terrific, Carlisle."

The thing is, I can dance. I pick up instruction like I'm remembering it. At the studio, I'm always in a level with girls several years older than I am, until there are no higher levels to get to but I'm still only eleven. My teacher suggests to Isabel that we look into the programs around the country offering more rigorous training. "Which I'm sure you know all about," she says, deferential. She knows who my mother is, of course. Isabel may call herself a mother first, and a physical therapist second, but when she comes to pick me up at the studio, her turnout becomes more pronounced, and her neck gains an inch. A Balanchine ballerina.

I'm twelve, thirteen, fourteen. The years ballet can become your identity, thank God. The alternative is adolescence. Ballet, at least, has rules you can understand.

There is a crucial devotion necessary for ballet. This seems obvious, but its parameters are not. Devotion is not precisely about love. A great dancer needs a mysterious alchemy of humility and obsession. It's a question of morals.

Do I have this? Not quite. Ballet is the right shape to hold my thoughts, what happens to me when there is music. It is easy for me to imagine, to dream myself into dance. In class, it's always a surprise when I struggle with something, since it's all perfectly clear in my head. My response to this should be to work harder. Sometimes I just dream more. I don't *quite* realize this is what I'm doing. I believe I am devoted.

At fourteen, I begin to campaign for switching to a boarding school for the arts just outside Boston, with a competitive ballet program. Going away to school is secretly stage one of a larger plot. Boston is a step closer to New York. I tell myself this is about dance. My goal is to gain admission to SAB, the School of American Ballet, like my mother had.

Isabel needed my grandmother and the basement apartment on West Eightieth, but this won't be the case for me, I'll have a place to stay. As far as I know, the idea of my living with my father and James has never been considered, but maybe only because I was too young, and it was assumed a young girl should be with her mother? I'll be fifteen by then. Who needs their mother at fifteen?

At boarding school I'll be just a train ride away from my father and James. I will demonstrate to everyone I'm talented and dedicated enough to be interesting, mature enough to be independent. After the summer workshop, SAB will surely accept me into their yearly school. I can finish high school in New York. Carlisle's Room will be Carlisle's Room full-time.

Isabel, when appealed to about the boarding school near Boston, proves less of an obstacle than I expected. *Yes*, she says. *If you can get a scholarship.* The timing is good: she's focused on Yuto. She knows what he needs from her. *I can't win with you*, she sometimes says to me. *I can't win with* you, I think. She's disappointed, my freshman year of high school, when I ignore the volleyball coach's efforts to recruit me. I hear her tell Ben, about my going to boarding school, "Managing things on her own could be good for her. You know how she's always in her head. *If* we can afford it."

There are concerns over money on both sides of my family. The Boxhill Festival has lost a major sponsor and my father is forgoing a salary in order to pay others. Isabel hasn't yet returned to work, and is it worth it, when daycare will eat up the salary? Ben's mother has MS and there are all kinds of things her insurance doesn't cover. I hear talk, on both sides, of hanging on to things, meaning homes. Both the maple boards of Bank Street and the wall-to-wall carpeting of the house in Ohio are less stable than I supposed.

The audition for the boarding school takes place in Cincinnati, at the same school I attended as a small child. It's more professional than the studio in Dayton. In the dressing room, I think all the other girls look prettier and more accomplished, but somewhere in the middle of class I realize I'm one of the best ones. Possibly *the* best.

I get the scholarship.

"Is this what you really want?" Isabel asks.

"This is who I am," I say. I see, for once, that I've impressed her.

The night before I leave for school, she gives me a family heirloom: a small crucifix on a gold chain she sometimes wore when she was in the New York City Ballet. (Our family's Catholicism has long faded, but Mr. B was devout; she'd have worn it to impress.) She also gives me a box of tampons. I've not gotten my period yet and wonder which of these items I'll need first.

Isabel drives me to the airport herself, without Ben or Yuto. When we hug goodbye, she surprises me by holding on. She feels small in my arms. I'm not prepared for her to be sad. The power of this confuses me. I hadn't known I could make her want more of me.

When I'd told my classmates in Ohio I was going to a performing arts boarding school, people asked if it was like *Fame*. I said yes, although my school is not gritty or flamboyant like that one. The campus is nice, and some attempts were made to make it feel like a New England prep school, although those pretensions buckled under the weight of a student body with no interest in preparing for anything but their chosen art. Not all the kids are obsessive and devoted, some are mildly talented but very rich and have done drama at a real prep school like Choate before getting expelled. They're in the minority; being on scholarship is a thing signaling extra talent and is respected. The college-bound want places like Curtis or Juilliard or CalArts; the rest of us are here to satisfy parental requirements of high school degrees before moving on to, if not immediate stardom, getting a gig.

I'm slow to make friends at boarding school but enjoy the routines. I work in the kitchen in the morning, preparing the scrambled eggs, learning to cleanly crack and separate two in one hand. I make my pointe shoes—so expensive—last as long as possible, coating them in shellac, setting them to harden on my dorm radiator. I'm startled by my art history class, notable for *not* being a perfunctory attempt to cram the bare minimum into academically incurious students. We're assigned John Berger's *Ways of Seeing*, and I underline passages about women, and how men look at women, and how women look at themselves being looked at. In art, in life. This feels important. Every day, I look at myself in the full-length mirrors of the ballet studio and watch myself dance. There seems to be a difference between the person dancing and the person watching herself dance. Is there a man, inside me, looking at me?

I still don't get my period (or boobs) but am propositioned by a middle-aged man at the local Dunkin' Donuts. He tells me he wants to lick my pussy. "What?" I ask, too bemused to be frightened. By the time I'd seen him looking at me, it was too late to prepare myself to be looked at, to be *ready*.

I imagine having sex—a highly impressionistic form of it—with the tallest boy in school, the art history teacher, Michael Hutchence from the band INXS, and Baryshnikov.

The ballet program is run by a lovely but fey French ballerina who has to get both knees replaced and shows up only occasionally. My class is taught by her second-in-command, a petty tyrant and bully who makes us call him "sir," and who likes to scream "Stupid!" and "Awful!" He takes a particular dislike to me until he abruptly reverses course and makes me his favorite, a partiality that costs me my few tentative friends. (He's of my father's generation, and I put his sudden warmth down to learning of the connection.)

It's possible to know one is gifted and yet feel one is horrible. James has already talked to me about this, but no one has explained hormones. I haven't read Judy Blume or the like, and such things aren't mentioned in Henry James or even Edith Wharton. John Berger doesn't talk about *girls*. I have first-timer thoughts about death, and trees, and Debussy. An aspiring actress two doors down from me is also worried about her height, and we drink coffee and smoke cigarettes together with solemn ceremony, as if taking a cure.

Isabel sends me a short letter, every other week. We talk on the phone twice a month, mindful of the cost of minutes. I go to Bank Street at Thanksgiving, on the train. My father and James say they wish I could come for Christmas. I've never spent Christmas with them. *Next year*, I think.

I discover I can jump. High. I can also move fast. It's about music, really. If I think more about music and less about myself, I sometimes finish a combination of steps and think, *Yes*.

In the spring, auditions for summer programs begin. I mention the School of American Ballet to my mother. "They're very specific about what they want at SAB," she says. I know what she means. The perfect body, like hers. But she doesn't know what I can do. She wanted me to play *volleyball*. "I don't want you to be disappointed," she says, adding that if I do get into the school, it might be best if I stayed with a group of students my own age. "Your father has always said you're welcome at Bank Street, but he'll be at Boxhill. We can't assume what will work for James."

I'm assuming like mad and it's wonderful. Summer with James at the piano, talking art, talking everything. Me on the library steps, listening. Us going to the ballet, to hear music, to bookstores. Me convincing him through word and deed that I should stay forever. Becoming indispensable.

"I might not get in," I say, to mollify Isabel.

"Don't take it bad if you don't. These things aren't fair."

The auditions are in Boston. I wear my best leotard and, on impulse, the small crucifix Isabel had given me. The woman running the audition is a former dancer with the company, also tall. She watches me with a little smile. I'm thin, I'm fast, I jump as high as the boys. I dance like I own the room. In later years, when friends talk about acts of teenage rebellion, I'll think of that audition.

"Carlisle, that's wonderful," says my father, when I phone with my acceptance news. "Though I'm not surprised. You're just the ticket. They're going to love you there."

He tells me he wishes he could be around more for my first full summer in New York. Perhaps I can come up with James to Boxhill for a weekend? He can show me the festival and I can keep James company.

"You'll have to come to Bank Street and have dinner with him while you're in New York," he says. "I know you'll make friends and want to do your own thing, but save some time for James too. Now, let's think about where you can stay. Or has Isabel arranged something already?"

My body understands the words first. Stomach sinks, heart thuds, face flushes, all the body things. My mind tries to square it, make it better.

"You know if it was up to me, you'd be here with us always." He speaks in a rush. "And you know James adores you. It's only that summer is the only time James gets to be on his own. He's not even teaching at Boxhill this year. He needs private time. To— Well, to be private."

"Totally," I say. "I totally, totally get that."

What I totally get is that my father loves James best and James loves my father best and Isabel loves Yuto and Ben best and everyone I know has someone they love best. I'm no one's best.

By the time we get off the phone, my father has gone so far as to speculate I might stay with Betsy. Betsy! Forget it.

Maybe I won't go to New York at all. I've also been accepted into the summer program at Pacific Northwest Ballet. They like tall girls there too. I could go to New York but never see James, not once, and not travel up to Boxhill either. Or I can spend the summer in Ohio, be super sister to Yuto and become the person he loves best.

"You can all quit and go be secretaries," my teacher sometimes shouts at us, when he thinks we aren't working hard enough. "You can go have *babies.*"

Those are both things my mother did.

The next day, a girl in my hall knocks on my door to tell me I have a phone call. It's James. He tells me he wanted to congratulate me himself. "And listen," he says. "I don't know what your arrangements are, and you mustn't feel obligated, but if you'd *like* to stay here at Bank Street, you're perfectly welcome. I'll be honest and selfish and say I would love it. You'd be entirely independent, of course. I know young people need to be free to do their own thing."

There is nothing I want less than to do my own thing.

"I'll leave it entirely up to you," he says. "You might wish to go to Betsy's, which *is* closer to SAB. Although I'm on the Upper West Side nearly every day myself in the summer, teaching. Anyway, I just wanted you to know. Oh. Robert's coming through the door now. He'll want to speak to you."

My father is awkward with me on the phone. He's been wrong-footed. James *wants* me. James wants *me.* I'm awkward too, almost contemptuous from relief.

"Well," says my father, before hanging up. "I'm so glad this worked out."

I arrive at the School of American Ballet. As far as talent or promise goes, I put myself in the middle of my class, not too bad considering the caliber. I tell myself I'll get to the top soon, once I've stopped growing. It's like my looks, which I do see are not great but should improve. Our teachers are either Russians who've been at the school for decades or former dancers of the company. The Russians are exacting and merry. They've seen so many of us. Their art is deep; they've survived revolutions. The retired dancers say mystical things in nasal accents and have signature accessories: a scarf, a flower in the hair, a skirt. I search for my mother in these Balanchine ballerinas and catch wisps. A kind of astringent beauty; an inviolate self-possession. The combination of pride and humility. The judgment. Perfume.

In class I receive no special attention or notice except from the portliest and most ancient of the Russians. She asks my name and, after a few attempts at pronunciation, gives up and simply calls me "de tall one." "Verrrrrry good, de tall one." "Do again little better, de tall one." "Try for me once more, de tall one."

Twice a week we have partnering class. The first day, the teacher plays matchmaker, leading girls by the wrist to waiting boys. The numbers are uneven so each boy receives two or three partners, who will have to take turns. When the teacher gets to me, he widens his eyes slightly, looks around the room, and sends me across it to the tallest boy. He's also fifteen and extremely skinny. The look on this boy's face, as I cross the room, will always be with me.

He can barely lift me.

For the second class, I'm moved to a shorter boy, but one who is two years older and stronger. This boy is eager to show how he's able to manage my size, and partnering becomes fun. "You're good," he tells me. And "Don't worry, I have you." The teacher sometimes asks us to demonstrate. I ask the boy if he wants to go to the movies with me. It's my first time asking anyone for a date (I've never been asked), and when he stammers and says, "Yeah, we could go in a group, let me ask who else wants to go," I pretend it's a yes and that he's shy. The next week, one of the girls takes me aside in the dressing room and explains how the boy likes me, but not *like that*. She thought I should know. If it was *her*, she'd want to know. The next partnering class, I'm icily polite to the boy, which seems to make him put his hand on my back more. Hope blooms in my chest and I smile at him. He takes his hand away. I feel I've learned something.

August comes too soon. On the last day, the ancient Russian approaches me at barre and pats my arm. "Don't worry, tall girl," she says. "Is okay." I have a very short meeting in the afternoon, where I'm told SAB is not inviting me to stay for the full-year program. They're concerned about my height, about my strength. "You're always welcome," they say, "to audition again."

I'm shocked, and humiliated. They think I'm weak. Huge and weak. I *am* these things. I've not pushed myself, proved myself. I've been living in a fantasy land. I've always known: if I'm going to be this tall, I need to be exceptional.

I return to Bank Street and reconfigure the conversation for James. "Oh, they want me to come back next summer, to sort of see how much I've grown," I say. "It's about not pushing me too hard right now." There's a jagged rock in my sternum. Maybe nothing is ever going to work out.

A few weeks later I'm back at boarding school. My junior year passes in a haze of hormones and joint inflammation. I wonder if maybe I should be another kind of artist, but dance is where all my thoughts—if not my body—come together. It's what I see. But I keep *growing*. The summer after my junior year I can't go anywhere: I get mono and spend the summer in Ohio, swollen and rashy and tired, quarantined to my room. I read a lot of books, and when I stagger upright, I'm six foot one. The height that— for a woman—is rarely allowed to pass without comment in the outside world, let alone the ballet one. I go back to school.

Teachers talk to me about theatrical dancing. "You've got

more of a showgirl physique." I begin to hear things about how my training might serve me in the future, in "anything" I do. Isabel presses for college.

My father seconds this. "It will give you time to explore your interests. You're a smart girl, you've got brains. And if you want to keep dancing you could take some modern dance classes, expand your technique. There are lots of different ways to work in the dance world. I should know."

"It's a chancy career at best," says James. He means it kindly.

The actress down the hall who I smoke with advises me to say fuck you to ballet. "You could be an actress," she says, and coaches me—an act of true generosity—in Helena's "How happy some o'er other some can be" speech from *A Midsummer Night's Dream*. (My singing voice is terrible; musical theater is not an option.) I go to one audition, for the drama department of a liberal arts college. I'm herded into a waiting room filled with other applicants. A person from the school wants to see us participate in a group "warm-up." We're instructed to pick an animal and improvise its behavior. The room—teenagers in jeans and T-shirts and sneakers—erupts into an enthusiastic menagerie. I find the exercise wildly humiliating and, furious in my full skirt and bolero jacket, give an imitation of the cat Olga when someone sits in her favorite chair at Bank Street. (Frozen posture, hostile stare.) This is also how I deliver my speech to the judges, a half hour later. Drama school, I decide, is out.

In the spring, I send photos and videotapes and attend auditions for every ballet company I can, large and small. Two girls at my school are offered apprenticeships, but I receive no offers. One director does keep me till the end of the audition, has me learn some choreography with two other girls who've also been selected. I think, *This is it.* I dance well and I know it. After, the director asks to speak with me and says, with great kindness, "You're gorgeous, Carlisle. I wish I could give you a place. But I'm afraid you'd pull focus in the corps. And I don't have any boys right now for your height." I thank him for his honesty, and he asks me out for dinner. I go, thinking he might change his mind. He doesn't. He's very clear he is *not* hiring me, but he does want to sleep with me and doesn't stop trying until the third time I say no. This incident, conceivably traumatic, doesn't register as such at the time. It was a *great* audition; I *nearly* got a job. Maybe someone else will say yes?

No one else does. No after no after no. They sometimes—often—say it with words of regret or praise, but all I hear is the "no."

James calls me up and we have a long conversation. "The ballet world is filled with most of the same prejudices as any other institution," he says. "Plus a few specialties of their own. This isn't a reflection of your dancing. You're so special. Don't give up on yourself."

But I do give up. I drag myself through classes or find excuses to skip them: exaggerating mild strains, inventing dizzy spells. I lie in my dorm bed, pinned to the lumpy mattress with self-loathing. It is clear to me my defect is not one of extra inches but of deficiencies in the soul. Real artists are brave, cannot be crushed. Look at all the obstacles *other* people overcome, much greater than mine. Look at me, lying here, a deserter from the battlefield.

An acceptance letter arrives from the college where I gave my horrendous acting audition. I think they must be insane but will later understand that every drama department needs at least one girl who can play the middle-aged woman, or old lady, and some combination of my size and fury pointed to these casting possibilities.

I'm seventeen. I feel like my life is over.

I decide to go to college. I cut my long hair and dye it red. When I visit Bank Street that summer, James gives me a copy of Uta Hagen's *Respect for Acting*—her studio is right down the street—and my father brings home videotapes of movies starring Lauren Bacall, his favorite actress. I show up at school with a suitcase full of lipstick and vintage men's suits I've hunted down in thrift stores. I've even acquired a gold cigarette case. I don't realize that costuming is not a personality. I adopt a mid-Atlantic accent and tell people I'm from "all over" rather than Ohio. In movement class, I hide my flexibility. I'm afraid people will pity the burned-out ballet dancer and think projecting a cool, sardonic confidence will be more impressive. I get so many things wrong. "You seem super guarded," an almost-friend tells me. I think this is a compliment until she adds that "we all have insecurities." I shrug, cross my pantsuited legs, and tap a cigarette against my case.

Do I tone this act down eventually? A little. But by then I've discovered the pleasures of solitude and acquired the habit of loneliness. These are hard to give up. I read constantly, add a minor in English, get a job at the library. I have sex but not boyfriends and can't tell if that's my decision or theirs. I survive my bouts of self-loathing by constructing and completing regimens of self-improvement. "You're so disciplined," people say. "So controlled." I have learned they don't always mean it as praise. I also know it's not true. I'm not disciplined, I'm frightened.

I want to belong to something but can't think of what. I like learning about dramaturgy, lights and sets, timing and motivation, more than I enjoy acting *inside* these things. I do well in academics but suspect I'm not a serious thinker, a true intellectual.

When I listen to music, I make dances in my head, but consider this a form of daydreaming only. I know what the ballet world is, got as far as the doorway and no further. Becoming a choreographer is not a thing I ever consider.

For a long time, I will tell myself that I didn't become as good a dancer as I was meant to be because I didn't become as good a *person* as I was meant to be. A question of morals. In later years, after dance and I have found each other again, I will say that I needed to grow up and understand myself before I could understand what I wanted to make. When I finally stepped through the doorway of dance, I will say, I did it as a different person. Yes. Maybe. At any rate, here I am.

But another doorway remained, as did that younger version of myself. She's here too. It isn't ballet she wanted to enter, but Bank Street. For her, it was always that.

Pavane

Afternoon in Los Angeles. I'm doing a pavane in my living room because of this job coming up where I need to provide Baroque choreography for a movie. I've been told strict historical accuracy isn't as important to the director as "wit," which could mean absolutely anything at all (including strict historical accuracy), so I need to have options ready.

I'm doing a pavane in my living room because I need to make arrangements to go to New York, and I'd much rather work. I'm also trying to calm down. You can be angry and freaked out *or* you can do Baroque court dances, but you can't do both.

Do I bring Robert and James something? A scrapbook from the past nineteen years? Videos of my work? An itemized bill for all the therapy I didn't have? Oh, petulance is no fun at my age. Flat-out rage has more dignity.

I'm going to work on this pavane. It's a simple processional dance, very useful for film actors, who often get a little hectic if they have to learn choreography. (I would never say it out loud, but it's easier to teach an engineer to dance than most movie stars.) What I should have ready is an arsenal of easy pavanes for the actors and a kicky galliard for the background dancers or in case one or more of the actors is coordinated. These are things I can do. Part of being a working artist is you work when you don't feel like it. I don't need to be inspired, or in the mood, or "not in pain."

Note: You can dance a baroque pavane with rage. But it's not musically appropriate and feels weird. The lute and the recorder are not instruments for fury.

I'm tired of carrying things I don't need to carry. I'm bored with my inner child and her resentments. I'm in my forties. Surely, I've developed more interesting needs.

Maybe not.

Fuck.

And now my phone is ringing. James. I'm working, I don't want to hear his voice, his suffering. The pain of James is not my subject anymore. A flume of panic shoots through me.

What if this is James calling to tell me it's too late? Robert is dead.

I can't answer. It feels certain. He is dead.

I missed it. Him. Here it is. The missing, the ending.

I stare at the phone until it stops ringing.

He's dead. We've all lost each other. This is what it feels like.

It's 10:00 a.m. on a Sunday. I'm working on a pavane. The structure of a pavane is A-A-B-B-C-C. We can understand counterpoint as—

My phone is ringing again. James. I have to. I have to do this.

"Oh, Carlisle, you're there!" James laughs a little. "I can hardly believe I'm saying that. To be able to call you. What a thing."

He's not dead. James would not sound like this if Robert were dead.

"I just got through to your voicemail," he explains. "And I hung up and thought I'd email you instead, but I didn't want you to see a missed call and— Well . . ." He trails off. I sit on the floor. It's a kind of sinking, really.

"You've always been able to call me." There is cold sweat on my arms, cold chips in my voice.

"I suppose what I mean is the relief that you answered." His own voice is quiet, humble.

I should tell James right now that I'll give Bank Street to him. He needn't tiptoe toward me with his pretty feet.

Except maybe I won't.

I betrayed him too.

I betrayed him *more*.

I'm not sure if he knows that.

I get to my feet.

"Listen," he says. "I don't know what your plans are for coming but please know you can stay at Bank Street. In your room. It's not—we have help that comes—I'm not asking you to do any of that. Caretaking. I just don't want you to think . . . I mean, you're absolutely welcome here and also, we're happy to put you up somewhere close. There's a boutique hotel we've recommended to friends. You'd be our guest there, of course."

"Oh thanks, but I'm staying with friends in Midtown." The lie flies out of me so fast it physically rocks me forward a bit. I grab hold of the mantel of my blocked-over fireplace, fiddle with the ornaments on top of it. Green bud vase. Brass bells.

"Of course. Good. I just wanted you to know—"

"How," I ask, stumbling. "How is he?"

"He wants to be home. It's all I can think about right now. Getting him settled."

"Right. Does he know—"

"That you're coming?"

That I'm coming. That he's dying. What really happened between us all.

"I'm waiting until you're here," James says. "Until it's certain."

I bend down and adjust the Deco fireplace grate I put in front of my nonfunctioning fireplace. I look around for something else that needs fixing or changing. I wish I still smoked.

"He does know he's dying, although we don't talk about it." It seems like James is keeping pace with my—confused—interior monologue. "He's a little anxious, about the obituary." I can imagine James shaking his head, casting his eyes up. "He's afraid they'll use that famous photo of him and LaGrange. And rehash that old story."

That story—my father's being ousted from LaGrange Ballet—is online, is the thing. None of us can control our story anymore. Algorithms are the new Greek chorus.

"He wants the photo of him from the first festival at Boxhill and our wedding photo. I shared the wedding photos with you, didn't I?"

"Yes, they were wonderful."

"I thought of you so often that day."

I should have been there. Robert could have written and said, *We're getting married and we want you to be there,* and the emotion of the moment, even its larger political significance, would have carried us through. His invitation would have been his apology, my presence would have been mine.

I've always wondered what they told people. *Where's Carlisle?*

People would know better than to ask, I guess. My father's famous absolutism.

I never invited them to see my work.

"The days are very long and very short," James says. "Everything takes forever. This slow, sort of numbing waiting and then rushing and taking care of this and that and then one gets to the end of the day and you want it all back to do again but also for it all to be over. The most absurd phrases come into my head. Grandiose poetry. And then I go to Duane Reade to get toothpaste. Death *is* ordinary."

My jaw hurts.

"I feel small," he says, with surprise, with intensity.

"I'll be there soon." I can't help it. The compassion slips out as easily as the earlier lie. I can see his face, beloved by me for so long. He must be so afraid. Of losing my father. Losing his home.

"I'm so glad, Carlisle," he says. "I can't tell you how glad."

He says he has to go. I promise I'll send my itinerary as soon as I have it. We say goodbye.

I feel small.

This is what he does—what he's always done. Bound me to him, to his feelings.

What an education it gave me.

I loved James so much, once. It's not been repeated, the *way* that I did. A person who was also a world, who *let me in*. Maybe this long separation has nurtured that sensation, kept it preserved in amber like a fossil. A treasure I don't want reappraised. Take that summer in New York. If it was a summer where certain illusions I had about my future were dashed, it was also a time of great magic. It was also the summer of James.

L'isle joyeuse

James, in the summer of 1988, is forty-five, forty-six? An odd age to welcome the constant company of a fifteen-year-old girl. I don't think about that. I'm determined to be seen as a kindred artist spirit. A true child of Bank Street.

In truth, James, in the summer of 1988, is a man in retreat.

The first treatment drugs for HIV have been approved. They are hard to get and wildly expensive if you don't have the right insurance. Not everyone can tolerate their side effects, which are sometimes ferocious. ACT UP is staging protests. President Reagan has finally addressed the issue in a speech. A quilt has been made, to honor the dead.

Every week, more names, more funerals.

My father and James have taken the tests. They need only remain faithful—or careful—to stay alive. Somehow this complicates things. Where there was choice, there is now survival, what was a matter of trust is now life or death. The balance of power between the two begins to tip back and forth, but violently, as when one person on a seesaw leaps off and sends the other player crashing to earth with a thud.

Will they stay together? They must. Are they staying together because they must? Who needs who more?

Robert says, of James, "He could have had anyone."

James says, of Robert, "It's something, to know you're another person's great love."

The one who needs the least will always hold the power.

They need each other too much, maybe. It frightens them.

The funerals don't stop.

They do love each other.

James is exhausted. He feels trapped, nostalgic, regretful. A midlife crisis? A return of his illness? It is hard to know what is depression, and what is an appropriate response to a plague on your house.

These are not things I understand the summer I'm fifteen, but I'm always pretending to be wiser than I am, and what James wants to do is talk. This is thrilling to me. I get along with the girls in my class at SAB, but without a common dormitory, there's not a lot of socializing. Or I'm not invited. I do see groups of friends forming, but I'm happy to take the subway back to Bank Street and let the stories unfold, hardly daring to ask questions for fear they will interrupt the flow. This isn't sympathetic listening, the compassionate ear of a friend. It's love and greed.

James doesn't talk about what is happening, has happened, to his friends and colleagues, old lovers, students, teachers. On the streets outside Bank Street, young men lean on canes, are helped up flights of stairs, wait for a visibly healthy friend to flag a cab. Inside, the more distant past is James's subject. What he wants me to know, to understand, to remember, of himself. He is forty-six and has survived, is surviving. He talks like a dying man. I listen. He pulls out photographs of himself from yellowed boxes, selects one, squints at the date on the back: "1947." I examine a small James holding a ball in his outstretched hand, striped T-shirt tucked into his shorts.

James tells me he was a happy boy. "I was *delightful*. Mother always said I had poise. A beauty pageant word, but she *was* from Louisiana. Frances Rose Patterson. She carried the South with her, but we never lived there so it was years before I understood her. I can't tell you the relief, when I saw my first Tennessee Williams play. Mother explained! She'd always been out of context."

I love the sound of clinking ice in James's gin and tonic as he waves it around, talking. He tells me stories about his mother while we cook together. I'm learning to chop properly, to be interested in food.

"Mother was a force. Everything was either a catastrophe or a sensation, although she was secretly quite competent. The best possible mother for a gay artist boy. Of course, I was also the best son for a lonely, beautiful woman. Some ghastly little straight boy, running around whacking things and shooting BB guns, would have been a tragedy for her. She taught piano. I played well for a child, won prizes, gave performances. A ten-year-old playing 'L'isle joyeuse.' Sensation! Only that was the extent of it. My hands got bigger, but my playing didn't. Now I'm much worse of course."

The books by my bed are *Howards End*, *The Pursuit of Love*, and *The Awkward Age*. I hear the characters in his voice. James never asks, "What's your point?" He tells stories with no purpose, taking his time.

"Once—this was in Bedford, Massachusetts—I ran into my parents' bedroom at night, with a nosebleed. I was seven or eight. Moonlight was coming in from the window above her bed—they always had separate beds, unremarkable for the time, you know—and she was lying there, in full negligee with some sort of plaster affair on her face. 'Frownies' they were called, to keep the frown lines from forming. Her lips were so pale, for a moment I was certain she was dead. And then her lips moved, and I saw her breathing. She wasn't dead, it was only the first time I'd seen her without lipstick."

There's no central air at Bank Street. James and my father's bedroom has an air conditioner, but James says the main room's windows are too beautiful to mar with a unit. He has a system for the fans and insists we swap bedrooms. "You need a deeper sleep than I do." Often in the morning I find him stretched out on the daybed by the piano. If there's always a gin and tonic glass on the floor by his side, it's also always on a coaster. Only occasionally do his words slur before bedtime.

Fourth of July comes. The cats are strangely undisturbed by the fireworks. "They've already seen the worst of a revolution," James says, referring to their Romanov pasts. To my surprise, he puts an American flag in one of the windows.

"My father was a pilot during the war. Then an engineer. I haven't the faintest idea of what he actually did, other than it was connected to planes. He never talked about the war. All of us who had fathers in wars say this. 'He never talked about the war.'"

He moves to the piano, plays a page of Scriabin.

"He hung himself in 1959, the summer I was at Tanglewood. It was Mother who found him. In the garage. He'd put down a tarp, underneath the ladder, below the noose. A tarp. For spills? To gather up his body? I don't remember who told me this detail. It can't have been Mother."

He moves from the piano, scooping up a cat.

"I'll find you some pictures. He was handsome. Away a great

deal. Whenever he returned there'd be a tremendous fuss, all his favorite meals and a new dress for Mother and I was trotted out to show him all my school reports and so on. He wasn't formidable. I liked him. He made these lovely and very gentle attempts to instill manly arts in me. One was taken fishing and so forth. Oh, there was never any question about what I was. From a very small boy I knew. Watching our neighbor Mr. Laughton wash his car from an upstairs window. Robert Taylor on the poster for *Ivanhoe*. One knows."

We walk to World of Video, on Greenwich Avenue, pass a scrum of men, nearly naked, drunk. There's a birthday boy, wearing a crown and sash. One of the celebrants shakes a boa at me. "You have a beautiful night, Princess!" "Happy Birthday!" I call out, and they all cheer.

These are the men, I think, who will like me.

James walks the streets of the Village, sometimes with a small smile, sometimes pensive, grave, his hands clasped behind his back, like visiting royalty inspecting the troops.

At Bank Street, we watch old MGM movies. James appears to enjoy the verbal sparring or romantic escapades but tells me, "A man kissing a woman never looks *natural* to me. There used to be something called the Hays Code. For films and television. What you couldn't show, and so forth. Absurd and racist and we lost all our most fun gay representations, but the single benefit was one wasn't *forced* to constantly watch heterosexual groping.

"You understand," he tells me. "I was *not* a tortured queer, not at all. I loved thinking about men, always. It didn't bother me to hide it. I wasn't ashamed, it amused me. Not that I took tremendous pains over concealment. It was more like hiding in plain sight."

We visit the Frick Museum, to look at the Whistler portraits

James admires. "There are more important things here, but I want you to see these." One of the women in the portraits stands like James, with her hands clasped behind her back. "I think she looks a bit like you," he says, and I feel beautiful and soft too, like the soft pinks and grays in the painting. I feel *painted*.

We return, again and again, to the subject of his childhood.

"Father got a job in Denmark. He kept being sent back and forth to Greenland, where the U.S. was involved in an air base, very controversial and much hated by the Danes, I believe. Mother fell in love with Copenhagen—so clean!—so that's where she and I settled. We lived in an apartment building, my first. The boy in the flat next to ours was my age and enrolled at the Royal Danish Ballet School. This was explained properly to Mother, as a thing of pride. Well, she loved anything with the word *Royal* in the title, so I was sent too. Those were the *truly* happy years."

James describes the red coats of the Danish postmen. How he used to watch men make nets at the harbor. The feel of cobblestones under bicycle wheels. The serenity and joy of ballet class. The power.

"It was all more fun for me than for Mother. If she was out of context in New England, you can imagine *Denmark*. Though nothing is more delightful, really, than Danish spoken with a southern accent. It sounds positively *Martian*. My mother befriended some British mothers, and they all clubbed together for schooling. I rubbed along well enough with the British children, but Oskar, my neighbor, was my real friend. We went everywhere on our bicycles together. In all my life there has never been anything more innocent, more perfect, than those bicycle rides."

James lies on the rug. Stretches his back—with a groan. Stares at the ceiling.

"Even now, I find myself thinking, *I'll go back*. As if one could pick up a life left at fourteen. There's no back *left*."

He asks if I want to come visit a friend with him. The friend is at St. Vincent's Hospital, in the AIDS ward. I say yes but am frightened. The disease lays waste to bodies, to minds. When the moment arrives, James says I shouldn't come. "I won't know what to tell you about what you'll see," he says. "There aren't enough rooms. People are in the hallways. It's hard." I'm ashamed of being relieved. The next day, in the subway on the way to class, I stand opposite a shivering man. He's wearing long sleeves and a scarf although it's summer. His scarf comes loose. Lesions on his neck, his jaw, black and thick. I've seen this before but always averted my eyes. Now I try to look and convey compassion, sympathy. Our eyes meet. He reads my efforts with fury, then contempt. Then he simply looks ill. I watch pain and fear consume all his attention. Later, I will fantasize about helping him, rescuing him, saving him. At the time, I do nothing. He gets off at the next stop.

Everywhere in the Village, on murals, on flyers, on signs: SILENCE = DEATH.

James takes up the story of his father's death and puts it down. Picks it up, puts it down. I gather the pieces, not quite putting them together. We go hunting among bins at the flea market for antique drawer pulls. We're refurbishing the furniture of my room. I think this is a good portent. I will not have to go back to school. We always stop for coffee at the same restaurant, sit at the counter. "I suppose everyone assumes I'm your gay uncle," James says. Secretly, I think we strike a romantic chord, mentor and protégée, something nineteenth century or European or, anyway, *interesting*.

He tells me about his high school years. His father's depression being explained as migraines. The sad leave-taking of Copenhagen and return to Massachusetts.

"There was no more dancing, once we were back in the States. Well, no more lessons. Mother and I had a sort of pact. After graduation I could go to Copenhagen or London and resume my training. At least for a year or two, before college, and in return I would *get along*. She was talking about discretion, about appearances. That wonderful southern way of dealing with oddities. She'd grown up with a beloved Bachelor Uncle who took her to concerts and cut out dresses for her paper dolls. He'd died an alcoholic."

Every block in the Village has something to say for itself. James Baldwin lived here. Jackson Pollock. On the six blocks of Bank Street alone: John Lennon and Yoko Ono, John Cheever, Merce Cunningham and John Cage, Patricia Highsmith, Willa Cather. A famous acting studio run by Uta Hagen and Herbert Berghof. I say, "Oh wow," even when I don't know the names James is saying. We step over the crack vials at Washington Square Park, watch the break-dancers, eat bagels on a bench, go to the Strand Book Store and Tower Records. We talk a lot about music. I can't play very well, but I read competently and sometimes sit next to James and turn pages. I think he plays brilliantly and don't understand what he means when he says he doesn't. This is also a part of his theme, his reminiscences, a general sense of having come just short of greatness.

"Oh, I had no illusions, not really. The piano was useful, for getting along, in Mother's sense of the phrase. I was let out of doing sports, on account of my supposed gift, and it gave me something to do at parties and school things. I really did think about music a great deal. *That* was sincere. I was always making dances in my room, but I thought I would do both. I went to Tanglewood, you know, the summer before my senior year. Leonard Bernstein. Pierre Monteux. Isaac Stern. Heaven for me in more ways than one. I was allowed to board in Pittsfield."

He makes ice packs for my aching knees—another growth spurt that summer. I lie on the couch, and he sits on the floor with his back against it. I watch his profile.

"Father didn't leave a note. What could he say? He was very gentle with me, on those fishing trips, and in backyard lessons. I think he was trying to show me how I might get along. That we were the same. It's rather touching when you think about it, a gay father tossing a ball with his gay son, not teaching him to catch so much as teaching him to *pass*."

He stretches out his legs, points his pretty feet.

"I never asked Mother about it. She said something to me, right before she died. That she blamed herself, always. Father had tried to tell her once, about himself, and she'd not let him."

His hair is thinning, in the back. I don't touch him.

"She loved Robert," James says. "I'm sorry you didn't get to meet her. She was here for every Christmas until the year she died, which was right before Isabel started letting you come back. I'll show you some pictures of them together."

But he doesn't move.

"Mother took Father's death better than one would have expected. Better than a Tennessee Williams heroine, better than Maggie would have taken Brick's. She drove over from Bedford to Pittsfield, and we went for a walk. She'd pinned a cherry brooch to her lapel. I remember thinking she couldn't be so very upset. You wouldn't be able to pin a brooch on if you were *broken*. I understood her bravery, too late. I just wanted to stay at Tanglewood, you see. I wanted to go abroad. I was almost free. But I couldn't leave her. Despite the cherries on the lapel."

We take the train to Boxhill. My father, waiting with the Cadillac. I talk about my classes. James talks about his classes. We talk about the cats, the neighbors, the hunt for drawer pulls. We both take pains to make it seem as if nothing in particular is happening.

What *is* happening? Only stories. Why the air of secrecy, of conspiracy? James and I not looking at each other, giving Robert all our attention. We both love him.

Why are James and I pretending we don't love each other?

James talks of us taking a weekend trip to Cambridge, where he went to college. I don't care about Harvard—I know I won't be going to university myself, because I'll be hired by a ballet company after high school—but love traveling with James. In the end, the logistics overwhelm him. He can't plan, he says. He just can't plan right now.

"But I adored Harvard. Of course, I found out right away I would *not* become a concert pianist. For the most part, one can only become as good a musician as one is meant to be. It's the same with dance. For every artist, there's a ceiling. As a teacher, your role is to make the very best of what is there. That's why I don't push my students. I explain. I say, 'Here is what it wants to be, here is what it should be.' They make of it what they can, or not. But one is always hoping. For that one student who transforms. Who takes your words and becomes better than nature intended."

James makes college sound fun although I think it can't be the way he describes anymore, if you go by movies. He digs out college photographs but flips through them quickly, not finding what he's looking for.

"I began studying dance again, in Boston. I'd lost some ground since my Royal Ballet days, but I never wanted to be a performer, not truly. I wanted to make dances. But then I became ill, you see, for the first time. Quite seriously ill."

Then he's back at the piano, playing furiously for a few minutes, breaking off. I lean against the window.

"I did tell Mother, before she died, that she needn't have blamed herself, for Father. Because when depression came for me, I understood there was nothing she could have done or said. I even understood the tarp below the noose."

What he understood, I don't know.

James in Denmark, James in Bedford, James at Harvard, quite seriously ill. James eventually making it to England and being hired into an opera ballet company. Wanting to make dances of his own, sneaking into theaters, London, the sixties. Ideas for dances not made. Explanations of why *this* choreographer is great, why this other one is second rate. James's brief job as a dance critic, for an arts journal. Feeling out of step with the times, the tastes. Not doing drugs. "All one's friends were older too, which does make a difference." Another illness, which sends him back to Frances Rose in Massachusetts. An offer to teach ballet at a studio in Boston. Choreographing his first ballet for a fledgling company.

James and me, lying on the floor by the windows, our feet in the air. "For thinking," he always says. I ask about the ballet he choreographed.

"I used Piano Sonata no. 2 in G-sharp minor. Scriabin. The music *was* difficult for the dancers. But it came together so beautifully. *Boats in the Harbor Sway* I called it. From a poem by Akhmatova. *I see the boats in the harbor sway / they didn't bring me a letter today.* There are certain poems you must read now, Carlisle, when they will make you feel seen. Later on, they'll make you feel invisible."

Our feet are nearly the same size.

"Robert Martin came to see my work and said he wanted *Boats in the Harbor Sway* for LaGrange Ballet. Sensation!

"Well, an invitation to work with LaGrange dancers, to be included in the season. LaGrange Ballet was really wonderful then, you know. When Robert left, he took all the good taste with him, but even when the company fell apart in the eighties, the dancers were still marvelous. So it was an enormous opportunity for me. I ought not to have been allowed, really. The first rehearsal, I vomited on the way to the studios. We should make a pilgrimage. I remember the alley."

He looks happy, though, remembering.

"Nothing, nobody, could have been kinder than Robert. He would come to the studio, in the afternoons, and watch from the corner. The dancers were so lovely. An incredible gift. Time and six dancers I liked. And Robert. Increasingly Robert."

I don't think—yet—about how all this was happening when my father was still married to my mother. Increasingly, James, decreasingly, Isabel. (And me.) At the moment, I'm only following a story of art and love growing together.

"LaGrange really was a dreadful choreographer, you know," James tells me. "We'll talk about that another time. Essentially Robert was forced out of the company because he had taste and sense and LaGrange became a fool the way men who put their names on things are always fools. Robert was everything good about the company. One could really talk to him, about dance. He understood what one was trying to do.

"When the Great Schism came, between Robert and La-

Grange, I withdrew my ballet from the company's repertoire. Well, I couldn't let them have it. My allegiance was to Robert. It needed to be total, you understand. My loyalty. Did I sacrifice my career?

"I could have made other dances. Of course, I could have. But it was a hard time. I became seriously ill again. The stress.

"There's no video of my ballet. I don't know if I should be glad of that or not. If I were to see it now, and find it dreadful, it would kill me off.

"And if I were to see it now, and think it wonderful, it would kill me off. Possibly faster."

I'm called into the SAB office a few days after this and told that I'm not being offered a place for the year.

James asks me if I want to take his class and I do. It's wonderful. Filled with professional dancers who seem unbelievably glamorous and cool. I love how they listen to James, laugh at his jokes, nod their heads at his corrections. I love the way he teaches, the combinations of steps he gives. They make me feel like I'm good, and I dance better than I have all summer. What has been missing? Encouragement or my own focus? Maybe if I'd danced with this confidence, I would have gotten an invitation to stay at SAB. James tells me I'm a fabulous dancer. "Really fabulous," he says. "Wonderful movement quality." Immediately I start constructing a new fantasy. SAB is out but James will tell my father I need to stay in New York and study with *him*.

I'm a talented fantasist, but this is a stretch even for me. I know I will have to go back to school.

My father returns from Boxhill, exhausted but happy to see us. He takes me to the Carlyle Hotel for lunch. It's quite different, being with him. I notice, for the first time, that my father and

James don't move through the world in quite the same ways. My father takes up more room, on the street, on the subway. People step out of the way for him, rather than the other way around.

The restaurant at the Carlyle is wildly elegant. I've dressed up: makeup, jewelry, a Moschino suit bought at a consignment store for fifteen dollars. It has a wild, bold print and is entirely too old for me—a suit?—but I know the designer is fancy and it fits me perfectly. "You're the shape designers make clothes for," my father says, with approval. "Those beautiful coat hanger shoulders. You look terrific."

There's a strange moment when I see a woman at a nearby table eyeing my father in a sardonic way. He notices my distraction, follows my gaze. When he turns back, his eyebrows are raised. "I guess you do look grown up," he says. When the waiter comes, Robert orders for me in a raised voice, beginning with "My *daughter* will have—"

He asks me about my summer, the old game: What were your favorite things? Instead I repeat capsule versions of almost everything James has told me. I don't intend to do this. It's me, claiming my share of James.

My father listens with a smile that changes degrees and angles. After a bit, it occurs to me to think of how he might be receiving this stream of information and, with a sharp retraction in my ribs, that I'm betraying James's confidence. Are all these things secrets? Will he tell James? I fall silent.

"James, James, James," my father says.

I blush.

"I know just how you feel," he says.

We look at each other. For a moment I almost feel sorry for us.

My father says what he really wants to do now is see a dumb movie. James never wants to go to dumb movies, he says, and he hates going by himself. "And you've had a summer full of high art and big talk." We choose *Die Hard*, as there's a Russian ballet star in the cast, share a box of Junior Mints, and have a ball.

When we return to Bank Street, he pauses at the gate outside and says, "It helped me a lot, knowing you were here with him. Thank you." He puts his hand on my back, and then hugs me. "I only wish I could've been here too."

The night before I leave, James comes to Carlisle's Room, where I'm reading, and thanks me for keeping him company. "You've been a true companion," he says. "And very patient with me. You're a wonderful person, Carlisle."

A Magic Egg

Afternoon in Los Angeles. I've abandoned the pavane for the day. I need to be a person capable of handling ordinary things. I must plan this trip to New York. Do I google "how long for deathbed vigil?" No. There's a hard crimp in my stomach. My agent calls and I hesitate over answering. I'm not positive I can make my voice sound normal. Only, it might be about this film job. Choreographers are the only people on a movie set *not* covered by a union. My agent has to hustle producers to put me on a "dancer" contract so I can get SAG benefits. I need this job to keep my health care. Maybe I won't have to sound normal on this call. Maybe I can be upset at American capitalism.

"Hi, Annika!"

"Check your email," she says, by way of greeting. "But let me just say, I have three words for you. Four actually."

She pronounces the name—three words—of a ballet company in England. It's on my dream list of companies I'd love to work with. I met the artistic director last year, at a festival in France where an excerpt from my ballet *Artemisia* was performed. A surge of adrenaline racetracks through my body.

"What's the fourth word?" I ask, but I'm already thinking, *Artemisia*. What if they want *Artemisia*? I'll be able to revisit, revise. Superb dancers. World-class lighting and sets. Full fucking orchestra. The director was lovely and said both smart and kind things about my work. The director was a *she*, which can sometimes work against one's chances, but I did feel like we connected. *Artemisia!* But maybe—

"*Firebird*," Annika says.

"*Firebird* what?" I'm almost crying, imagining the curtain rising on a fully realized *Artemisia* and the opening gesture and none of this has anything to do with my dying father and—

"*Firebird*, the ballet. Check your email."

I move from kitchen to bedroom, where my laptop is. Goddamnit. Some scandal or weird thing has happened, and Annika is calling to gossip. Her list is mostly hip-hop and modern choreographers but she's a true ballet fan and follows everything.

Just when I think I've gotten hope calibrated in my body so it doesn't exhaust me, something like this happens.

I open the email she's forwarded and read.

This company in England, that I would love to work with, that I *must* work with, is interested in commissioning me for a new version of *Firebird*. They'd like to hear my ideas.

"Are you reading?"

"Yes," I say.

I walk with the phone back to the kitchen and open a cupboard, look at my dishes. I move to the stove and turn a burner on and off. I scratch my knee.

"Carlisle?"

Most of my work runs about twenty minutes, and while everything I do is an exploration of relationships, I'm not a storyteller choreographer. I've only made two full-length narrative works, *Artemisia* and *My Friend*. I've never touched any of the big classical ballets.

The music for *Firebird* is Stravinsky. *Early* Stravinsky.

Annika starts saying things about time lines and how she's set up a phone call for Friday, but it will have to be morning because London is eight hours ahead.

I always think of *Firebird*—well, I never think of it, but if pressed—as a kind of budget *Swan Lake*, shorter and with a happier ending. Something a company can shake out of the repertoire every couple of years to showcase their powerhouse ballerina and get butts in seats.

"*Firebird*," I say.

"I know! This is the breakthrough thing."

Everything I've done in the past five years has been the "breakthrough" thing.

"*Firebird*," I repeat, because I can't stop saying it. "*Firebird* is like—"

Annika has an encyclopedic knowledge of ballet. She's probably more familiar with *Firebird* than I am. It was a signature role for the first Black female principal dancer of ABT. There've been—

Wait.

"Oh my God," I say. "I haven't seen a full production of *Firebird* since I was a kid. I think in twenty years I've only watched a few excerpts or read reviews. I don't *know* it."

"Okay, well, you have almost a week to get up to speed, but I think that's fine," Annika says. "It's not *Swan Lake*, it's a one-act. And this company knows your work. They'll be open to a new interpretation. They'll want that. I mean, my first thought," she says, "was you're *perfect*."

I pull myself together. It is a fantastic opportunity I need to seize with both hands.

"You don't have anything going on right now, do you?" Annika asks. "You can use the week to focus?"

"Of course," I say.

She says congratulations and she'll send on details about the call when she gets them, and we hang up.

I have six days to come up with some ideas of how I might interpret this one-hundred-year-old ballet I don't remember, and be ready to discuss whatever my ideas are, in such a way as to convince them I am indeed perfect. Somewhere in these six days, I will see my dying father.

I'm not a feeble thing. I can do this. And in ten minutes I've found a red-eye for New York for tonight, booked myself three nights in a hotel in Midtown, and reserved a space for my car at the Park 'N Fly at LAX.

There. See. And if my hands are shaking it's because of *Firebird*, a huge commission if I can secure it, if I can make something of it. I move to the case where I keep my reference books and pull out *Masterpieces of the Ballet*. I dropped it in a bathtub at some point in the thirty years I've owned it, and the pages crackle as I turn them. I do remember the story, basically.

A Prince Ivan gets lost in a mysterious forest. Meets a magical creature, a Firebird. Captures her. She begs for freedom and when he grants it, the Firebird gives him a magical feather. Prince Ivan continues on in the forest, where he encounters dancing maidens, playing with apples. Falls in love with one, a princess. (No name for her.) She explains they're all prisoners of an Evil Sorcerer, Kaschei, who rules the forest. Kaschei shows up and summons his monster minions to attack Prince Ivan. The prince uses the magical feather to summon the Firebird. She shows up, puts monsters and Kaschei to sleep with her powers. Ivan kills Kaschei by smashing his soul, which is in a magic egg. Everyone is freed from spell. Prince marries Princess.

This is traditional, classical ballet. Far-away realm. Magical creature. Handsome Prince. Beautiful Princess. Bad Sorcerer. Monsters. Maidens. Conflict. Resolution.

Classical ballet doesn't traffic in your bullshit.

There are several iterations of the score, Stravinsky's original 1910 version, and shorter suites he arranged later. I've never used Stravinsky in my work. It's not that I dislike him, it's almost like an allergy. I acknowledge he's great, and he makes me a little sick. I choose a recording of the full score online and lie on my rug, with my legs in the air, for thinking.

The two full-length ballets I've done were both about women, so they might be coming to me because they want a sort of feminist *Firebird*. There is, when you think about it, quite a lot of vagina-adjacent imagery in the plot. Enchanted forest. Maidens and apples. A magic egg. It's also a plot I don't care about.

I can't stand this music. I mean, I hate it. Fuck. What the fuck.

I watch some *Firebird* videos online. A re-creation of the original 1910 choreography by Mikhail Fokine, sumptuous and unapologetically magical; Dance Theatre of Harlem's version, streamlined and elegant, set in a Caribbean jungle. Another from a famous French choreographer where the Firebird is danced by a man who is meant to be either Jesus or a communist. I read about a splashy new production, by one of the leading choreographers—also a man. I'm sweating.

The timing is not great. I'm not in my best mind or body.

I need to pack for New York. I need sleep.

Isabel is calling. She will—I think—have been feeling bad about our last conversation. I suppose I want her to feel bad, which is an unpleasant thing to recognize. I answer the call and jabber on about *Firebird* and accept her congratulations and, yes, yes, it comes at a difficult time, but anyway didn't she dance Balanchine's version of the ballet?

"I was a monster," Isabel says. "In 1970. When we did it again, I was a Maiden. So, did you figure out when you're going to New York?"

"Tonight." I move to the bathroom cupboard, where I keep a bag of travel-size things. "Got a cheap red-eye. What were rehearsals like?"

"For *Firebird*? They were fun. Won't you be tired, flying all night?"

"I'm giving myself a day to settle before I see them. I'll do some research at the Performing Arts library. So I sound, you know, intelligent and prepared and all that when I talk to the people in London."

"I'm sure you will. You're not staying at Bank Street?"

"They offered, but I thought that might be a little stressful. For everyone." I move from bathroom to kitchen, to get vitamins. Dying is no excuse to let one's regimens slide, especially when you're not the one who's dying. "I can't say I'm crazy about the score for *Firebird*. Or the plot."

"The music is brilliant," Isabel corrects me. "And plot isn't important. I once heard someone ask Mr. B what a certain ballet was about and he said, 'It's about time, dear. It takes twelve minutes to dance it.'"

"Ha."

There's a little silence. I think maybe I need to stretch my back again.

"*Firebird* closed the opening night of the Stravinsky Festival in 'seventy-two," Isabel says. "I was pregnant with you when I danced it. I was glad of the Maiden dress. We didn't get a lot of forgiving costumes. I was worried about showing. The funny thing was, there was one step Mr. B always told us to do 'like pregnant lady.'"

"That's funny." I lie on my back and press my hand into my pelvis.

"I felt you move for the first time during *Firebird*," she says. "Onstage."

I take my hand off my pelvis.

"I thought it was a sign I should stop dancing," she continues. "But I guess it was really just you complaining about Stravinsky."

We laugh. In my mind, I search out her body. To think of Isabel is to pull one's shoulders back.

"Do you have any ideas about your *Firebird*?" she asks. "What you might do?"

I'm surprised. She's never asked about my process much. Yuto is more interested in what I do, and he's a policy officer for the UN.

No. I always do this. I skip over the great moments. She has come to see a lot of my work. After she saw my *Artemisia*, she grabbed my arm and said, "I would have loved to dance that. Your dancers are so lucky."

"No," I say. "I just got the news and I've never really thought about this ballet. I'm a little— Well obviously there's sort of a lot going on. I'm trying to—"

What do I even want her to say? What do I want *any* of us to say?

"I know," Isabel says.

She does?

"I've been thinking since we talked," she goes on. "I guess this sort of thing brings up the past. Fragments. I never wanted to dwell on all that. New York days. Dance. Your father."

I wait. I stretch out my legs, point my feet. My feet are good, but I didn't get her superbly arched insteps.

"I guess I never talked too much about that time," she says.

She didn't. We have a family talent for not saying things. The exception was my aunt Pat, who I only got to know at the end of her life. She lived in Nevada, but when she got sick, she came to Los Angeles for consultations at Cedars-Sinai. She stayed at my apartment for a week, refusing sympathy and telling family stories in which she alone possessed common sense. Unsentimental, confident in her prejudices, often terribly funny.

"Grandma told me a few stories. And Aunt Pat."

"Oh really?" A sigh, but then, with asperity, "I don't know what *they* knew about it."

Isabel's relations with her mother and sister were like those knots you get in necklaces. You try to tease them out and end up putting the chain back in the jewelry box.

"I was curious," I say. "Honestly, I always felt like I couldn't ask you much."

"Oh, I would have told you anything."

This is, I suppose, true by her lights. *Rehearsals for* Firebird *were fun.* There, she's told me everything. But for once, she's in the mood for reflection.

"Robert was always supportive of my career. Mother acted as if she were my greatest champion, but it was really Robert. You know when we met, he was completely running LaGrange Ballet."

"I know. Although he never talked about that."

"Your father and LaGrange were funny together. Robert was sort of the straight man. I guess that's funny in retrospect. LaGrange was the kind who'd say, 'I don't care what it costs! I want the tutus to look like they're on fire,' or whatever. You know, when Mr. B didn't have money for costumes, he just had everyone wear practice clothes and it became a *thing*. I heard someone once say that LaGrange was the favorite choreographer of people who didn't know anything about dance. Or music, really. But your father was so loyal. He always did his best. That's why the ending was so humiliating for him. I think some of that was my fault, though. It all kind of combined."

I ask, gently, what she means.

"I had a little bit of a hard time after you were born. And things were starting to get rough between Robert and LaGrange then. Maybe I could have listened more or tried to help. LaGrange had them lock the doors on Robert. There was a lot of gossip about that, in the dance world. Everybody turned their back on him. Except for James."

And just like that, I don't want to hear any more. I stand. There are things I need to do.

"Your father didn't cheat on me," Isabel continues. "He wouldn't have done that. He cried when he told me about falling in love with James. I didn't want to listen or understand or anything like that. I just left and I took you. People say the first two years with a child are the most important. For the bonding. They mean the mother, but they could mean the father too, I don't know. You and Robert missed that. So maybe that's why— If he'd felt like more of a father. If I hadn't taken you away—"

"You were young," I say. I could almost stamp my foot. "He was nineteen years older. And he married you and got you pregnant and then you had postpartum depression. He fell in love with James. What were you supposed to do?"

"Well, what was *he* supposed to do? He fell in love. He begged me not to leave him. I was selfish. I know Mother thought I was doing the wrong thing, and Pat. I didn't listen."

I don't want to hear about my father begging her not to leave him. I try to keep my voice calm.

"You didn't do anything wrong," I say. "What happened between Robert and me, it wasn't because of things you did and didn't do. And if you hadn't left, you wouldn't have met Ben, and had Yuto. Become a physical therapist and helped a lot of people."

"Right."

"Grandma and Aunt Pat had their own agendas or whatever."

"That's true."

"Nobody did anything wrong. People make choices."

Silence.

I get it. Things so seldom feel like *choices*.

"I guess we all have things we wish we'd done a little different," she says.

It occurs to me, not for the first time, that she *knows* what happened between me and Robert and James. It's why she wants me to give Bank Street to James. Atonement. Hers is the flintiest moral code I know.

My father's voice, some of the last words he spoke to me. *I know your mother didn't raise you to behave like this. I know I certainly didn't. Isabel would be horrified to know what you've done.*

Shame lets you know you're in the wrong, which is why you should trust it.

Incorrect. Shame is the bullet of judgment and anyone can wield that gun.

Has my mother been waiting for me to confess? Waiting for me to become a better person?

I tell Isabel I will call her from New York, let her know how things are. "Yes, you have to get ready," she says, something of an understatement.

I put on another recording of *Firebird*. I don't need to fall in love with this music, but I need to understand it, be interested in it, find something in this story I can tell.

I go to the bathroom and consider myself in the oval mirror above the sink, adjusting the dimmers to a level a few degrees below Harsh Reckoning. Has Robert looked for me online in the past nineteen years? I don't look like either of my parents, it's a patchwork. Perhaps I no longer look quite like myself either. The gray hairs get dyed and the frown line between my eyebrows had a collagen injection. Being six-two can be a cool flex for me now, but I'm not off the hook more than any other woman. At this point, it's all about looking like I care while not looking like I'm trying. Despite all those diversity panels, directors of ballet companies would still rather commission a piece from one of the flirty young lads, the swaggering dudes, the boys with attitude. There are fewer ways for a white woman in her forties to be considered cool.

What will Robert think when he looks at me? He was always on the watch for ways I could be seen at my best. Not in a fussy or judgmental way. He praised. "I saw this, and I thought, no one will wear it better than Carlisle."

I used to joke I'd escaped the curse of the male gaze because so many men have to physically look up to meet my eyes. But the male gaze is a God's-eye view, which is to say omnipresent and internalized.

There's still a man in the mirror, watching me look at myself.

The desire for Robert to say, one last time, "Don't you look terrific," takes me by surprise and is so powerful I lean over the sink, catching my breath. The sink, above which are brass Art

Nouveau sconces he might have picked out himself. I'm seeing myself not only through his eyes but through his lighting.

I move into the hallway, where Isabel still waits to catch Balanchine's eye. I don't have any photographs of Robert up, although there's an archival box in the closet I haven't opened in ages. We were still using film cameras when the last ones of us were taken. I type my father's name into Google. The first image that comes up is one of him in 1963 with Leonard LaGrange. This is the famous photo, the one he doesn't want in the obituary. LaGrange is slim, diminutive, neatly bearded, holding up his hands with splayed fingers like he's demonstrating fireworks. In the background, on a chair near the piano, is my father. He's wearing a suit and has his arms folded.

This is my legacy. I come from people who are in the back of the photo. This is my inheritance. To know the precise distance between oneself and greatness.

I press my fist against my sternum. *I never wanted to dwell on all that,* Isabel had said. *New York days. Dance. Your father.* She'd used an odd word for her memories. *Fragments.*

I need to pack. What do you wear to your father's deathbed? Layers?

I enjoy packing. I do it well. I can live for months out of one duffel. I can fold a coat into a fucking tote. What do I need for this trip? Will there be one big meeting and then a dismissal? Will I be sent to a lawyer, asked to sign over papers, giving the deed or—fuck, I don't even know what *comes* with property—to James?

How can they ask that, of me. How can I refuse.

I try, again, to picture my father's body. The last time he hugged me went unnoted by my brain and I have no memory of it.

I remember his words, at Bank Street. Telling me to go.

Something in the music of *Firebird* distracts me. Mad piccolo and flute with string action underneath. I close my eyes, see nothing, feel nothing.

I stand in front of my closet. When I travel for work it's all about clothes I can work in, plus one fantastic suit for anything official, which I wear on the plane and then immediately take off and steam upon arrival. Robert always steered me toward colors, belts, low necks, high waists. "Don't hide an inch."

Oh, James, doesn't Carlisle look terrific?

Infuriating, to be dressing for this dying man. This dying male gaze.

The first time I went to Bank Street was with Isabel. The grand reunion. I received the first of the teddy bears. Was lifted up in his arms—so high!—and told to leave the bear on the shelf for my return. "Your mother says you can come and visit me now, so we'll leave Bear here to keep me company and guard the room." But James was already living there.

Absent, that day.

I try reassembling that visit from Isabel's point of view, imagine her distress, her regret. How had *she* dressed for reconciliation?

Now I see her in her Maiden costume from *Firebird*, smoothing the skirt, hoping the child inside her is not showing. Scared at the movement inside her? She hadn't said so, but she wouldn't. Today was the first time I'd ever heard her speak of that "difficult time" after my birth. She wanted to tell me something, reveal her feelings, and I rushed her through them, the way she's rushed me.

My favorite thing in my closet is this tailored red suit—consignment Dries Van Noten—with this blue chiffon blouse Freya gave me for my birthday. It makes no apologies for any inch of me and there's something so perfect about the colors against each other. I try it on to make sure I still love it. In the mirror

I look at the pale indigo blouse against the cherry-red suit and recognize the color combination for what it is: an exact match of the Strawberry Thief wallpaper at Bank Street. Understanding carves a flume of absurdity into my anger. I imagine standing before Robert, literally blending into his wallpaper.

I take the suit off.

Jesus Christ, the music for the appearance of Kaschei's monsters is bananas. This would be the part Isabel danced in 1970.

This music, I like. There's something here.

What is this ballet about? What is anything about? Balanchine had it right.

It's about time, dear.

Bank Street. Bank Street. I see the front stoop, the windows, imagine the feel of the brass doorknob under my hand, the old-building smell of the foyer, like dusty leaves. Stepping into that room.

Stop it. It's an apartment in the West Village, it's not Manderley, it's not Howards End.

What if I fought for it?

Me, living in New York. Bank Street. A real home. Taking possession, literal possession, of my past.

Money. If I sell it, money.

I haven't even walked on that street in nineteen years. No reason to, it's all residential. One floor of a brownstone in a prewar building in the Village. What will it be worth now? Over a million dollars. Two million?

Held for me in trust. Funny phrase.

Firebird is reaching its big conclusion, almost martial in triumph. The big canonical ballets are like opera, or Shakespeare. At the end, people are either dead or married. Mostly dead. *Firebird* has an unusually happy ending. The Evil Sorcerer is annihilated, everybody shakes off the spell, the Prince and Princess get married. The Firebird is free.

My packing is done. I walk around my apartment, which now appears to me as something flimsy and insubstantial. Cobbled together, transitional. What am I doing here in Los Angeles? Other artists I know have spouses, houses, children. Look at Freya. Here I am still living like a child, being promised the next thing is the breakthrough thing, always organizing myself to be okay with disappointment. Making work that might be no good at all.

I turn off *Firebird*. Find something in that ballet I can understand and tell? Find something in my *life* I can understand and tell.

Fragments. They're all we can have of each other.

War Games

Fragment.

My first Christmas at Bank Street. 1988. I'm in my junior year of high school. The year before, I'd gone back to Ohio for Christmas, but that's a costly plane ticket and we're all saving money for next year, when I'll be auditioning for companies. Maybe even going to Europe.

It's wonderful to be at Bank Street, but I'm having insomnia. So is my father. He says it's quitting smoking. We both try reading, give up, meet in the front room and watch old movies on television. The set is kept in a cabinet low to the ground, comfortable to watch only if you're lying on the floor or on the yellow daybed. My father takes the daybed and I make a nest on the floor with cushions. There's a new kitten. Beloved Olga has died and been much mourned. Now there's Tatiana. Maria is teaching her how to hunt the Christmas tree. At least once an evening, we all jump up and rush to the rattling fir in an attempt to save an ornament.

My father and I don't often talk while we watch the movies, but I feel a new closeness with him. It's because of the strange hour, and being alone together, and having the same problem. He must feel it too, or perhaps it's the sentiment of the season, because for the first time he talks—a little—about his past to me. It starts during a movie, an old World War II story. He surprises me by identifying the planes. "That's a Grumman F6F Hellcat." "That's the P-51 Mustang." "Bf 109." I ask him how he knows. He tells me his uncle Howard flew a Hellcat.

"We all admired him. My brothers especially. They couldn't wait to be old enough to join the Navy." His voice is soft. "I had to play a lot of war games when I was a kid. I thought it was terrifically boring, so I always volunteered for dangerous missions and got killed early. Then I could lie there and think of other things. I used to make up paintings, in my head." He laughs, remembering. He tells me his faked enthusiasm was too convincing and earned him toy weaponry every Christmas and birthday. "An arsenal."

I want to hear more about his brothers, but he'll only commit to "Good people," before turning back to the screen.

"A *prominent* Michigan family," James will tell me, when I ask him. "'Prominent' being what old money rich people say instead of rich."

I say that Robert had described them as being good.

James considers. "It's a *type* of being good. The kind who are only as good as the box they've built for themselves. Frictionless morality. It's not hard to feel you're a good person if you ignore any semblance of an inner life. Oh, I'm maybe being unfair, not to mention obscure. I did meet the brothers once. The youngest one, Jerry, has a sense of humor. They make Robert a little sad.

You see, they were so very much what *he* was supposed to be. He wanted to be that too. To belong to that."

Fragment.

My father says to me, "I have no memories of high school whatsoever."

"It's enough," James tells me, "for boys like us to have survived it."

Fragment.

I know my father started dancing late, in college. He had a kind of mentor, called Aunt Daphne, who encouraged him. Her portrait hangs near the dining table at Bank Street. "Meeting Aunt Daphne" is part of a set piece, a monologue my father performs if anyone asks about the portrait. It starts with a college spring break trip to New York, the host family coming down with the flu, being sent to stay with an aunt in the city.

"Greg tells me to watch out because his great-aunt Daphne is an old gorgon and will probably drag me to the ballet with her. Well, I'm dying to see the city, so I say okay, that doesn't sound too bad. I take the train in and get myself up to the address of this Aunt Daphne, which is on the Upper East Side. Everything looks terrific. The doorman sends me upstairs. I'm thinking I'll offer to escort her for a walk, if she can walk, but when I get to Aunt Daphne's door, this *tiny* little gal in a turban opens it up, takes one look at me, says, 'My goodness, aren't you a colossus, I hear you like art,' grabs ahold of my suitcase, *hurls* it backward into her apartment, and marches me straight to the Modigliani show at MOMA. I thought, *Well, shoot, this is really* New York."

It's Aunt Daphne who takes Robert to see his first ballet, and they'll be friends until her death. In her portrait above the dining table, she wears a lime green cape, gumball pearls, and gloves. She was a major benefactor for Boxhill. "For better and worse," James always says, "art in America has always relied on gorgons."

Fragment.

Stories from Betsy, my father's old college girlfriend. I don't see her every visit. She works in the film industry, mostly with a Swiss director with whom James says she's "involved." One time, she has me over to her Upper West Side apartment to see if I want any of her clothes before she donates them to Housing Works. (Betsy's eight inches shorter than me but my father thinks I should look at her scarves.) Her apartment is stylish in a different way from Bank Street. Foreign film posters and low bookcases and all-white furniture. I'm intimidated by her and also her scarves, which I want but don't know how to wear. Betsy gives me tea in a white mug and shows me a picture of her and my father from college. Smiling in sweaters.

"Humphrey Bogart only giant," Betsy says. She speaks fast, has a natural rasp in her voice. "People called him Big Bogie. He was very shy unless he was doing something like track or glee club." She was a few years younger than my father, and the only one who knew when Robert started taking ballet lessons at a local school.

"We came from the same kind of family but were both out-siders. Didn't know it, but we were. Bobby came back from New York like someone who'd got religion. He'd seen ballet in what we still called 'pictures'—*The Red Shoes, On the Town*—but this was different. Much more real. He couldn't stop talking about the *dancers* and what they could do. Knew that whole world was for him. Said his brothers were like that, but with the military. The uniforms and the planes and the drills. All the language. The salutes. The flag. Romance. Emotions. It was *just* like that for him, only with ballet."

I find the comparison startling at first, and then I see it. Even the language and structure carry over. Corps de ballet. Marine corps, corps of cadets. Hierarchies. Boot camps. Discipline. Then the romance, just as Betsy said. The specialized language. Sacri-fice. Devotion. Costumes. The desire to serve an ideal.

My father's family will never concede the equivalency. (My father's family? My *country*. It's one thing for a man to love guns and the flag. That's American. It's not American for a man to love ballet.)

"Ballet made Bobby feel normal for the first time," Betsy ex-plains. "Because he had something that seemed right for him. I encouraged him to dance, to take lessons. We'd both go down to Chicago to see the dance companies passing through. He dis-covered he was good at arranging things, which almost nobody is. When the woman who ran the dance school wanted to give performances, he'd get musicians from the university, or the light opera to lend costumes, or people to donate. His teacher wanted him to perform, though, and gave him private classes. She told him, 'There is always a place in ballet for a boy who can lift a girl.' And you know she was right because after college he went to New York and started studying with LaGrange and joined the company." She lowers her voice. "He loved that company. He would've gone to war to protect it."

I take the military analogies to James, who agrees with them. "Your father is a man who needs devotion. I mean, he needs to be devoted *to* something. If ballet hadn't gotten him, religion might have. Or maybe he would've joined the military. I think we can all agree ballet was the best option."

Fragment.

I'm seventeen, about to graduate high school, and I've come down from school to New York for the weekend. Robert and James have been gifted tickets for Bernstein conducting the Vienna Philharmonic at Carnegie Hall. "It will be a pomposity fest," says James. "But you've never seen him live and goodness, this may be the last time." (Indeed, Bernstein dies later that year.) Outside the theater, my father's in a rare nostalgic mood. "I took my first class with professional dancers in a studio here," he tells me. "I almost didn't do it and just watched from the doorway. I knew I was going to be told I was no good. But I wasn't. It turned out to be the day my life really started. I was invited in. Everything changed that day."

I ask what his family said about his dancing and he smiles and says they were good sports.

"His family were good ostriches," James corrects during intermission, while my father goes outside to smoke. "When he went to New York he told them he was going to take a year or two to explore opportunities in 'arts management.' He gave them a way they could ignore what was happening. Not lying, just clan maintenance. He was terrifically smooth, and they all looked the other way, after some teasing about Robert being the black sheep. Oh, I'm sure they knew they weren't being told the whole story. Maybe they hoped his secret was being a Democrat."

Fragment.

A book I read in college: *Rare Birds: Mavericks and Visionaries of American Ballet.* There's a chapter on LaGrange Ballet. I see the famous photo of my father behind LaGrange. The chapter traces the beginnings of the company my father helped build, which starts with a tour in 1955 sponsored by, of all things, the Freemasons. I learn about Leonard LaGrange, who serves in the Coast Guard during World War II and studies ballet on the GI Bill, a thing many male dancers of his generation do that seems impossible now. I read how the fledgling company tours in a donated Chevy Nomad Wagon with a Shasta trailer containing all the costumes, sets, and luggage. It's ham-shaped and green. The dancers call it Le Cochon Vert. There's a picture of the Shasta. I read how from the beginning my father acts as both dancer and company manager. He runs the tape player, rehearses the local musicians, hangs the lights, distributes paychecks, rents the motel rooms, and communicates with local volunteers and Lodge members. Occasionally the dancers arrive at a theater to find a wooden floor waxed to skating rink levels of slippage and Robert is the one to coat the stage in a layer of Coca-Cola to save their necks. If the venue is a high school, it's Robert who rearranges the biology lab to serve as a dressing room. If there are no stagehands, Robert makes an early exit from the last number in order to ring down the curtain. Sometimes the ceilings of the stages are so low, when Robert lifts lead ballerina Guinevere Porter, the top half of her disappears from the audience view.

Included in this account is a photograph of my father in tights and leotard, partnering Guinevere Porter in a publicity photo. My father is lunged forward, arms outstretched. Guinevere is perched on toe, one leg swept behind her in an arabesque. Robert looks strong and slim and elegant. So young. In a few years he hangs up his shoes and officially takes over the management of the company. They leave Le Cochon Vert behind, begin touring Europe, have their first New York seasons. He'll never talk about any of this.

Fragment.

Bank Street. Another Christmas visit, just after college. Betsy and I are shivering and smoking on the front stoop, tipsy from champagne. She's reminiscing about her early days in New York, when she'd lived at the Hotel Martha Washington ("My parents thought the Barbizon too fancy"). She tells me she and my father were once engaged.

"We got engaged when he went to New York," she explains. "We didn't know what we were doing. We were late bloomers. Not born sophisticated, like James. We only knew we were different. My family had no interest in the arts. Bobby's liked things like boats and sports. I thought being an artist was sitting on the floor to eat and drinking wine out of jam jars. Neither one of us was experienced. Anyway, my point is we really loved each other, it wasn't a cover-up. *He* wanted to be married. I didn't. I figured that out. Marriage is always kind of a net loss, for girls."

"After Betsy came your mother," James says. "Robert's family was thrilled. I suppose at that point any girl would've been fine, but they adored Isabel. Those legs. That hair. And the timing was perfect because LaGrange was already throwing power fits with Robert about the company. Your mother was someone who he could be devoted to, and really help. Or thought he could. He did *love* her."

F ragment.

On the phone with James, just after President Clinton signs the Defense of Marriage Act. "Such a depressing day," James says. "You know, marriage wasn't ever what I dreamed about but it's what Robert wants. As a young person he thought the only kind of gay you could be was a terribly camp buffoon or a tragic pervert. That's how we were portrayed."

I press a little. Was it that my father didn't know he was gay, or didn't act on it?

"You know, dear, he's a little older than I am." James laughs his third-glass-of-wine laugh. "Not a different generation but almost. And a quite different family. I've gathered he had a furtive something with a boy, in high school, which he more or less suppressed entirely. The less said about the fumblings with Betsy after glee club, the better, I should imagine. Even when he moved to New York and started studying with LaGrange, he was quite chaste. I've extracted precisely one story: a LaGrange tour through Germany in 1960 where he was introduced to the work of Herman Hesse and some preliminary sodomy by a waiter at the Hofbräuhaus. Robert being Robert, what should have been ein tryst turned into secret trips to Munich, until he realized he wasn't the only lover. He still hates Munich because of it. He really wanted to be married."

F ragment.

A few years earlier. Bank Street kitchen, the newspaper open to movie listings. We're looking for a showing of *Four Weddings and a Funeral*. I ask my father if he saw the recent *Philadelphia*, where Tom Hanks plays a lawyer with AIDS who gets fired from his firm, with the reluctant Denzel Washington taking on his case. "Yes," he says. "We both did. James was angry about it, thought it terrifically milquetoast. Using *us*"—he makes quotation marks in the air—"for tears. But I thought the actors were great. I always like Tom Hanks."

I'm a little embarrassed. When I'd seen the movie, I'd cried so hard the person sitting next to me asked if I was okay. But the opening is there. He'd used *us* for gays, if in quotes.

"Hey, Dad," I say. "Your family knows about you, right?"

For a moment I think I've offended him. He's sometimes hard to read.

"Who do you mean?" he asks.

His brothers, I explain. Their wives, their kids. Did his . . . parents know, before they died?

"Oh. I don't know what they knew or know," he says. "I never asked."

I turn this over in my mind, not sure if it's admirable or sad. There's a new directive for the military this year, a don't-ask-don't-tell policy on sexuality. Will this keep people safe, or prejudice alive? I'd thought it noble of my father to distance himself from his family—at least financially—when they'd not supported his career. But now I want him to have fought harder to make them accept his identity, his nature. See him for who he truly is. I don't see why he hasn't insisted on this. He's not a man afraid of a fight.

"Loyalty isn't only about sticking by someone no matter what," he says. "Loyalty is also about making sacrifices for the other person. That's what makes a family."

"So you decided," I say slowly, wanting to get this right, "not to give them more information than they could handle?"

He looks impatient. "I wasn't thinking of what *they* could handle."

I'm confused, but afraid to press further.

"If they'd not accepted James," he says, "I would've never spoken to them again. It would have hurt James terribly and I refused to let them do that. I wouldn't give them the chance."

Now I understand. When my father speaks of "loyalty and sacrifice," he doesn't mean to his parents and brothers. It's why he'd been confused when I'd asked what his *family* knew. When my father says the word *family* who he's thinking about is James.

Flight

Los Angeles airport. I find a corner of a bar and order a Bloody Mary, which I think I bloody well deserve. I'm going to call Freya. It's what I should have done immediately, right after James called me. In what weird game do I rack up points for *not* calling her?

A Bloody Mary is an excellent airport drink. I wonder, if I have two, will I be able to sleep on the plane, even though that's never happened, including on flights to Asia. It's eight hours ahead in London so, early morning. A bad time to call, and the idea—very reasonable—Freya won't answer the phone is unbearable. I send a text: *At airport in LA. Going to NYC to see Robert and James. Robert is dying. Flight boarding soon. When is a good time to call? Sorry for dramatic wording.*

Freya's my first true, deep friend, made at the age of thirty. I think my friendships before her were like my general knowledge skills: wide but shallow. I'd been in love only once.

Freya is a playwright, brilliant and odd and English. We meet at an artists' residency—I can't believe I've been accepted at one—in Washington. Her boyfriend—also English—is trying to break into American movies and television, and she came with him to Los Angeles out of curiosity to see the American West and because she thought she might also try writing for the screen. She has the right attitude toward LA, one that took me some years. "It's so big, so ludicrous, and not embarrassed of itself. Everyone is always looking the other way, or at themselves. It gives you space to work."

Freya is exactly the kind of artist and woman I want to be: strong, strange, funny, elegant, opinionated. We talk about things: ambitions, ideas, books, religion, art, sex. Some nights we grab a studio and I improvise movement to lines from one of Freya's plays as she reads them out. I get her up and moving with me (the inspiration for my later suite of duets for one trained dancer and one not). Our residency romance continues when we return to Los Angeles. Her boyfriend is beautiful but dumb. She calls him The Last Hurrah. "Something to get out of the system so I can move on to the dependable man I love dearly."

One day she calls me up and asks if she can come over and walks straight into my apartment and talks and cries for hours. Nothing specifically traumatic has happened, it's a conjunction of various stresses: her work not going well, old shit with her family surfacing, The Last Hurrah can still be hurtful even when she doesn't love him, a friend of hers from conservatory days is doing well and it's wretched to be jealous. For the first time in my life, I don't listen to another person with observant greed, I listen as if I'm inside her body while she's talking. When she takes a long shuddering breath, I do too, and we burst out laughing at the same time.

We go away together to the desert for the weekend, get high and soak in hot tubs at night. I tell her the full story of what happened between Robert and James and me the summer I was twenty-four. She's quiet until the very end. "Fucking hell, darling," she says. We don't laugh this time but look up at the sky and continue talking and I no longer feel like screaming.

Freya gets an offer to teach at a drama school in London, goes back to England, and falls in love with a Welsh painter. I get a commission, the biggest I've received, the year she leaves. I'm able to use Meredith Monk's music for it, the first music I listened to where I fell in love with the sound of the female voice. My question for the work has to do with female friendship. It's because I miss Freya. Sometimes, you make things to keep yourself company.

What does friendship look like, in ballet?

Modern dance has always been better than classical ballet at depicting emotional nuance. There are women all over the stage, all the time, in the big story ballets, but those have tragic heroines, not besties. Men sometimes get a "friend"—there are Mercutio and Benvolio. Juliet has her nurse. In the classical repertoire, there's a motif of large groups of women, often dressed in white, but they represent a kind of moral authority, beautiful or terrible, but not personal. You see the friendship between women only in the rehearsal room or the wings, when women are chatting or laughing or checking in with each other, released from the obligation of being divine representatives. I suppose you could superimpose a friendship libretto on some of those mostly all-girl Balanchine ballets, but Balanchine adored women, and adoration generally doesn't include examination of an inner life. I can't imagine he was interested in how women felt about *each other.* Isabel agrees. "Mr. B was a genius, so he didn't have to make things be about things. *Every* ballet is about how fascinating and beautiful and powerful women are. That's what he saw and that's how he made us feel."

Is there anything other than sex that differentiates a romantic relationship from a friendship? Is the absence of sex replaced by some other thing? Is there something that happens only in friendships between women? Are any of these questions *danceable*?

The ballet I make—*My Friend*—isn't "about" Freya and me. For the purposes of the piece, I imagine a larger and more conventional narrative arc: two childhood friends who grow up, grow apart (men), come back together, grieve, comfort, sustain each other. I would like to use something more subtle and interesting than men as the dividing factor, but choreographing the other reasons friendships fall apart—for example, a series of unprocessed misunderstandings or resentments—is hard to do balletically.

There's a section that's all Freya and me though. The "She" character runs straight onstage into the arms of the "Her" character, driving her backward, then forward. They stay locked together for a sequence of steps, one woman freaking out and suffering in the arms of the other woman, who contains, mirrors, and partners the movement. It gets bigger and wilder—I have wonderful dancers, very open—but I can't figure out how to end it. The first time they perform what we have all the way through, the emotion of the room fogs up the windows, and when they get to the stopping point, the dancers burst out laughing. It's not embarrassed laughter, it's something else. They laugh and catch their breaths and touch each other's wet shoulders. "I'm sorta crying," says one.

I'm so grateful to them. "That's it," I say. "There's no ending for this moment. You'll get here, and then whatever happens between you happens. If you laugh like that, great. But you don't have to force it. You can just look each other. Or breathe. Find it together. Then we'll go to blackout. Let's *try* it. But not now."

I don't want them to get self-conscious, re-creating it, so we leave the ending of that section alone until dress rehearsal, and I've discussed the cue with the lighting director. The dancers have, over the course of working, become so alert to each other that when the moment arrives, I realize I've done them a disservice, thinking they will balk or try to prettify it. They have thought themselves deeper into the roles than I know, have secrets I haven't given them. They are exultant. I'm in awe.

It serves as answer to my puzzle: What is the thing that happens in a friendship that isn't an absence of sex? The thing added, that's maybe only between women. Not a matter of our organs or whether we were born with them or what we do with them. It's this: a particular kind of glory that happens when we share our suffering and are seen. There's a rising—a cry, a rush, a beating of wings together. An exaltation. I'm loath to connect womanness with suffering, or suffering with greatness, but there it is.

Freya comes to the premiere in Toronto. I'm too nervous to watch sitting down and stand in the back of the theater until the end, when I run around to take a bow with the cast. I think I can pick out Freya's voice, cheering. She comes backstage and I introduce her to everyone. "This is my friend," I say. I don't think about Robert or James once all evening.

My phone rings. Freya.

"Carlisle."

"Hey."

"Hold on one second." I hear her saying something—presumably to her husband.

"Carlisle."

"We don't have to talk long now," I say. "My flight will be boarding in a bit and I'm sure you're getting the kids—"

"Nick is coping. Let's talk as long as you can. How—what—"

"I just wanted to hear your voice," I say, in a rush. "I've been in this weird mind space, like I'm narrating everything for a documentary. Do you ever have a thing, like you're afraid of having one of those experiences where your life flashes before your eyes, but it won't be your life you see because you're just a blank space looking out? I know that doesn't make sense. And you wouldn't have that. You have a life."

"Okay, you have a life too, but you know that. Let's not worry about your thoughts right now. I mean, let's not judge them. You can have every weird feeling and crazy thought. Tell me what's happening. Is he in the hospital? Did James call you?" I take her through the details I know.

"Isabel offered to come with me," I say.

"Wow." It's so wonderful she knows exactly how that felt.

"I know," I say. "I'm having that thing where you realize the greatness of your mother."

"Oh God, that's awful, isn't it?" I can imagine Freya ruffling her short hair, tugging at the roots. "I mean, even if mothers are terrible, the world is still worse. Is she coming?"

"No, but I'm okay."

"I'm going to look up flights. I can come if you want me."

"Oh no, no. Thank you. I can do this."

"Not everything is a test," she says gently. "Of how much you can stand on your own."

"I'm saving you for after. For picking up the pieces."

"Just so you know, there's not a crying limit. Or asking things limit."

"I don't know what I want to happen," I say. "Something that's

not an awkward, mostly unsatisfying thing I'll process for another twenty fucking years."

"You're not at the mercy of fate here," Freya tells me. "Or him.
Them. You have some control."

"I have some control," I repeat. "Some."

"Are you staying there? Bank Street?"

"In a hotel for a few nights."

"That's good, I think. That's good?"

"There's more. Isabel told me there's a trust and Bank Street
comes to me."

I picture her thinking, biting her lip.

"I know," I say.

"Don't sign anything." Her voice is urgent. "I mean, in the
emotion of the moment you might feel like—they might want you
to promise—I'm sorry, it's *not* my place—"

"I don't know where to put my shields." Oh, I *am* going to cry
maybe. "I feel like I'm going into a battle and I don't know what
part to protect. Or who. I keep thinking, *Well, everyone had a part
in this, it's not just me, but I'm still outside. I'm somehow* still outside."
I would like to get down on all fours and howl but I'm so close to
actually doing it that I scare myself.

"I'm not doing this well," I say, desperate. "I want to meet the
moment and I'm failing. I can't even cry."

"When Nick's father was in the hospital, Nick got up at four in
the morning to wax the floors. For a week. You're okay. There's
not a right way to do this. What can I do to help?"

"Come up with a kickass concept for a ballet?" I ask. "You have
until Friday."

I tell her about *Firebird.*

"Fucking hell," she says.

"I know!" I thump the bar, and two businessmen look up at me in surprise. I stare them down and, for good measure, stand.

"But also, that's the most fabulous thing," Freya says. "I want to be leaping about and then, you know, googling *Firebird*. *Oh, Carlisle*."

They're calling my flight. I tell Freya I'm okay, I'm not going to lose my shit on the plane. She makes me promise to Skype when I get to New York so she can see my face.

"I'm going to look at flights from London to New York just in case. I love you."

"I love you too."

It's not quite the moment from *My Friend*. The exaltation. It's because her body is not in front of mine, and we are not alone together, and life is not ballet.

Because I can't let my body go forward, run, release. Not yet.

I put in my earbuds and cue up the opening of *Firebird*. "Kaschei's Enchanted Garden." Seductive murkiness. I think about stepping into Bank Street and what it will look like, feel like. What I might find there.

I stop. I've been here before. I did these same things, nineteen years ago. An overnight flight to New York. Two Bloody Marys at a bar. I maybe walked this same stretch of institutional carpet, imagining Bank Street.

And if I could retrace those steps, would I do it all differently?

Firebird's entrance plays in my ears and I turn her off.

This is where betrayal began, nineteen years ago.

I suppose it's time to think about Alex.

Personal Assistance

It's 1997. I'm twenty-four, and have been living in Los Angeles since college. I've stopped dressing like Lauren Bacall, but have yet to settle on a new identity. I secure a (fairly low-level) agent, who says I'm a Lucy Lawless "type." I get a pair of leather pants and assign myself episodes of *Xena: Warrior Princess* as homework but am mostly sent out for Lady So Tall It's Funny roles. I try on this persona, don't get many auditions, but attract more friends. I'm rarely asked out on dates. My new friends say I'd be good with someone older, but I'm maybe not a top-choice younger woman in Los Angeles. Too tall, no status. I do not live in hope of love. When I'm in a restaurant, my eye scans the menu for the least expensive item and doesn't consider the rest. Love, like lobster, is for people who aren't always worried about the bill. (Or the mess.) All my energies are for self-preservation. I have lost at dance. It's enough to lose, for a lifetime.

I still make up ballets in my head when I listen to music. I assume it's what everyone does, who grew up dancing. It doesn't make me Balanchine, or Tudor, or Ashton, or Robbins, or Forsythe, or any of the others. The Great Men.

The guy who delivers pot to my employer's son tells me his cat sitter also did ballet. My employer is an enormously wealthy widow who runs a charitable arts organization. James was right: art in America has always relied on gorgons. This is the West Coast version. I'm her personal assistant, a job that entails a lot of listening. I am good at listening but also good at seething. One year turns into two, into three.

I begin to understand I might be depressed, have possibly been depressed for a while. I can't afford therapy but borrow some books on mental health from the library. I find smoking pot to be helpful, and then not. My employer, who knows about my background, says she doesn't understand why I don't still dance. "Just for fun." She's always telling people I used to be a ballerina. In lieu of a Christmas bonus, she gives me a yearly class pass to a dance studio. I complain to everyone in a funny way about this gift and tell no one when I start using it. My body shakes with effort at things I once did easily, but I go again, and again. There's no point in trying to get back into shape, I think. I take a few classes a month. "You're dancing for yourself," one of the girls in class suggests. I don't know what this means.

When I describe what dancing feels like now to my friend Yves, he says it sounds like going to lunch with an ex who broke up with you. "You are hoping he will find again his love for you and beg for you to return. Even if you don't like him anymore. But he never does. Later, you must drink."

Yves runs a French cabaret-style weekly show in Hollywood. He tells me I could be a burlesque star. "You are built," he says, "for the solo." This seems true on many levels.

This year, 1997, Robert and James have been offered the use of a house in Sanary-sur-Mer for most of September and October. I'm joining them in New York for a week and then two in France. I haven't had more than a few days of vacation since leaving college. Because of money but also because I don't understand exactly what I'm trying do, or why. No rest for the baffled.

As wonderful as the trip sounds, I'm anxious about presenting myself to my father and James. My circumstances are unimpressive. I'm always hoping to come to them with *more*.

My father has generously paid for the tickets to France, and I've got a cheap red-eye to New York. I get to the airport early and splurge on a Bloody Mary at a bar. "Let me guess," a guy says when I take a stool. "*You* never have to ask for help reaching a shelf." I give him my smile-grimace. "Hey, no offense," he assures me. "I like tall women. You can even wear your high heels around me." I will not be allowed to read in peace. He has many things to say about how tall I am. Blessedly, his flight is called before mine. I order a second drink. By the time I make my way to the gate, a little tipsy, I've remembered I like myself so much more when I'm at Bank Street. I picture stepping through the front door.

At the airport in New York, it's not my father who is there to meet me. It's James.

For a moment I'm struck only by his loveliness. He wears his summer uniform: a white Panama to keep off the sun, cream linen drawstring pants, a linen messenger bag slung crosswise across a long-sleeve white button-down. Standing stock-still in filthy, chaotic LaGuardia, he looks like he's wandered in from the set of a period film. Or like a pale idol abandoned by customs. Very few people stand with their arms hanging loose at their sides. They cross their arms or put their hands in pockets. (We're still not yet at mobile phones.) James is one of the few people I've ever known who can—and does—stand in complete repose.

His face breaks into a smile when he sees me and he takes off his hat and hugs me long and close, not his usual style at all. When he draws back, I see his face is gaunt and the line between his eyebrows is so deep it looks like a scar. He looks at me with a helpless expression and something in me funnels backward. James, crossing to a window at Bank Street. My father, covering the mouthpiece of the phone, looking up with a face full of outrage and grief and guilt. Saying, "It's Danny."

My spine goes cold, an actual running zipper of ice shooting up and down.

"What is it?" I ask, and when he doesn't answer right away, the zipper of ice tightens and spreads to my rib cage. "Where's Dad?"

"Boxhill," James says, in a tight voice. "A little crisis with the main stage and a new floor. Also. Things are a little rocky. At present."

"But it's not—" I can't say it. "He's not sick?"

I press a fist against my sternum, and James grabs my arm. "Oh! No. He's not sick. I'm not sick. Not like that. I'm sorry to scare you."

Of course they're not sick.

"But something's wrong?"

"I'll tell you when we're home." He pats my arm. "Do you really only have this one bag? For France and everything? You're so clever."

In the queue for a cab James asks me questions about my life, with a hectic air. I don't think either one of us cares about my answers. What is happening?

Not sick. Not like that. I hadn't worried about either one of them getting HIV or AIDS for a long time, since it became known how it was transmitted. They are together; they are safe. I'd not imagined infidelities, don't picture their erotic lives more than any other child does of a parent. They've never been demonstrative, but their appreciation of each other gestures to an abiding physical connection. "James wore his new suit with the blue tie you gave him, Carlisle, and was the most handsome man in the room." "I told your father he can't put a hat over that gorgeous head of hair."

Is my father sick in some other way? He's now sixty-six; not in the best of health and beginning to show it. He moves his large frame around stiffly and takes a number of medications for his heart. "Lose weight, don't smoke, drink less alcohol, no red meat," he'll say with a shrug, after ordering a second drink and stepping outside a restaurant to smoke before his steak arrives. On my last visit I'd seen him cross his legs with a slight groan and been struck by the appearance of his calf, visible from a rucked-up pants leg. The flesh was mottled and thick. He got out of breath climbing subway stairs.

In the taxi, James tells me about Alex. I don't realize he's telling me what's wrong. I do notice he's gotten thin. It's not a trimness. More of a wasting.

"I started working with a dancer in June" is how he begins. "A promising young person, from Atlanta."

"Twenty-two. Younger than you. Straight."

"It's a working relationship. But a meaningful one."

"This is my *work*, the one gift I have."

"Alex left two weeks ago. Back to Atlanta. Well, this weekend he'll be in Mexico, performing at a festival there. But he lives in Atlanta. *He doesn't even live in New York.*"

James falls into a funk and I wait for a bit, then prod. *What happened?*

Nothing happened. James and Alex have been sending letters since Alex departed. Emails, James explains. This surprises
me. My father is an early adopter of technology, but James much
less so.

Robert, it seems, read the emails.

"I didn't know he knew my password," James tells me. "He
helped me set up my account and must have memorized it? I never
imagined he would read my personal correspondence.

"He 'happened upon them,' he says.

"He sent Betsy over, with the spare key, when he knew I was
teaching. God knows what she was meant to be looking for.

"She left her cigarette lighter. Like Iago's handkerchief.

"He's very angry. He is colossally angry."

I've seen my father angry, a few times. He looks like a baby
when he's angry.

"James," I say. "The emails that he read? Did they . . . reveal
something?"

"It doesn't matter." He looks out the window. "No, they don't
reveal anything. There's nothing to reveal. He's a straight boy.
He's a child. It's an innocent correspondence. But it doesn't matter. If a person wants to see something, they will. I feel *awful*."

I'm confused. Are the emails truly so innocent? My father is
an obdurate man but not, as far as I know, a jealous one. James has
said the kid is straight.

I have no experience of them at odds with each other. And now,
a selfish pang. Our wonderful trip to France might be spoiled.

"But *why*?" I ask. "Why is he acting like this?"

"To punish me," James says. "To punish himself. He has so
many hurts. He needs a crime to justify the wounds."

I'm struggling to process this when James starts pulling
books out of his bag. Iris Murdoch's *The Sea, the Sea*. Shirley Haz-

zard short stories. "I got these for you," he says. "I can't remember if I told you to read Shirley Hazzard or not.

"I haven't been sleeping well," James says. "I'm sorry." He leans back in the seat, rubs his arms, and shuts his eyes. I gather the books up and look out the window, momentarily distracted by that New York feeling. A sense of homecoming mixed with a sense of having missed my chance. James reaches a hand across the seat to me, another unusual gesture. His hand is much stronger than I expect, the pads and fingertips thickly callused. For a moment all I want is to lean my head against his chest. I've never done anything like that with him.

We hold hands. The shock absorbers of the taxi are completely shot, and my body hasn't unkinked from the plane, but by the time we lollop down Bank Street, I'm almost asleep.

Bank Street. It's here I realize how serious things might be. This isn't an enchanted kingdom I'm stepping into but an X-ray, revealing damage. The dining table is heaped with laundry and newspapers and grocery bags. Highball glasses and mugs of half-finished tea on every surface. Curtains drawn shut. The rooms look not just disorganized but dirty. I set my bag down in Carlisle's Room—the bed is covered with the paper contents of a filing cabinet—and return to the main room just as one of the cats—Tatiana or Maria—leaps from the mantel and sends a decorative plate crashing to the ground with a flick of her tail. James moves to collect the pieces and studies them without expression.

"A portent," he says.

James can't keep still, won't stop prowling. He picks up things to do: the laundry, the tea, a scattering of bills and circulars, but only sets them down somewhere else. My languor has been replaced with a jangly, dry-eyed fatigue. It's too hot, too dusty. James says he can't bear the noise of the fans. He's found two quiet enough for his nerves, but they're inadequate. We don't take up our positions at the piano and library steps. I watch from the couch as he paces.

"Something did happen this summer," he says. "I started to *breathe* again. In a way I hadn't for years. This dancer—did I tell you his name? Alex. Alex came to me with so many questions. We'd break things down, talk. He'd never been talked to properly. About dance or anything else. He's very bright, very quick. He's had a terrible education, but his instincts are sophisticated. In trying to answer his questions, I began to— Oh, I suppose a kind of loneliness lifted. We'd part, in the evening, and I'd come back here, and I wouldn't be able to calm myself. I'd put on music and dance in the living room. Me." He laughs. "Dancing." He looks around the room, following this improbable vision. But I've seen it, a shift in the weight of his body. Something that's been contained within him, a beauty I didn't know. James as he was meant to be seen.

Jealousy blooms in my chest. It really blooms: I can feel petals unfurling, a prickly stem snaking down my sternum. This Alex ignited something in James I never did. That my father, his love, his lover, did not inspire. We might be many things to James—my father and I—but we aren't his muse.

"It wasn't that I was remembering what I wanted to do thirty years ago," James says. "I was having new ideas. I thought, I could walk into a studio tomorrow and make a ballet again. I want to do that. God forgive me, I started to dream." He lifts his arms, beats with soft fists against his temples. I can see his ribs through his shirt. "I'm not entirely an unknown figure. There might even still be people in Europe who remember me. My generation isn't *all* dead, though God knows there are few of us left. I even thought— maybe I could work on something at Boxhill. Bring Alex over, continue working with him. He should be seen by more people anyway. One day, in the studio, I started to give him some steps."

For a moment I think he's going to demonstrate, but he only picks up a heavy book from a side table and then drops it back. The smack startles me and also a cat, whom I hear hit the ground from some unseen perch. James moves to the couch where I'm sitting, then decides on a chair opposite.

"Carlisle, it started flowing out of me. Old work. New work. I was so grateful to Alex. Immeasurably grateful."

Foolish James, to not see how my father would be jealous. To *not* be the muse of the person you love most? Or am I confusing my father's jealousy with my own?

"You told him all this?" I ask. "My father, I mean?"

James sits back in the chair.

"I didn't. It felt—oh, not like a secret but like a spell I was afraid to break. And then, when Alex left, I'm afraid I started to feel my old trouble returning. I suppose—in the emails—there's something of me struggling. Emotions. I've told Robert, many times, that *nothing* ever happened between Alex and myself that was improper. No question of an affair, or my running off, or anything like that. The notion is absurd."

"Maybe if you explained it to him like you did to me?"

James kicks off his shoes and stares at them bleakly. "I tried. He thinks it's all lies. Please understand, he really can't help it. Do you remember that summer when you came to New York?"

My summer. My perfect, terrible summer.

"Robert always hated leaving me to go to Boxhill. He hated it so much, he'd perversely insist on it. How I *must* have my solitude. We had quite a big fight over your coming because I assumed you would stay here with me, and he wanted to insist I needed my precious time alone. We were having a bit of a rough patch. He can be possessive, you know. He says protective, but the distinction can be tricky. Anyway, he was angry with me, for wanting to be alone. He always thinks I might *do* something."

What, I ask, does my father think James will do?

"Oh God. Everything and nothing. Leave. Get sick and die. Come apart. He has a fear, and then this compulsion to make the fear true. He won't be talked out of it. I really think it's death he's afraid of me running off with."

Maybe I make a face. A protest of the melodrama, but James misreads it.

"I apologize," he says. "That must have been a *miserable* summer for you. I wasn't well. Poor you."

It wasn't, I tell him, a miserable summer. For me.

James leaves the chair, moves to the window, twitches at the curtains. I look at the outline of his shoulder blades through his white shirt.

Tatiana and Maria make their appearances, emerging from unknown stalking locations. Tatiana stares at me balefully before headbutting my shin. Maria ignores me entirely and sniffs the shoes James has abandoned.

What, of any of this, do I believe or understand? I only know I'm not prepared for there to be a split between my father and James. A split won't be a wound, it'll be an amputation. My father will not tolerate disloyalty. I'll be obliged to lose James. This must be fixed.

"It was strange to have it come back to me," James says, from the window. "My work. It did make me feel, how to explain? That I was a *man*."

He faces me. He looks defeated and exhausted and ill. Our eyes meet. His are blue and pellucid.

It's all real, despite the unreal language. But their pain and their love are inaccessible to me. Despite my size, I'm a small person, with a small heart. And here is the old fear. I will lose this, lose Bank Street, lose my father and James.

I have to fix this.

James turns back to the window. "It's not the same, of course, but I keep thinking about my father. Alex is only a little older than I was, when my father died. The pain never goes away. I promised your father I'd never communicate with Alex again so I've just stopped returning his emails, his phone calls, everything. Alex's father abandoned him, did I tell you? One doesn't get over such things. And now I've done almost the very same. If only I could explain."

I suggest, tentatively, that despite the promise, perhaps one explanatory letter would be okay. James says he doesn't think so. But he can't stop thinking about his own cruelty. There's something he'd like Alex to have, but how to get it to him? It's too precious to send in the mail. Alex is at this dance festival in central Mexico and may be going to Europe after, to audition for some companies. He's not terribly happy in Atlanta.

James moves to the piano. Sits. He tells me about the moment when you realize you won't achieve the dreams of your youth. How he wants the things he cares about to continue, otherwise they'll all die with him.

"You know what's more terrible than giving up a dream?" he asks. "To discover you *haven't*.

"It's not about this boy," James says. "You do see that?"

And then—

"Is it worth it? All this—" He shuts his eyes. "All this *wreckage*."

I'm not sure what he means by *wreckage*. Himself? His career? His relationship with my father?

Perhaps he only means *life*.

"I'll talk to him," I say. "My father, I mean. I'm sure I can make him see it's not, not a betrayal."

I'm not at all sure about this.

"Maybe he will listen to you," James says. "Maybe you can help him find a way out."

I feel, for once, at the heart of something. I'm inside their union, their family. James has come to me for help. My father must be shown that however jealous or possessive he might feel, James has done nothing wrong. Everyone needs to be understood. I will do this.

It takes all day to reach my father. I make some attempt to clean up Bank Street, but it's too hot. James plays Scriabin and I go outside to smoke cigarettes. James tells me to lie down in their bedroom, where there's air-conditioning. I nap. We walk to Balducci's to get fish. When I reach my father, James is making dinner in the kitchen. I move the phone as far as I can into the main room. My father barrages me with questions, as if he's got a list by his phone. Did I find someone to fill in for me at my job while I'm away? What kind of luggage did I bring? Do I know how to pack a hat properly? He tells me, at some length, about the problems he's having with the crew working on the main stage. I'm afraid he will end the conversation before I've had a chance to say anything of value and interrupt him with a clumsy "Hey, Dad, James told me what happened."

Silence.

"I mean, what didn't happen. I mean, what you thought—you know. His student. And how—"

"Is he there?" my father breaks in. "James?"

"Yes. He's in the kitchen."

"Everything is fine." I can hear him lighting a cigarette, the sharp inhale. "It's over. We're moving on."

"Dad—"

"This doesn't have anything to do with you and we won't discuss it further." He does not—quite—hang up. He says things about needing another week at Boxhill, and how he'll get his travel agent to rebook our tickets to France. I should tell James not to do the packing. He will do it. And then he does hang up.

I move to the kitchen, where James is arranging smoked salmon and cucumbers onto plates. I repeat my father's words about everything being fine. *It's over. We're moving on.*

"Ah," James says. "Well. There it is. Good." He looks devastated.

I'm angry with my father. James let me in, came to me with their troubles. My father has said it's none of my business. I review my side of the conversation with my father, with guilt. I'd not tried very hard. A few weak words.

James has lost the thing that made him feel he was an artist. He's lost dance. It's enough to lose, for a lifetime.

"James," I say. "What can I do?"

He lifts his head. "You've been kind to listen. There's really nothing to do. Alex is in Mexico. I just want to feel I've ended things on a less horrible note. I've had a life of interrupted things, you see. Perhaps I can't bear to have one more part of myself go unfinished."

This sounds terrible to me too. I must do *something*.

I say I have a friend from San Miguel who is back living there now. She's not in the city where Alex is performing, but close. This is true. We haven't talked in a while, but maybe it wouldn't be so weird for me to call her up. I'm mostly thinking out loud, wondering if maybe this friend could get a message to Alex somehow, but James lights up.

"Do you know I had this completely mad idea of sending you down to Mexico for a night or two? Or maybe it's not so mad.

Robert is still in Boxhill till next week. You could talk to Alex and give him this thing I'd like him to have. Oh, you should see something of the festival too, it's quite a good one. Then, we can all go to France. Put this behind us."

He shivers. "It's probably a ridiculous idea. So much fuss. I can't ask this of you."

I'm a little taken aback but also moved. I feel desperately sorry for him. And for the boy in Mexico, who has lost James. Enough to lose, for a lifetime.

"Of course I'll go," I say. "Of course."

Memory of Lightning

Only an hour into this flight to New York and my legs are cramping. It's the alcohol from the Bloody Marys, the salt. I shut my eyes and focus on my muscles. Something deep in my right hamstring is pinging. An old memory.

These foolish men, I think. *These foolish old men. My father, the angry baby. James, the swooning sylph.*

I was foolish too.

The flight to Mexico. 1997.

I have all the self-importance of a messenger god, but none of it feels right. It *isn't* right. I have a thick padded envelope, to give to Alex. It feels like it contains a book. Something rare? The envelope is sealed. It's in my duffel along with the name of the theater where Alex will be performing and the address of a hotel where James has booked me a room. I hadn't been able to reach my friend in San Miguel but left a message. I'll be here for two nights. James has given me cash to exchange and pay for expenses, meals and things. The amount is generous and I'm frankly hoping to hoard as much of it as possible. What am I doing? James's words at the piano are still in my ears. His desperation. His pain. The look in his eyes when I said I would do this thing for him. How much I want to be the person James is grateful to, his true friend.

The diffidence in the proclamation *I'm just the messenger* is not correct. The messenger is a powerful role. The messenger always has the power *not* to deliver the message. To alter it. To destroy.

My duffel appears on the carousel at Del Bajío Airport in central Mexico with a rip and a few items spilling out. I almost lose the envelope there, without meaning to. A portent, James might have said. I've been advised to reject offers of taxis. On the bus, flustered, I try to hold my bag together and consult a map, my neck snapping back and forth as I fall into sudden fits of sleep and miss my stop, something of a feat as the central plaza could not be more central. I stumble off the bus, clutching my damaged bag to my chest, in front of a marigold basilica.

It's hot and still, the hour of siesta, though not quiet. There's a terrific racket of dogs barking, but I don't see any. It's almost ridiculously beautiful. I wander through a few streets, approach a shady restaurant, order a café con leche, and sit. This isn't like me, or the new me. The past few years have made me practical, efficient. I'm now the person who finds the hotel, sorts out where the theater is, strategizes about how to contact people. Instead, I plop the bag at my feet and smile at the waiter, who smiles back and returns with plastic bags and duct tape. He rigs a fix for my bag and then scrawls an address on a piece of paper. A leather store, I gather.

There are banners in the streets, promoting the weeklong celebration of the composer Carlos Chávez.

"Alex knows about you," James had said. I imagine going to the performance tonight. Sending a note backstage. Waiting for him after. He'll know which one I am. It's easier for me when they know to be expecting someone my size. What I'm meant to do is sit Alex down and explain the whole anguished drama. I don't want to do this.

I'm angry at my father but will not make him look like a fool. I'll not make James look like a fool either.

I might actually be angry at them both. What is in this precious envelope? What is James giving to Alex that he never wanted to give to me? Perhaps I need to take matters entirely into my own hands.

"I happened to be in town," I might say to Alex. "On vacation, visiting my friend. James told me I had to see you perform." I'd wait for whatever reaction, probably something like "Is he okay?" or "Yeah, I haven't heard from him," or something like that.

"Yes!" I will say. "He told me you worked together over the summer. He thinks you're great but also, he's really against teacher worship. He thinks it's bad for artists. I hope he didn't break things off with you in a rude way. If he did, you shouldn't take it personally. Like, if you got in touch a few years from now, he'd be thrilled."

I'll congratulate him on his performance and fade into the night.

"I told him everything," I will report to James. "He understands but he really wants to stay as far away from all the drama as possible. He has to think of his career. He thanks you for everything you did and wishes you well, but he won't be contacting you again."

I'll give him the envelope. That will be quite a fine moment for me, not having given in to the temptation to open it, make sure it's only something like a rare edition and not a packet of love poetry.

Am I capable of this? I'm not sure.

My hotel room is blue and white and yellow. There's a china dish on the dresser and a brass bedstead and a tiled floor. I tell myself I'm on an adventure. I'm at the heart of a matter.

I find the theater—a splendid nineteenth-century affair topped with statues—and approach the box office; receive a folded pamphlet. Guest artists from companies around the world have come to present ballets choreographed to the music of Chávez. Alex is on the bill for all the performances, but the entire weekend is sold out. James hadn't thought about that; a New Yorker's belief that only New York City requires reservations and hustle.

I can still wait by the stage door, but I've no idea what Alex looks like. James had not described him physically other than to say he was tall and dark, very butch and not handsome. I ask the woman at the box office if it would be possible to get a message to one of the dancers. I'm told to come back closer to performance time, no one is in the theater now but the cleaners.

I head back to the plaza, notice a group of dancers, their posture and gaits as unmistakable as a musician carrying an instrument case. It makes me stand like that too. I'm filled with longing, the vines of jealousy straightening my spine, snaking down my hips, turning them out, reaching the arches of my feet.

I wander curved alleyways, step inside the marigold basilica and stare at a bejeweled Virgin Mary, return to my hotel and sit on my balcony, too keyed up to eat. I write a short note:

Alex—James Sogard said I should look you up. Will try and catch you by the stage door after the show to say hi. —Carlisle Martin

The bathroom is the exact size of my wingspan. I take quite a bit of trouble over my appearance.

Outside the theater, I scan each departing dancer. A tall guy appears, with dark wet hair, and scans the crowd, but doesn't seem to notice me. He drops a canvas bag at his feet and ties a bandanna over his head. I see that he wears a leather cuff bracelet. He straightens, cigarette in hand, nods at someone calling out to him. "Yeah, man," he says, in an American accent. "I'll catch up with you later." A woman sidles toward him, program and pen extended. He smiles and signs. This has to be him.

My first emotion is relief. I'd been worried James's insistence on the straightness of Alex had been exaggerated. In a similar vein, I was hoping not to meet an awkward waif, or an earnest young artist. I watch him interact with the fan. I may not have had a career myself, but I've been around professional ballet dancers all my life and I recognize the type. He's ballet's version of a dude.

He must be a very good dancer. He stands like a hot guy. I watch him look up and around, squint and cock his head at me. This looks like performance. He knew exactly where and who I was.

"Carlisle? I got your note."

We shake hands.

"I wasn't able to see the performance tonight," I say, to explain my lack of compliments. "I was hoping to get a standing room ticket but even that was sold out."

"I can probably get you a ticket for tomorrow if you want." We're the exact same height, eye to eye. I'm wearing a skirt and a T-shirt and sandals. I'm glad my T-shirt is black because my back is sweating, always a tell for me. I have on a lot of red lipstick, my go-to armor.

"Let's get a drink," he says. "Everything's open late here. Stage manager told me of a place."

At the bar, Alex suggests a tequila shot, which I pretend not to loathe. I drink two glasses of wine. Alex ballet-man-spreads on his side of the booth and complains about the girl he's partnering in the piece, how she has a crush on him. It pisses him off. She keeps acting helpless, which is totally the wrong way to attract him. Doesn't she know that? The piece they're dancing was choreographed by the director of an important company in Germany. The director is here for the festival too. Alex wants to dance for him. He says American companies are shit. Short seasons, no money, no pensions, shitty union. He wants to dance in Europe. The company in Germany would be perfect. He could start building an international career.

"Wow," I say.

He talks about the repertoire of the German company. "Just an incredible mix of classical and avant-garde. America doesn't even know what avant-garde is, like what's avant-garde in the U.S. is *nothing* in Europe." Then he switches from sophisticated artiste to kid from Florida. He's just a kid from Florida, he's not a fucking elite anything. He's of the people. I wonder how or why James tolerates all this. Perhaps this is only how Alex talks to girls.

Or James is in love.

Alex seems to buy the idea I was visiting a friend in San Miguel and decided to catch some of the festival, a tale I managed to get in on our walk to the bar. "Yeah, James didn't tell me much about you," Alex says. "Except you're 'unusually bright.' And the height." This appears to have covered the topic of me.

He's doing a lazy flirt. He might actually try to sleep with me, although he won't try very hard.

I watch myself behave as if he's saying interesting and impres-

sive things. Something about him has pressed both the MUST-
ATTRACT and the UGH-WHATEVER buttons. It's appalling. I hate
myself. What am I doing here?

"So, things are sort of a mess with James," I say, cutting off his
thoughts on whatever the fuck he's saying. "My father—Robert—
thinks you and James had some kind of affair. Maybe somebody
suggested it to him, I don't know. I know it's not true, but for now
James wanted me to say sorry. He sort of sent me here, to say
that, and there can't be any communication between you two for a
while because he needs to focus on Robert. My, um, dad."

I've not covered for my father or for James. I've made us all
look ridiculous. I pull some bills out of my purse. I touch James's
envelope in my bag but leave it there and stagger upright. My
unsteadiness is alarming. I've had way too much to drink.

Alex is no longer sprawled in the booth. He's hunched over
crossed arms. Then he looks up at me, some kind of appeal in his
brown eyes.

"I don't know what else to tell you," I say. "That's the situation."

"I'm sorry," he says. "It's messed up. I never learned—I mean
nobody teaches you. How men are supposed to love each other."

Am I supposed to be enraptured by the display of sensitivity?
Feel sorry for the confines placed upon poor *straight* men? Tell
him how to love James?

"Oh for fuck's sake," I say, and walk out of the restaurant.

It's super exhilarating to be on the streets, to find my way
back to the hotel. What a rush! What a dick!

By the time I get to my room, I'm in a panic. My sloppy behavior. What a bitch! James will be upset, and I've probably made
things worse. What did I even say exactly? I can't remember. I
finish a bottle of water and think about returning to the bar, trying to find him. I smoke cigarettes and reimagine the evening,

making Alex worse and me better. I drunkenly try to read a Shirley Hazzard short story. Maybe I'll leave another note at the theater tomorrow. *At least*, I tell myself, *I didn't fuck him.*

The street outside my window is noisy, and I have jet lag. It was a mistake to smoke those cigarettes, especially at this high altitude. I doze, but then a headache wakes me up in the morning, sharp edged and vicious. I crouch in the shower trying to get enough tepid spray to wash my hair. I finish another water bottle and almost throw up several times. I try to reach my friend in San Miguel again. Her cousin picks up the phone. In a mix of Spanish and English I learn that my friend is in Costa Rica with her boyfriend. She won't be back until the end of the month.

I won't see the town, I decide. I'll go to one of the plazas, get a café con leche, and spend the day in bed reading. Tonight, I'll leave James's envelope at the stage door for Alex, with a note. Tomorrow, I'll go back to New York. It's so uncool to be this bad at adventures. The need for coffee is great.

I find Alex perched on the sidewalk railing across from my hotel.

"It's weird," he says. "I've been here for, like, fifteen minutes. I was thinking about what to write. And now here you are." He holds up a piece of hotel stationery and a pen.

"How did you know where I was?" My thoughts fly to James. Alex had called, told him how I behaved. James had provided the address.

"I followed you last night. I wanted to make sure you got back okay."

I press the inside corners of my eyebrows, where my headache is threatening to burst out of my skin.

"I need to get some Tylenol or something," I say. "And water and coffee."

"It's the altitude," Alex says. "I feel like shit too." He points to the plaza across from the hotel. "Sit over there and I'll get the stuff."

"Give me the paper," I say. "I'll write your letter to me." He laughs and hands it to me, along with the pen.

There are little iron tables and chairs in the plaza. I find a shaded spot. It's cleaner and more charming than Los Angeles, lighter and more intimate than New York. Still, the invisible dogs are barking like mad.

Dear Carlisle, I write.

I'm leaving a ticket for you at the box office. I hope you enjoy the performance! I have absolutely no memory of last night (tequila!), but I seem to recall James wants me to know we can't talk or send emails right now, and of course I understand things between couples can be weird, for all kinds of reasons. If I could do anything to reassure your father that my relationship with James was absolutely and strictly professional I would, but I can see how that's difficult, maybe impossible. James is a great teacher and I loved working with him. Please let him know I totally understand.

PS: you seem like a cool person.

Alex returns with two plastic bags and a coffee in each fist. He sets them down, lays out water, Tylenol, two bananas, and a large pink crusted roll.

"Thank you very much."

"You're welcome."

The building behind Alex is cerulean blue. He's wearing a

green bandanna today, but the same leather cuff. There are yellow flecks in his brown eyes. *Poor James*, I think. *Poor, poor James.*

"Don't you have a matinee?" I ask.

"I have an hour before I need to be at the theater. Can I read my note?"

He nods at the piece of paper. I slide it across the table and watch him read.

"That's how you spell it?"

"Which word?" I ask.

"Your name. I thought it was with a *y*."

"No. That's the hotel."

"You're named after a hotel?"

"No, after a character in a book. Only my father can't remember which book. He just remembers there was a girl called Carlisle in it, and he always loved the name."

"Where's the hotel?"

"New York."

"That's cool. Do they have matchbooks and stuff with your name on them?"

"The different spelling though."

"Right. I'm not stupid, just kind of hungover."

He returns to the letter.

"You have really good handwriting."

"I know."

He stretches out his legs, beats his quads with a fist. Drinks half of a bottle of water. I watch the people moving about the plaza. Some obvious tourists. It's becoming crowded, lively. I feel cocooned in my hangover. A piece of my headache softens. The coffee is sweet.

"This coffee is sweet," I say.

"I told them to add sugar. I think it helps."

"It does. Where are all these barking dogs? I hear the dogs, but I don't see any."

"They're on the roofs. Have some concha."

I tear off a piece of concha and eat. Bread and sugar. Some portion of my headache flares and subsides.

Alex turns over the piece of paper, writes, and slides it across the table. His handwriting is also very neat.

Dear Carlisle,

You seem like a very cool person. I'm glad you explained everything. Would you like to take a walk with me sometime, like now?

He's written *yes* and *no,* and drawn circles underneath them, as if we're in grade school. I smile.

"I need a hat," I say.

"There's a place a few blocks from here." Alex points. "I passed it. I almost bought one, but I look stupid in hats. I have a really big head."

"Me too."

We stroll, our big heads level with each other.

"I'm sorry I was such an asshole last night," he says. "I could hear myself talking and I was like, *What a dick*, and everything I said kind of got worse."

His hand bumps mine.

"It's a weird situation," I say.

"Yeah."

His shoulder is almost touching mine.

The narrow streets are cobblestoned, the pastel paint of the buildings charmingly flaked. Each little alley presents some diverting staircase or series of shops.

"It's like Europe," I say. "Or, I guess, like colonialism."

"Fuck those guys," he says. We laugh.

"I've only been to a few places in Europe," he confesses. "On tour last year. I don't know the fuck about anything."

We laugh again and then he says, not looking at me, "I'm glad you came. I mean, thanks for explaining. I thought I'd offended him somehow."

I stop. We're in front of a used bookstore.

He asks if I want to go in. The proprietor, a middle-aged man with a perfectly round belly under a pale blue Cuban shirt, greets us. Alex chats with him in Spanish while I wander down an aisle. Alex catches up with me. I hold a book up to my nose.

"Books don't have different scents the way people do," I say. "It seems like they should."

"Maybe dogs can tell the difference between books," he suggests.

I feel weird. It's weird to feel happy.

"Did James give you books?" I ask. It's like we're talking about a shared lover.

"Yeah," Alex says. "But I'm a slow reader. I don't mean I have a problem reading, I just take a long time. I'd rather have, like, James read it and talk to me about it."

"He's a good talker."

"He gave me a lot of books on dance, though. And art. He's really generous."

"Yeah."

"It wasn't, like, a seduction."

"No, I know. Let's go look at some hats," I say.

Trying on hats is not a cute activity if you have a large head. A too-small hat is a humiliating object, not funny. At the shop, Alex grabs a soft white large-brimmed hat off a hook and sets it on my head. It fits perfectly. I pull a straw cowboy hat from a shelf and hand it to him. It also fits.

We look at each other, in our hats. I smile.

"Well, that's done," he says. "Wow."

Alex wants to buy my hat, along with his. I let him, feeling oddly something. Girlish? Concubinish? Some strange sensation.

Alex puts on sunglasses. I watch him adjust his posture slightly, to match the hat and shades. Gunslinger on vacation. I think, not for the first time, that if the body I had was male, I'd have a career. If I was this tall, and had my brain and the talent I know I have, what *wouldn't* the world give me?

"He showed me some of his choreography," Alex says, when we're back on the street. "For his ballet? *Boats in the Harbor Sway?* He taught me one of the solos. And passages from all the sections. And some other stuff."

We stop to let a car go by. Alex reaches out and tweaks the brim of my hat, so it dips over one eye. We're standing quite close together.

"What was it like?" I ask, humbly. Alex doesn't know how humbly.

"Crazy beautiful. Dramatic. But not that fake drama thing where you do a bunch of steps and then do drama at the end, so everybody knows it's supposed to mean something. It was better than any new thing I've been asked to dance."

"Sensation!" I say lightly, in James's voice. Alex laughs and steps back.

"Sensation!" His imitation of James is not as good as mine.

"But he's sort of easily defeated? He said he didn't want to, like, investigate it."

"'Juvenilia,'" I suggest, still using my James voice. "'Pale imitations of better men.'"

"That's it," Alex says. "God, you sound exactly like him. You're lucky you got to have him all your life."

We resume walking, but the sidewalk narrows and for a while we're single file. I look at Alex's back.

I can see it. The lunches, the walks, the conversations around the piano. James unfolding his ideas, his anecdotes, his theories. Of course, I can see it. I'd had those lunches, those walks, those conversations.

We turn onto the street leading to the theater. Now we're shoulder to shoulder again. Literally. You could balance a ruler between our shoulders our heights are so exact. My arms are a little longer. We pause for another car. Alex twists the leather cuff around his wrist.

"I miss talking with him," he says. "I used to think I didn't like most people. But it's more that I don't like *myself* around most people. I'm way more interesting and smarter around James. We'd separate for the night, you know, and I'd walk back to my place feeling like, I don't know. Like I was a part of art or something."

"I know," I say. "I think he felt the same. You inspired him."

"So, I don't want to say it wasn't a romance." Alex looks me full in the face. "It wasn't anything sexual. We never slept together or kissed or anything. He never touched me, and it feels really shitty to say that. Like, cheap. It seems cowardly to say it wasn't love. I know I had that feeling. Romeo after Juliet says good night. It's not just sex. It's leaving someone thinking, *Okay, the world is less lonely and*—" He makes a gesture, recognizable to me from the balcony scene of the ballet. Not the full pose, only a slight twist of the shoulders, a lift of the rib cage, one hand curling toward his chest. In a cowboy hat and sneakers.

Oh, James, I think. *I get it.*

"I'm really, really sorry," Alex says. "I totally didn't want to make trouble. I mean, that's your dad. You must kind of hate me."

I tell him it's not his fault, and he's not responsible. We reach the plaza in front of the theater.

Alex says he'll arrange for a ticket for the evening performance, but it might be standing room. I realize my headache is gone. We part, and I go back to my room and sleep for five hours. When I wake up, I see I have a message from the front desk. Flowers have been left for me, with a ticket attached and a little note. *Hope you like it. See you after?* He's being charming.

At the theater, I lean against a railing in the dark and watch him move across the stage.

"So, you can dance," I tell him, when we meet at the stage door.

"Do you think so?"

"I do. Very much so."

"I was nervous."

"I think it's the performer who is supposed to get flowers," I say. "Not the audience member."

"Oh right," he says, not smiling. "I just thought you should get flowers is all." He's not just being charming.

It's a brass bedstead, and only a full-size bed. We spill outside of it, falling off, grabbing at the posts, the frame, the rickety bedside tables, putting one foot, two feet on the floor, which is tiled and shockingly cold. Our legs are hot and tacky with sweat. I am the brass slats, and the rug, and the floor, and also myself, laughing, and also Alex, smiling and intent, saying into my neck,

"God." And me stretching out, making myself taller. I've never felt so satisfyingly large.

If it's just my body calling the shots, I think I could fall in love. If Alex and I fall in love, it will solve everyone's problems. Alex will be made safe in my father's eyes and James will be able to keep his muse. I'll be happy.

It's not about this boy, James had said.

The Black Shoes

Mexico, 1997. We wake early, with the sun, and roll around on the bed, dehydrated and horny. "We have to stop fucking," Alex says, after a while. "Or we'll never stop fucking. And I need to take class or I'll be shit tonight." He lifts one of my legs from the bed, rotates it into turnout, and sculpts my foot into a point. "Nice. James said you could have danced professionally if you wanted to. You should come to class. It's informal. Just some of us meeting onstage."

It's a shock how much *if you wanted to* gives me a pain. A woman left at the altar doesn't want to hear she wasn't abandoned, it's that she didn't love the groom enough. Even if it is true. Not my height but my heart.

The anxiety of this propels me off the bed and to the window. I remind Alex I have a flight back to New York in the afternoon.

"New York?"

"I'm going with my father and James to France, like a week from now. Anyway, I don't have shoes for class."

"You can borrow from me." He joins me at the window, positioning us side by side. "Look, we're the same size. We're perfect for each other." Some of his body is ordinary: the size of his cock, the moles on his arms. Standing next to him is so easy.

"Except on pointe I'm a giant," I point out. "*More* of a giant. I'd be too tall for you on pointe."

"I didn't mean," he says, "for dance."

He presses against me.

"Come take class with me," he says.

I wear leggings and a camisole. Alex gives me an extra pair of shoes. His feet are larger, but the slippers are brand-new and haven't been stretched, so they fit me perfectly. On the walk to the theater, he takes my hand. I never hold hands with anyone.

Alex introduces me to the girl from National Ballet of Canada who is teaching. I want to explain that I'm not really a dancer anymore, out of shape, a nobody even when *in* shape. Instead, I make a weird self-deprecatory gesture and take a place behind Alex at one of the barres spaced out across the stage. I feel gauche and nervous. It will suck to dance badly in front of him. I put on his shoes and stretch, a little tentatively, my hamstrings. I'm sex-drunk and unmoored from all my circumstances and it's giving me a weird clarity. How have I allowed my life to happen the way it has? My daily rounds in Los Angeles, my ugly apartment in the large building, my job in the "arts" that's mostly being a paid companion to a sentimental gorgon. Apathy.

What am I going to say to James?

It's been a month since I've last taken class. I look at the bodies of the other dancers, stretching, chatting. About thirty are here, a mix of languages, the bodies whippet lean, but varied in skin tones and proportions. There's even one other woman near my height; I'd seen her dance the night before and she was wonderful. I'd not realized how tall she was, since her piece was a solo. A modern dancer, from a company in Prague.

I wonder if I can make it through class without blowing a hamstring.

I look back at Alex, rolling his shoulders, thumping his quads with his fists. At a certain level—a professional level—*everyone's* technique is good, even wonderful. With the great ones you see the step and the dancer but also something else. A style, an oddity, a quirk, a flourish, an embellishment. Like with Baryshnikov. Other male dancers of his generation—not so many but they existed—could do the same technical feats, but they couldn't do them with a quality so personal and specific, that communicated so much. When I'd told Alex, *So, you can dance,* I wasn't talking about the steps. He was special. You could see he was after something when he moved. It made you want to keep watching, to see if he found it.

The girl he was dancing with was lovely, but she'd only been serving the music and the choreography. Alex was serving himself. She was lovely; he was great. These things aren't fair.

How do you get to have the humility to submit yourself to dance and also the ego to transcend it?

We're joined at the barre by Alex's partner. I remember that first night and him complaining she had a crush on him. He introduces us. Her name is Laura. She's all pretty points: pointy chin, nose, nipples, collarbones. I calculate she's six inches shorter than I am, the perfect partnering height for Alex. She's also from Atlanta Ballet, a company I auditioned for and was not accepted into. She deserves it, there's no mystery, no unfairness as to why.

She's gifted and strong. Great feet, high legs, good turns. A little bland, but that's unfair because she was dancing next to Alex and for all the supposed primacy of women in ballet, nobody coaches girls to have more ego.

No one had ever talked to me about my dancing, my qualities, what I might bring to the work. I'd not had a James.

I'd *always* had a James. Only I'd never been his Alex.

Class begins and I surprise myself by being able to do more than I expected, possibly because we're not in a studio with mirrors but on a stage, and I can't see myself, can't *size* myself. Since I have no future in dance, I stay in the present. The girl who is teaching must have burned this CD in advance. Instead of classical music it's all pop. Madonna, Toni Braxton, Michael Jackson. At each new song, people laugh but settle into work. There's a little clowning. A surprising number of Europeans know all the lyrics to TLC's "Creep."

I do not, let me be clear, become magically fabulous, but by the time we get to center practice, some sleeping part of my brain is up and dressed and dancing well. The music is classical now; the girl from Toronto is giving very dancy combinations, with lots of rhythm changes. I can see a few dark shapes in the audience, watching. Ushers maybe, or people who work in the theater.

When we change groups, I watch the other dancers with a smile on my face. I can't help it. I'm happy. I'm with my people. The tall woman from Prague grabs my arm when we line up for jumps on the diagonal. "Yah, do in my group with me," she says. "Usually, I jump with boys, but now I have sister to jump with."

The houselights are raised. I notice a man in the first row, sitting with his legs crossed, watching. I follow his gaze to Alex, who is dancing on a level that has everyone watching him. Alex is the real thing. I look at the other dancers on the stage, all real things. I don't envy these better dancers. I love them. I'm proud of them.

I want something. I can almost feel what the something is.

I'm also aware that I'm only *just* not hurting myself, dancing like this. I don't care. I will deal with the pain later.

Class ends. Alex says he needs a shower. We arrange to meet in the plaza in twenty minutes. He is glowing, keyed up, cocky. A little of the asshole from the first night has returned. Maybe this will make leaving easier? Yes, it will. Anyway, I want to go away and continue my thoughts. It seems like I'm almost having real thoughts, about something.

I know I need to think about what to say to James.

I follow the girls to a communal dressing room. I'm sodden and glad I had the foresight to put a hotel hand towel inside my bag. I've sweated so much I feel dry inside. Several of the girls ask where I dance. This is enormously gratifying, to have it assumed I dance somewhere, professionally. The tall girl from Prague asks me if I've studied modern and when I say not really, she says, "Oh. But you are musical for a ballet dancer," and all the ballet dancers in the room laugh. We exchange names and she asks where I studied. I run through the schools and say that both my parents were dancers. It's been years since I've been this comfortable talking about my background. I listen to myself say easily, "My mom danced for Balanchine and my father is the director of the Boxhill Festival. So, I grew up with dancing. But I never became a professional."

"Oh, wow, Boxhill," she says. "That's cool. My girlfriend was there this summer."

I bend over to take off Alex's shoes and a muscle deep in my back seizes. I'm able to straighten, but this and the rapidly hardening something happening in my hamstring and a jammed sensation in my ankles are all bringing me—retying me—back to earth. Possibly I've fucked myself up, but as long as I can walk, I can walk away from Alex with dignity. *It won't matter if my body is a mess in my real life,* I say to myself. *I don't need my body for my real life.*

I repeat this thought to myself in the shower, testing the shape of its sadness. There's definitely something wrong with my life—pretty much everything—but for once I'm able to do more than take the temperature of my sadness. I rotate slowly in the shower and think, *That was probably the most fun I will ever have in a ballet class, but I don't need to be onstage, and I don't need to be* that.

For a moment I feel as drained of ambition as I do of sweat. It's bliss.

There is dance in my head. Yes. It will probably always be there. I don't have to do anything with it. Although.

Making dances.

I hear James, in my head, talking about choreography. Choreographers. Petipa, Fokine, Bournonville, Balanchine, Ashton, Tudor, Ailey, Forsythe, MacMillan, LaGrange, Joffrey, Cranko, Kylián, and so on. All men. The only living women choreographers I can think of are from the modern dance world. Where are the female classical ballet choreographers? How do you even become one? There's no school or program for it, that I know about. People do it after dancing in a company and making a name for themselves that way. Or they have mentors or money or something? My father is the person to ask. He's always inviting new choreographers to Boxhill. He could help me, introduce me to someone who needs an assistant or let me observe.

It's not a dream. Why shouldn't I make dances? Not everything on the program I'd seen the night before had been great. Lots of it wasn't great at all. It had only been done. By people who hadn't dreamed of it, they'd *done* it. Men, to be specific.

Is there an opposite to "enlightenment"? An endarkenment. Not some stupid butterfly emerging from a cocoon. I feel myself inching slowly forward, to some real place inside me. Something lost in dreams of flight.

I'm sick of dreaming. I'm so fucking sick of dreaming.

I dress in a daze and am thinking so hard that when I step into the square, I'm surprised to see Alex. He's chatting with an older man, an obvious former dancer from the carriage of shoulders and motion of hands. I hang back, watching their bodies talk. It occurs to me the older man might be the artistic director from Germany, the one whose choreography Alex is performing. I know his name but not his face. His work was the best of what I'd seen the night before, a lot of it truly special.

Who wakes up and thinks: I can make ballets? *What made him think it?*

They are very chesty, these two men, talking to each other. It's like a sternum-off. Then Alex dips his head, with modesty. He's putting on a little of an act. That's fine. I'm reminded of where his head was, last night, and how beautiful it looked between my legs. I walk over to an iron bench and wonder how much sitting down and standing back up will cost me, physically. The adrenaline from class has faded and retribution has started. I'm going to be very, very sore.

My flight is supposed to leave in three hours. James will be looking at the clock, wondering if I will call from the airport.

I hear my name. Alex and the man are walking toward me. I stand, somewhat precariously. Alex says, "This is my girlfriend, Carlisle."

I immediately guess that the use of the word *girlfriend* is a straight-guy reflex. Alex wants to make his sexuality clear to the man. I'm flustered anyway.

It's indeed the artistic director from Germany. I tell him I love his work. His face is intelligent and foxy. He peppers me with questions and agrees with my answers as if I'm getting them right. "Yes, you live in Los Angeles." "Yes, six-foot-two is one hundred eighty-eight centimeters."

"I can see you were trained very well," he says and folds his arms. "And you have a beautiful movement quality. Sensual. You will come to Stuttgart."

There's a wild moment when I think he wants me to come dance for him and I say, "Oh my gosh!" with a huge smile before he turns and pats Alex's shoulder. "You will come visit," the director says. "This fellow."

Luckily, my reaction is appropriate for this too. Alex nods and bites his lip. Now I see he wasn't putting on an act. Perhaps this is how he is around James too. Diffident, almost bashful.

"I just got my dream job offer," he says to me, with a sidelong smile at the director, who again claps him on the back and says the name of someone who will be in touch with Alex, who will help with "papers." He strolls away. I congratulate Alex, who picks me up and spins me around. I point my feet. It's been so long since anyone has lifted me.

"Holy shit," he says. "Oh my God, my *life*."

I'm thrilled for him, I'm envious, I'm excited. His arms are the right everything. He kisses me because he's so happy and we kiss and kiss.

After a bit he says, "I wish I could tell James."

"I'll tell him," I say. "He'll be so pleased for you."

My hamstrings are aching. *What will I say to James?*

"Do you have anywhere to be," Alex asks, "right now?"

I remind him about the airport. I should leave soon.

"But do you have to go back?" He grabs my hand. "You're not going to France until next week, right? And I don't have to be back in Atlanta until the week after. Let's stay in Mexico for a few days and be stupid? Who knows if it will ever be like this? I never fall for someone fast like this. I want to—"

He puts a hand over his sternum. He puts his other hand over my sternum. *It's euphoria*, I think. *It's ego.*

I want to say it too. *Oh my God, my life.* I want to have one.

"My ticket," I say.

"I'll change it. Give it to me."

For the first time in my life, I don't want to go to Bank Street. I reach into my taped-together bag and give him the ticket. He sprints back to the theater. I make my way to a bench, cantilever myself down gently. I put my bag in my lap and peer at its contents in a daze. I didn't bring many things to Mexico with me, leaving what I'd packed for France back in Carlisle's Room. I'll have to wash underwear and things in a sink. Am I really doing this? *Any* of this?

And here is the envelope James gave me.

I open it, almost idly. As if there were hardly any point in standing on ceremony now.

It's a journal, a choreographic journal. Not the steps. Dance *has* a formal notation system, but it's not used very often in ballet. Nowadays there's videotape, but before that, choreography was passed down verbally, physically, collective memory of the dancers who performed the roles and the directors and coaches who rehearsed them. Even with video, people still rely on this tradition. "Mr. B said this step was like shaking snow off your boots." "Alice is doing the wrong arm in the video. It's *supposed* to be on the three." James's ballet, *Boats in the Harbor Sway*, exists only in whatever he, and the dancers he taught it to, remember of it.

The journal starts with a kind of libretto for that ballet, outlining the sections with accompanying notes, in his tiny, precise lettering. There are also lists. Ideas for other ballets. Music he wants to make dances to, with thoughts on what they might be. Poems, some attributed, some not. Line drawings. References. Descriptions of ordinary movement.

Once, I would have devoured every word. The day before, I would have. My only thought at this moment: *Oh. This all makes sense. I can do this.*

I see my name.

Carlisle walks with her fingers splayed when she's thinking, like she's blind, like she's wading through invisible tall grass. Use.

I flip through. At the back, pages marked *Alex.* I see the word *love.* A few more phrases, a poem.

I don't want to read this. I don't want to know this.

I look up. Alex is making his way toward me. He's smiling. He holds out his arms.

I want, I want, I want.

I put the journal back in its envelope, and back in my bag.

"All done," Alex says. "The gods have spoken. They want us to be happy."

Which gods? But when Alex kisses me I stop caring.

I call James, later, from a downstairs cubicle in our hotel. The cubicle has flocked wallpaper, and a little rotating stool. I run my hand, so recently against Alex's bare skin, up and down the wallpaper, as if petting it. Or my conscience. James answers on the first ring.

"Carlisle? Is that you?"

His voice is so anxious. I'm sweating.

"I saw Alex," I say. "I explained everything to him. He totally, totally gets it. He sends you his best."

"Oh. That's an enormous relief." He doesn't sound relieved.

"Listen," I hurry on, with the story a corner of my brain has been working out since Alex rushed off with my ticket. "My friend? The one in San Miguel? She's actually getting married this week, here, and she's begging me to stay for it. Like, her whole family offered to put me up and everything—"

"Oh how fun," James says, after a beat. "Of course you must."

"I said I had to check with you." I'd prepared for everything but this absolute concession and can't put on the brakes. "I'd be back before we go to France, of course, but also I don't want you to feel, you know, abandoned, and it's really all right, I mean, with Alex. I mean, I hope you feel—"

"You stay and have fun," James says. "You enjoy yourself. Young people need to be with young people. No, really, I'm glad this worked out."

What does he mean by that? He knows. Does he know?

"Alex's going to Germany," I say. "He told me he got into a company there. So, like, in a way that solves things too, right?" For a moment, he doesn't answer. *He knows. How could he not?*

Well, what did he think would happen?

"Can I ask?" Something humble, meek, in his voice. I can't bear it. "Did you give him the envelope?"

"Yes, yes," I say. "I gave it to him. It's safe with him. Are you sure it's okay if I stay?"

"I'll miss the extra time with you," he says. "But I think this will be better. I can collect myself. Get sorted out." A small pause and then he continues in a lighter tone. "Oh dear. I'm afraid I have another favor to ask."

"Anything," I say, wildly.

"Would you not mention to your father that you're down there? If you happen to speak that is. He's up to his eyes, sorting out the mess with the builders. Anyway, if he knows you're in Mexico, he won't believe you're with your friend. He'll guess this has something to do with Alex, and that I'm up to no good. It'll be a mess. And just when we've solved it all."

I promise. Who knows better than I how James will not be fucking Alex this week?

He tells me he loves me. "I love you too," I say.

I will think, many times in the next four days, of insects, of cocoons and carapaces, of wings, legs, hearts.

I move to Alex's hotel. I buy a notebook of my own. A notebook and a box of Band-Aids. I see Alex dance again. I drink with the dancers at a bar, Alex's arm tight around my waist. Someone buys us a good bottle of something. I ask a Belgian choreographer what he looks for, in a dancer. "Look at the back," he says. "The shoulder blades. They are the eyes behind us. They are the windows to the soul, not the eyes. The shoulder blades cannot lie. They will tell you who that dancer is, in their soul." I put this down in my notebook. I write lists of composers and works I want to make dances to, ideas for ballets, people I know who might help me. My employer has connections at the opera. There are my theater friends from college. My friend Yves and his cabaret.

Alex asks me what I'm going to tell James and Robert. *Loyalty isn't only about sticking by someone no matter what,* my father had said. *Loyalty is also about making sacrifices for the other person. That's what makes a family.*

"I don't know," I tell him, and we drop the subject, though Alex says, more than once, after I've offered an opinion: "You sound like James."

Telling lies interferes with my ability to feel I'm not doing anything wrong, and this is the only aspect of the week that's neither thrilling nor sexy.

I check my voicemail twice a day in the little phone cubicle. There are no messages from my father and only one from James, left a few hours after we'd spoken. *I can't thank you enough,* he says. *Robert isn't back until Saturday so if you're here by Friday, it will all work out perfectly. Have a wonderful time. I do apologize for the drama. You've been a champion.*

It's not about this boy, James had said. *It's not about this boy.*

I've never experienced someone acting as if they were wildly in love with me. It's like Alex and I have eloped. We attract attention when we're out. He holds my hand, wraps his arms around me, kisses me on corners, at restaurants, everywhere. He sings me songs in the shower, runs out every morning for coffee and flowers. *Is* it a performance? On our third night together, he tells me he's in love with me. He says he's known it since we put on the hats, our first morning. "You smiled at me and I think I said something like *That's it,* or *That's done,*" he explains. "I meant my heart. Like, I was done for."

It's the most romantic moment of my life.

He talks about my coming to Germany. I get drunk and tell him about wanting to make dances. Why not, he says. If a guy like him could get a job dancing ballet in fucking *Europe,* why couldn't I become a choreographer? Come to Germany, he says. Come to Atlanta first. His contract there runs through *Nutcracker,* so he won't be able to leave until next year. He should go see his mother before he leaves, in Florida. She will cry. She's a crier.

It's the first time a man has said he loves me, and I say it back and then have to stop myself from saying it over and over.

He doesn't want to go to Germany alone. I know this. It's a much bigger company, a foreign place where he knows nobody and doesn't speak the language. He's not sophisticated, his confidence has large holes, despite all the talk of establishing an international reputation. It's always been a fight, for him. An absent father, a needy mother, friends who called him a "faggot," the loneliness of wanting something nobody in your life understands, the anxiety of wanting something at all. America. James was the person who made it all feel possible. Now there is no James, but there's me. So, come to Germany, he says. Come with me.

I don't want to do it alone either. I may look like I'm built for the solo, but it's not how I feel inside. If Alex looks at me and sees a version of James, well, he's not wrong. Anyway, does it matter? I'm high on love and sex and ambition. Why not go to Germany? Why not everything. Oh my God, my *life*.

Sex and ambition. Love and ambition. "Who knows when it will ever be like this?" he asks me. How did he know?

I became a choreographer. It's the love that outlasted all the others.

Maybe it was the shoes, I will write in my notebook. *Alex's shoes. Magic shoes. Anyway, I've danced in a man's shoes and now I know what it feels like, I'm never going back.*

Trio in E Minor

Early on the morning of my return, I slip down to the cubicle to check messages one last time. I don't want to go to New York. Or France. I want only to return to Alex, still sleeping upstairs.

I have messages.

Carlisle, this is your father. Either he's coughing or choking or the connection is poor—the next sentences are truncated. *You need to— You have to— I don't know where exactly you are.* Then, distinctly, *I came back early and I caught him,* which is interrupted by another rattling sound. It's not static. It's my father's smoker's cough, mixed with something else. *I caught James.* It sounds like he's trying to yell but can't because he's crying.

The message ends. The next three, also from my father, are clear.

James has tried to kill himself.

He's at a hospital, in New York.

He's alive.

My father relays these facts in staccato, like a telegram. He ends each message with *I don't know where you are. Call.* In the third he says, *I've contacted your mother. No one is clear where you are. I'm worried. Please call me.*

I'm so angry I nearly slam the receiver down. I want to throw something, break something. Fucking James. Fucking James. Tried to kill himself. You have got to be kidding me.

Shaking with rage, I listen to a message from Isabel. She says she's heard James is in the hospital and Robert has not been able to get in touch with me. *You can let us know where you are,* she says. *When it's convenient.*

I sit down on the little stool. I'm sweating. Cold sweat. Fear. I've swung into wild contrition. I call Bank Street. The machine picks up. *I'm so sorry, I just listened to my voicemail, I'm not in New York, I got invited to a friend's wedding, I'll be there tonight, I'm so sorry, I love you, I'll be there soon.*

I want to throw up. I should immediately come clean.

Do I need to cover my tracks? Which of these tracks are also James's tracks?

My brother, Yuto, answers when I call Isabel. Yuto is twelve. If anyone were to ask me, *Are you jealous your mother loves him best?* I would say *No, I would love him best too.* He's thoroughly charming and funny and smart. He doesn't dance, but he's socially grace-ful, an equally rare talent. I hear him shout, "Mom!" and then a muffled "Carlisle." They're in a new house, which I've never seen. I hear a dog bark. They have a dog now.

I get very little out of Isabel. "Robert indicated James is in the hospital." She doesn't need to know where I am, or what I'm doing, only that I'm okay. My relations with her, since college really, haven't been close. She tiptoes around me, which I find extremely irritating and seems designed to make me be exactly the kind of touchy asshole she's trying not to provoke.

Isabel tells me it was Robert's understanding I was in New York. Robert said things of mine were at Bank Street, but I wasn't. He was, she said, starting to panic. James had suffered some sort of breakdown. I was missing.

"It was all last minute," I tell Isabel. "A friend's wedding in Mexico. James didn't want me to miss it. What did Robert say about James? Is he okay?"

She tells me she has no details other than James is in the hospital but he's going to be fine and is not in any kind of critical situation. Her voice has the clotted texture it always has when speaking of my father and James. I tell Isabel I'll be at Bank Street later that night. I rush through an abbreviated set of lies about my whereabouts. I can hear Yuto laughing in the background, and the dog barking. "Right," Isabel says. "Right."

My hands are shaking. I replay my father's first message. Maybe he was trying to say he *caught* James from dying, in time. Or maybe the doctors *caught* him, in time?

James might have left a note.

Is my father angry with me? Or just worried? Possibly, the time to worry about my father's anger and fear was before I came to Mexico to meet the man his lover is in love with.

Tried to kill himself over.

From the moment I opened that envelope, I knew it was always about love. *It's not about this boy.* Come on.

James has tried to kill himself.

He planned it, all along. It's why he gave me the notebook.

How dare he. How dare he send me down here to give over his precious possession to a straight boy he has a crush on and then try to kill himself in some bullshit fashion.

No. I was supposed to go back to New York. He was waiting for me. Maybe he thought I'd give Alex the notebook, the declaration of love, and Alex would fly to his arms. And instead Alex had flown into mine. And somehow he knew it.

The notebook is still in my bag.

I walk outside the hotel. I'm wearing Alex's jacket, which has cigarettes in a pocket. I light one. For once, the dogs are not barking, and then, just as I notice the silence, they start up again.

I finish the cigarette and go upstairs. I brush my teeth and fit myself into bed next to Alex. He sleeps in a sprawl, like a man dropped from a building. He turns over and settles my head on his chest. Our feet hang off the end of the bed.

I wanted what I wanted. I still want what I want.

Alex half-wakes. I tell him I will come to Germany. He laces our fingers together. I'm shaking. *I didn't know*, I tell myself. *I didn't know this would happen.*

"You're cold," Alex says, and wraps himself around me.

I shake into Alex's chest and say nothing. He begins to kiss me, growling, sweet. He thinks we're at the beginning of our lives.

I will make it so. I will.

At the airport, Alex asks if I'm going to tell James about us.

"Maybe not right away," I say.

"I think he'll be happy for us," Alex says. "I think they both will. It sort of fixes everything, right?" My flight leaves before his. "I'll see you soon," he says.

On the plane, my body suffers immediate withdrawal. I could claw the fabric of the seat, my own arms, from longing. Have I been drunk all week? I can't read more than a few sentences of my book, which anyway is the collection of Shirley Hazzard short stories James gave me. I pull out the notebook I was using to write ideas for choreography.

I have done the wrong thing, several wrong things. I need to think seriously about the situation. The moment I tell myself this, it leaves my head instantly. Fantasy, my old friend, comes to the rescue. I'll dream of something else. Alex and me happy together.

What will be helpful is music, big earwormy love songs, but I left my folder of CDs at Bank Street and have only the one in my Discman: Shostakovich Piano Trio no. 2. All week, Alex had been playing me the music he liked: Fugees, Shaggy, Bob Marley, Sade. He said he still liked cheesy pop sometimes because his claim to fame in middle and high school was he could do all the background choreography from music videos. He said he got into Caribbean music because his dad was from the Dominican Republic, even though he hated his dad. His white mother likes the Beatles and he loves his mother but hates the Beatles. Flipping through his CD holder, I spotted Scriabin piano sonatas and knew James must have given these to him.

I shut my eyes and listen to Shostakovich. Three instruments, three characters. Shostakovich is in a grim mood. How would I approach this as a choreographer? The notion feels wildly self-serious. Delusional. Maybe if I were on my feet I could improvise something? Sure, but that doesn't mean I can be a choreographer.

Except, what's the difference between improvisation and choreography? Repetition, and refinement. Those can't happen unless you take the first step. The first step isn't physical, it's the belief that what's inside you is important enough to repeat and refine. Where does it come from, this belief? Why should being serious about myself feel wild? Are these things that can be taught, muscles you can exercise or grow? Or is it something you are born with?

James, talking about setting *Boats in a Harbor Sway* on La-

Grange Ballet. His first ballet. *I ought not to have been allowed, really.*

But he was allowed.

Maybe it's something you're born with *and* something you're given. Maybe it's why all the ballet choreographers I can think of are men. We give them things. *I* give them things.

I shift in my seat, cramped and compressed, dry-eyed, horny. My hamstring still aches, and my ankles are still a little jammed. I pretended to be less sore in front of Alex. Of course I did. I turn up the volume on the Allegretto. It feels like a chess game to me, although there are three instruments and chess has only two players.

I shut my eyes. Now that I'm consciously trying to make up a dance, I see nothing. How did I do it before? Did I imagine a studio, a theater? Some nonplace? I stop the music, restart the Allegretto from the beginning. Chess is a game for two people. They play each other. A third person would play them both. A third person would have no pieces but reach out a hand and move the others'. No one can make a strategy. The two players will have to kill this third. Games are no fun unless the rules are constant.

I stop the music, play from the beginning again. Again. Again.

When I arrive at JFK I check my voicemail, but there's no message from my father. Still at the hospital? I have no idea which one and don't have keys to Bank Street. Well, there are coffee shops, a few friends I can call. I climb in a cab, mentally running through my funds. I spent all the money James gave me. My head is still moving in trios, a mad chess game.

James, Alex, me.

James, my father, me.

My father, James, Alex.

The cab is at Bank Street too quickly, I've not assembled any kind of plan or way to handle the situation. I loiter in front of the brownstone, looking at the lit windows. The sheers are drawn shut but not the heavier curtains; I trace the shadow shapes of the tops of furniture, a vase on the console, the corner of the piano. While I'm still looking, the light above the front door snaps on and the door itself opens. My father's shape fills the doorway. I take a step back. He doesn't see me yet, is already lighting a cigarette. I move closer. He jerks his head up, a New Yorker's defense ready. His expression shifts only slightly when he sees it's me.

"And here you are," he says, as if concluding a thought.

He holds the cigarette in front of his chest and doesn't move as I step forward.

"I'm so sorry," I say. "I'm so sorry, I'm late getting here. I just got in."

There's movement behind us. Betsy, at the door. She props it open with a foot and folds her arms. She doesn't hug or kiss me, or even say hello. She lifts the fingers of one hand in a simulacrum of a wave and looks at my father.

"Bobby?"

"Carlisle, you better go on up with Betsy," he says to me. He doesn't hold out his arms. His body is a dark bulk, closed. In anger? Pain? I will make this all okay, but I need to understand what has happened. I put my hand on his arm and he nods an acknowledgment but then moves to smoke.

I follow Betsy in and up the stairs. The choreographer in Mexico told me I could learn a lot about a person by looking at their shoulder blades. Betsy's are visible underneath a thin gray T-shirt, but they tell me nothing. Once we're inside, she grabs a bulky tote bag.

"I was going to spend the night," she says. "But I think it's best if I give you two time alone." She doesn't leave though. She follows me into Carlisle's Room. It's been cleaned since I was last here, all is swept and polished. My swimsuit and dresses and the things for France I'd taken out of my duffel are in a stack in the closet. Betsy sits on my bed.

"He's not upset with you," she says. "We didn't know where you were. Your father said you finally got in touch and you went to a wedding?" She gives me one of her shrewd, measuring glances. "Bad timing. Although a part of me thinks James sent you away so he could try again. Not that it's your fault for agreeing."

Okay. So James did not leave a note, or confess everything in remorse. All my father knows is that I wasn't here. And James? *Did* he send me to Mexico so he could do what he intended all along, or did his decision come when he heard my voice on the phone and guessed what had occurred? I run Betsy's words in my head and realize I've missed something.

"Try *again*?"

"This has happened before," she says.

Another boy? I nearly say it out loud.

"These are old—" She stops and shakes her head. We've grown friendlier over the years but not closer. She has never been impressed by me, or perhaps I mean she's never thought me better than I am.

But Betsy betrayed James too. She spied on him. And now she's sitting on my bed, hunched over with her chin in her hands. Like a gargoyle.

"Years and years ago," she says. "After what LaGrange did to James. James took some pills. That was a close call too."

"I thought—" I shake my head. "What did LaGrange do to *James*?"

"Listen, it was all a mess." Betsy straightens. "LaGrange was mad that your father hired James. I guess Robert sort of went over LaGrange's head. LaGrange went to a rehearsal of James's ballet and came back and said a bunch of shit about it to Robert. Like the ballet was a mess and would never be staged. There was a big fight and LaGrange gave Robert the boot. James took some pills and nearly died."

"James told me something different. He said—" I stop. I won't betray him further.

"Listen." Betsy waves her hands. "Your father and LaGrange were already fighting. The split was always gonna happen."

"But it was a good ballet," I say, although why I'm fighting this particular corner now, I don't know.

Betsy shrugs. "Obviously James had other problems. And LaGrange apologized to James, like a year after it happened. He even offered to stage the ballet. LaGrange was an asshole, but he had good moments too, I guess. Well, nobody is one thing. Except maybe Robert. I say that with love."

There's a warning in her eyes, but I feel, if anything, relieved. This isn't about the boy. This is James and depression and old things between him and my father. Alex and I are not a part of this. *He doesn't know.* I sink into a chair. It takes me several seconds to be ashamed of being relieved. James is in the hospital. All I've been thinking about is how to get away with the lies I've told. A betrayal no one knows about is still a betrayal.

Betsy rises from the bed, crosses to me, grips my shoulder, hard, and shakes it. I don't know if the gesture means *wake up,* or *be better,* or *it's going to be okay.*

She leaves. I sit, listening for the front door, and eventually hear my father turning the locks, putting his keys and lighter down on the console. He coughs and walks down the hallway, past my open door, and straight to his and James's bedroom. The door shuts. I stand outside it.

"Dad?"

Movement. Coins plunking into a dish on the dresser. The wooden groan of the bed frame.

"Dad? Are you okay?"

"Go to bed, Carlisle," he says. "We'll speak in the morning."

The bathroom is spotless and smells powerfully of bleach instead of my father's Proraso aftershave and Vitalis hair tonic. Why bleach? James wouldn't, I think, have tried to slash his wrists. I try to make the attempted suicide smaller in my head. It was a couple of aspirin or something. I glance up at the ceiling light fixture, remember James describing his father's death. *I even understood the tarp.*

I caught him, my father said.

I go to bed in Carlisle's Room and listen, for several hours, to my father's heavy tread, the opening and shutting of the front door as he goes outside to smoke. I listen to Shostakovich Piano Trio no. 2.

Trios.

Jealousy, anger, guilt.

Lust, love, shame.

Attack, defend, obscure.

Sensation

Bank Street, the next morning. My father has the television on and is ironing shirts. Neither of us has slept and we look it. In the daylight I can see how the entire apartment has been thoroughly cleaned. The main room is so tidy it looks as if they've been robbed. I've never seen my father clean anything except dishes.

I stand in the doorway, waiting to be noticed.

"I'm taking things to James," he says. "The hospital is cold." I move farther into the room. The piano, which I've never seen shut, is shut. No sheet music on the rack.

I say my lines about being sorry I wasn't here, the last-minute invitation, James urging me to go. When my father looks up at me his expression is unreadable, smudged, as if his features have been pulled in different directions, like dirty clay.

"Betsy tells me that no one is to blame," he says. "That people will do what they want to do. They'll find a way, if they're really determined."

He clears his throat and swings the cord of the iron out of the way with an easy, graceful gesture. I always forget there's a dancer in my father's body.

"It's a very selfish impulse." His voice is off-key, in some weird register. "Very. He wasn't thinking clearly."

He becomes brisk, practical. James is out of intensive care and has been moved to the psychiatric unit but is not being committed. James's doctor is pulling some strings. James will be moved to a bed in a regular room. My father resumes his ironing. "I'm going to the hospital when I finish this," he says. "He needs something to wear home."

There's coffee in the scrubbed kitchen, a *New York Times* folded to the completed crossword. I remember James's story of his mother coming to tell him his father had died. She'd pinned a cherry brooch to her lapel. *I remember thinking she couldn't be so very upset. You wouldn't be able to pin a brooch on if you were broken.* But he'd been wrong. *I understood her bravery, too late.*

Tatiana traces infinity symbols around my ankles, purring. I pour myself coffee and return to the main room, watch Robert finishing the cuffs on a shirt. On the television, a news anchor tells us about upcoming specials. More things about dead Princess Di.

My father selects a new shirt from a pile, shakes it out, and smooths it over the board. He looks terrible, leaden and lumpish. I ask if I can come with him, to the hospital. A cloud of steam poufs up from the iron. I'm impatient. This studied ironing, his refusal last night to talk to me, is getting on my nerves.

"Of course." He flicks the iron cord again. "You can see, can't you, why I was alarmed. I come home and I find James, as he was, and I see clothes in your room and as far I know you're here— somewhere—but nowhere to be found."

I apologize and trot out my story again.

"You didn't see any signs?" His voice slides up into that thin, metallic register again. "You felt comfortable leaving him alone in a terrible state?"

Okay. Here it is. He *is* angry I left James alone.

"He was upset about everything that's been going on," I say, through a tightening of my throat. "The accusations."

"The accusations."

"Well, I think he was exhausted and, and, overwrought, by you not believing him."

I can't quite believe what's coming out of my mouth. Am I trying to pin this on him? It does sound like it. We stare at each other.

"The 'just friends' business," he says. "Alex, his little friend."

"It wasn't sexual. It wasn't *cheating.*"

My father grips the iron, I grip the coffee mug. We're mirror images. I'm aware of the angry bulk of his body. Of mine.

"He said it was mentorship," I carry on. "It was creative. It made him feel like an artist again."

"I would never try to take that from him." The ironing board totters under his hands. He steps back. "I *want* him to have that. He always tries to make it seem like he gave everything up for me. The truth is, *he just gave up.* This depression thing he talks about. It's not my fault he didn't become the next Antony Tudor. I told him, anytime he wanted to, he could come to Boxhill and choreograph. I told him, over and over, I would support him. *It's not my fault.*"

This comes out in a complete flow of words. He's been saying this to himself for a long time. It also sounds like the truth. Maybe because it's what I want to say too. *It's not my fault.*

"I think." I clear my throat and try another voice, something calmer. "I think the depression just overwhelmed him and made everything confusing. But he definitely didn't cheat on you and he's not still secretly seeing Alex or any of that. He needs you to believe him, Dad."

Why am I defending James? Oh, because I've wronged him.

"If I hadn't come back early, he would be dead," my father says. "He would be dead, Carlisle. He meant to do it. He cleaned the house. He left stacks of things, to leave to people. He put his clothes in boxes." His voice trembles, squeaks. His neck flushes a heavy purple. "As if I would just throw them out."

I still don't believe it. A line from *As You Like It* pushes itself into my brain. *Men have died from time to time, and worms have eaten them, but not for love.*

My father resumes ironing. After a minute, his hands become steady. He quotes Betsy again: it's nobody's fault. He says I should stay at Bank Street while he goes to the hospital. "I need to take care of this," he says. "I need to look after him." After he leaves, I chain-smoke on the street and call Alex from a disgusting pay phone on a too-noisy corner on Eighth. Alex, just back in Atlanta, is wired and chatty. He doesn't know whether he should tell his boss he's leaving after the winter season. Better to wait until he gets the official contract from Germany, right? He got a German phrase book at the airport. He tries out a few sentences, laughing.

I need him to be desperately in love with me. I need to be desperately in love with him.

I see his life, the current one and the future, folding up around him, enclosing him, like fronds. The thing to do is to get inside, get enclosed with him. But they are his fronds, his enclosure.

"How is James?" Alex asks.

"Good," I say.

"Are things better between him and your dad?"

"They are," I say. "I haven't told them about us yet, but I think it'll be cool."

I smoke more cigarettes. Robert calls Bank Street from the hospital, late in the afternoon. They aren't releasing James until tomorrow. Can I bring a pair of sweatpants? I fall over myself to say yes, to find some ground, be useful, be *something*. A daughter. I pick up some gerbera daisies at a bodega on the way. *They'll get over it*, I think.

"Cheer up," says a man standing next to me.

I'm mortified. Am I talking out loud? No. The guy's just giving me a variation of the demand to smile. Usually, with me, they just—

"Hey, how tall are you?" he asks.

"Tall." I clutch the daisies.

He waits until the light has changed and I'm crossing to call me a bitch.

The entrance of the hospital looks like a formerly elegant, now dilapidated hotel. I expect to be struck by immediate horrors. What I'm given are a series of instructions and linoleum corridors. I watch my feet go down them, watch nurses turn on their heels, watch a patient partnering an IV glissade around a corner. James doesn't have a private room but is currently the only occupant of his double. I find him cross-legged, curled over, forehead touching his ankles. No Robert. The television is on, set to the same channel Robert was watching this morning. James's shoulder blades triangle through the shirt he's wearing. What do they tell me? He's alive. I realize—at last—this almost didn't happen.

I squeak forward on the linoleum and James straightens at

the sound. His skin is pale where it isn't mottled red, with violet patches under his eyes, but I don't see any marks or bruises. The lines of his skull are too pronounced, cheekbones, temples. The top buttons of the dress shirt my father was ironing earlier are open. He licks his lips and blinks.

"Carlisle."

"Hi, James."

I lift my offering.

"How pretty," he says. "Thank you." It's a ghost version of his voice.

I don't have a vase. There's a much larger and more beautiful bouquet on the table next to him, in a vase. Some more thoughtful person than I, one who didn't decide against a more expensive bouquet. Remorse on a budget.

"You just missed Betsy," James says.

"Betsy brought you these?" I put my dumb flowers down.

"Yes. Poor Betsy. She never liked me." This seems valiant.

"She's never liked me either." I find I'm able to meet his eyes.

"No. We're lucky she's so bad at disliking people. She actually kissed me."

We ghost-laugh at this.

"I brought you some sweatpants." I hold up the bag.

James moves himself out of the bed in a series of exhausted jerks, painful to watch. The shirt he's wearing is not one of his normal summer ones, it's blue and white and needs cuff links, so the wrists are flopping open. No bandages. He's not wearing pants, just briefs. His legs are finely muscled.

"Sweatpants and a dress shirt. I'll look like a Republican on a bender."

I hold out a T-shirt.

"Robert's gone to get us some dinner and more blankets and to badger people about getting me out." James unbuttons his shirt. "We've both spent far too much time here."

I'm not familiar with his naked chest, his rib cage, his stomach. James and Robert are always modest around me. James's torso is pale and lovely.

James gets back in bed, resumes his cross-legged position but under the blanket, pulls a second blanket across his shoulders like a shawl. My expression sits tensely on my face, a sort of compassionate and concerned half smile I never make. I pull up a chair, unsteady. It's a mockery of our usual positions: me on the library steps, James at the piano bench.

A nurse comes in. "You're so flexible!" she cries at James's position in the bed. "Look at you!"

He introduces me as "my partner's daughter." There have been so few occasions for these kinds of introductions. We've never been fully in each other's worlds. Or I've only ever been in theirs. *Friend or family member?* they had asked me, at reception.

Even now, I long for Alex. It's unthinkable to give up Alex. I guess it was for James too. Who knows about men dying for love if not my father and James?

Would I die for Alex? I haven't even made any dances yet.

The nurse gives James something to swallow and puts my flowers in an extra water pitcher. We watch her leave. James begins to talk to me. He says he doesn't want me thinking I could have prevented anything if I'd come back from Mexico. It's not my job, my responsibility, to prevent anything. That Robert knows this too.

"I was relieved," he says. "When you said you wanted to stay down there. I wasn't planning this. I just wanted some time alone. I can't explain how it works. One gets a clarity. But it's the wrong kind. It feels right. It's not voices or anything like that. I just thought—with great certainty—this was what I needed to do. I know it's hard to understand."

Everything is hard to understand. I think of my chessboard, the game that can't be played because there's a third party moving the players.

"You tried to help me, and I repaid you very cruelly," James says. "I'm sorry. It won't happen again. I've promised Robert."

"Okay," I say, quickly. "That's good. Don't worry about anything. I mean, you don't have to apologize."

We're quiet for a moment.

"Will you tell me how he is?"

"He's ironing!" I say. "He's sneaking cigarettes. He's overfeeding Maria and Tatiana. You better get home quick."

James closes his eyes. I fiddle with the edge of the blanket. He works a hand from under it, holds his palm up. I put mine on top of it. Both our hands are cold.

"He's going to Germany," I say. "He got an offer to dance there. He's very happy."

"Yes, you said."

I could tell him Alex didn't deny the importance of their relationship. That it *was* love. How Alex described parting from him like Romeo parting from Juliet, thinking the world less lonely. I could have told him that on the phone six days ago. He would not have tried to kill himself with such knowledge.

"I know it's an insult," James says. "To the men here now, fighting for their lives. I feel terribly guilty. I had a dream this morning I was in Bellevue. I remember when they first set up an AIDS ward there. It was next to the cafeteria and some of the staff were upset because they didn't want to eat next to us, to our disease. But others were such angels. Here too."

"James," I say. "What happened? What was the certainty?"

He looks away from me, at the window. "I just had a, a vision, I suppose you could call it. You remember how he told you it was over and we were moving on? I saw then how it would be. Robert would never forgive me. We'd never leave each other, but he'd never forgive me, and I wouldn't ever be safe again. There didn't seem to be any point. I convinced myself, in the horrible way one can, you know, that I'd be setting him free." James squeezes my hand and withdraws his own. "I think if you're lonely too long, your sense of the world warps, and you can never find the right shape again. Robert doesn't—he can't—he doesn't have the right size heart for an ordinary world. It has to be everything, with him. *I* have to be everything."

It sounds like an accusation.

"It's not his fault," James continues. "My mother understood what I was. My poor father, I think he understood too. I found my people, my tribe if you will, quickly enough. You were *born* into yours. But Robert, he was alone."

My father, at the airport many years ago, telling me that James was not like "us." And now James, in a hospital, explaining to me how it is my father who is not like "us."

Perhaps I don't want to be like either one of them.

"We have to find a way he can get through this," James says. "I did *not* choose a very good way."

"You're saying you did this for him?" I hate his air of thwarted sacrifice, am relieved to find something in him to hate.

"No, no. It was my own weakness. But now I think, there's maybe some good in it. You see, if he can be angry at me for this, then he can forget about the other thing. Alex. This crime, which is real, which is *worse*, he can forgive."

How can they *afford* to be like this, to play these complex games?

"You make him sound like a monster."

"We're all monsters." James leans forward and grabs my wrist. I'm surprised at his strength. "That's important for you to know, Carlisle. We are all of us monsters. Even the failures."

He's right. It has not made me a better person, to be a failure.

"You know he wants you to have everything," I say. "He wants to support your work. Alex said the choreography you taught him was amazing. Incredible. It needs to be seen. You can do everything that's in your head. You just have to believe in yourself."

His grip slackens and something in his eyes retreats. How can I blame him? *You just have to believe in yourself*? Jesus. And now I'm hating all of us, and all our petty tragedies. My mother, the dancer whose career had been cut short by pregnancy and then injury. My father, exiled from the inner circle of New York ballet. James, whose masterpieces were never to breathe form, in order not to make my father unhappy.

My own lack of will and guts.

"I have to make things right with your father," James says. "And that's between me and him. It's not your responsibility, Carlisle. We've burdened you enough. *I've* burdened you enough. The best thing for you to do is to take a little break from us. Go live your life and let us sort out our nonsense between us."

"Do you love him?" I ask. And then, in case it's not clear, "Do you love my father?"

"He's my life." James takes a deep breath. The muscles in his neck stand out sharply. "He's my life. And I'm his."

I reach into the bag I brought and pull out James's notebook. I put it in his lap. He turns his eyes to the ceiling.

"At any rate, I live," he says. "Sensation."

The Flood

My father and I walk back to Bank Street together. He'd been gentle with James, in front of me, but a little remote. He'd talked about France. James and I had both watched him carefully.

"Is he really okay to travel?" I ask, as we cross Greenwich Avenue. "Medically?"

"It was an overdose," he says. "He took sleeping pills and got in the tub. That's where I found him. If I hadn't come home early, he'd be dead. But I did come home early. So in a few days, he won't be dead, he'll be in France with me."

We walk the rest of the way home in silence. I imagine he's repeating that sentence to himself, over and over. *If I hadn't come home early, he'd be dead.*

He doesn't like to smoke while walking and waits till we're at the gate in front of Bank Street to shake a cigarette from his pack. I pull out my own.

"That makes me sad," he says. "It's a filthy habit."

"I'll stop if you do."

He doesn't smile. He takes a deep, bitter drag. He smokes with his fingers on top of the cigarette, like a character from a noir film, a giant Humphrey Bogart.

"Did James tell you what happened?" he asks.

"You mean—?"

"I mean why," he says. "Why he did it."

"He said he got a certainty, a kind of feeling, but it was the wrong one. It's depression, Dad. He got anxious. He was so sad about everything that happened between you two. Desperate."

"But you didn't know how bad it was when you left?"

"No, I—"

"What you're saying"—he jabs his cigarette in my direction—"is it's my fault for not believing him. I drove him to it."

It seems to be what I'm saying.

"That's rich," he says, in the metallic, remote voice. And then, "I know you're both lying."

It's too theatrical, I almost laugh. I feel sick. Of course, he knows what I did. Of course.

"What would we lie about?"

"Stop it," he says. "Stop lying. I can't bear it anymore. You left your passport in your room this morning. You were in *Mexico*. What a coincidence. James's little friend was down there too."

"You went through my things?"

He mimics my words back to me, horribly. Now I'm angry.

"Okay, yes, I went to Mexico. I knew Alex was there, and I decided to go and find out the truth because I love you both. I talked to Alex. He gave me his notebook. James did. To give to Alex. Alex loves James as a teacher. That's all. It's innocent. That's the truth."

"He gave you his notebook to give to Alex." The hand holding his cigarette is shaking a little. "What notebook?"

"With his choreography notes." Oh God. What have I done?

"You were gone a week."

"I went to a friend's wedding down there. I told you."

He takes a deep drag of his cigarette, appears for a moment almost contemplative.

"I'm sorry," I say. This comes out in a whisper. "I should have told you the truth. I'm sorry."

"So the wedding part was true."

I use smoking as an excuse not to say anything and nod my head.

Robert swipes his cigarette out on the grate. I do the same and follow him up the stairs. He walks down the hallway, to their bedroom, and I follow him there, leaning on the doorframe. He has James's white shirts lined up across the bed, folded flat. James's pants in tidy rolls. His own shorts and Breton striped shirts. Sandals. Sun hats. Bathrobes. There's a stack of boxes, emptied and broken down flat, leaning against the narrow window. I remember my father saying James had boxed up his clothing, before trying to kill himself. *I even understood the tarp.*

My father takes things from a large Duane Reade bag on the dresser and puts them in two Dopp kits. Tatiana tries to enter with me and I shoo her out. She will pee in their closet if she sees the suitcase.

My father almost looks cheerful. Cheerful? Determined, maybe.

"So, am I coming with you?" And now it's a child's voice, coming out of me. "To France?"

"I'm just trying to figure out," he says, "who told James that you and Alex had an affair."

I shake my head and am about to issue a string of denials, but he holds up a hand.

"Which is it?" he asks. "James tried to kill himself because I didn't believe his innocence? Or James tried to kill himself because he sent you to Mexico to explain his heart and instead you broke it?"

"No, I'm not trying to say, to blame—"

"I don't believe this story about a wedding," he spits out. "You were with Alex the whole time."

"No," I say, although why not admit it to him? At least he'd know James hadn't cheated. Maybe I could do *one* good thing. "That's not—"

"Just say it," he yells, and it's sudden and loud and it feels like everything in the room jumps. "Just say you and Alex are having an affair, or fucking, or in love, or whatever you are. Stop lying. I can't bear to hear you lie to me."

"Okay, I won't." To shout this gives me a delicious, sickening release. Hot and cold. Vile and happy. "*We're* the ones who fell in love. *We're* the ones who want to be together. *I'm* having an affair with Alex, not *James*. We didn't mean for it to happen, but it did and we're in love. He wants me to come to Germany with him. It's *real*."

There's a moment, I swear it, when I think this has solved everything. My father goes so calm. No angry toddler at all. The lines in his face smooth and he watches me the way I've seen him watch dance, with a still attentiveness, almost a smile, something secret inside finding purchase.

"I haven't been very happy," I say, almost dizzy with confession. I sit on the edge of their bed. "For a long time. I want to change my life. It's part of what I figured out in Mexico. I had this epiphany, or whatever. I mean, I think I want to start choreographing, or trying to, or getting involved with that in some way. And I want to be with Alex."

"You want to be with Alex." Yes. He's calm. He's taking it in.

"James doesn't know," I say. "I mean, he knows I went to Mexico, but not what happened between me and Alex."

"He knows."

"No, really," I say. "He doesn't. He can't."

"Because you're such a good liar?"

I can't read him. I don't—I think—*know* him.

"I found him in the bathtub," my father says, looking at James's clothes. "Passed out. Cold.

"I had to pull his body out of the bathtub. They had to pump his stomach. James *knew*, Carlisle."

He lifts his head. I stand and take a step back.

"I pulled him out of the tub"—his voice is rising again—"and they pumped his stomach and he was delirious with pain and, and grief, and he said Alex's name. And he said, 'They must be laughing at me.' I didn't know who he meant. The world, I thought. But it was you. You and Alex. He knew. He *knew*. Someone must have told him. All those people from our world down there? You're not invisible." He points a shaky hand, gestures up and down the length of me. "Someone saw you together and told James. You broke his heart just like you're breaking mine."

I think, with a jolt, of the director, and Alex calling me his girlfriend. Or maybe it was the Belgian choreographer. One of the dancers. We *weren't* invisible. We didn't try to be. Alex didn't know we had anything to hide. I look at my father.

"You went behind my back," he says. "And then you had an affair, behind James's back." He's really shouting now, worse than before. I can't see his face; my eyes are swimming.

"You tried to make me think it's my fault." His voice is so loud it feels like the room is ringing. "That James was depressed because I didn't believe him. James was innocent and you were innocent. You almost killed him, Carlisle. You almost killed him.

"Now you announce you're going to Germany and you've had an epiphany. *You're* gonna be a choreographer. What have we ever done?" His voice breaks. "What have we ever done to you that you would betray us both like that? And then you stand there and say you didn't mean for it to happen. As if you had no responsibility."

"I didn't mean to betray anybody." This comes out in a whisper.

"You knew this would hurt us both and you did it anyway. A mistake, I could forgive. Bad judgment. This is more. This is malice. Now you're going to go off to Germany."

"It's not," I say. "No. I didn't—"

"Why, Carlisle? Why?"

"This is stupid," I shout.

"Stupid? You think it's all stupid? Because we're just some old fags? Because *your* love is real love? You knew that to hurt James is to hurt me. You knew I can't live without him. Why would you even *go* to Mexico?"

Why did I go to Mexico? Why would I do that?

"Betsy came to Bank Street," he shouts. "I knew James was a mess. She said the place was a shambles. I thought I could trust you. I thought you would listen and you would help. You can't tell me you didn't see what a wreck he was."

"He wasn't—"

"He gave you his life's work." His voice breaks again. "He gave you his life's work and told you to bring it to someone he loved. You could have called me. You could have said, 'Dad, James is suffering and confused and he wants me to do this thing and I don't know what to do.'"

I could have done those things.

"Why, Carlisle? Why did you do this?"

The question fills the room, nearly shoving me out of it. My father's face is shining. He straightens to his full height. Something has been released in him. A kind of euphoria, a chemical. I'm transfixed. I think, *James was right. He needs a crime for the pain. Only James had the wrong crime. This is the right one.*

"Until you understand why," he says, "I don't want to hear from you. Until you figure out why you would do such a thing to us, and until you can explain it to me, you are no longer welcome here."

A choky kind of laugh comes out of me. He bends back to the packing.

"You're kicking me out?"

"We're leaving tomorrow." He won't look at me. He speaks to the clothes. "You can stay here tonight. You should say goodbye to James. I trust you'll not say anything to upset him. You'll tell him you have a work emergency. Or I will." He screws up his mouth. "Obviously, I can't trust you. I ask you, to say nothing to upset him."

I don't know him, I think. *I don't really know him. I thought I did.*

"Isabel would be horrified to know what you've done," he says. "I know your mother didn't raise you to behave like this. I know I certainly didn't."

You didn't, I think, *raise me at all.*

"I can't *make* you a person of integrity," he says, with finality. "Think about your behavior, about the kind of person you want to be. Think about what you did and why. When you have an explanation, I will hear it."

I say nothing. I go to Carlisle's Room and shut the door. There doesn't seem to be a reason *why* I did what I did, other than I *wanted* to, which apparently is not a reason. I don't know how to think about my behavior, except how to justify it. But there's no one to tell but myself.

James had not acted like he knew what happened with Alex. Or, if he knows, he doesn't blame me. James will help my father get over it. It's fine. It's all going to be fine. It's the emotion of the moment. I'm his daughter.

I repeat this to myself all night. I wonder what my father is telling himself.

The next day my father brings James home from the hospital. James tells me he is sorry I can't join them. The story of a mysterious work emergency has apparently been accepted. James is affectionate but distracted. He helps my father finish the packing. Laughter comes from the bedroom. They touch each other in the hallway. My father doesn't ignore me. His attitude, I interpret, is one of expectation, and innocence. Anything that happens now, happens because of what I will do, have done, am doing.

James catches me in the kitchen and squeezes my shoulder.

"Carlisle, everything is going to be okay," he says. "He's forgiven me. I'm flooded with relief."

Why should a *flood* of relief be a good thing? Floods are bad. You have to send relief when there are floods.

"I'm happy for you," I say. I search his eyes for reproach. It's not there.

I don't know what to do, exactly. Call the airline. Go back to LA. Go to Atlanta? Betsy is coming later, to pick up the cats. Tatiana is so vengeful, but she will not misbehave at Betsy's. I walk to the pay phone on the corner, call a school friend and ask to stay on her couch. When I return, my father is outside, with their suitcases. I move to touch his arm and he pulls it away. We both react as if we've been slapped. I run inside. James is coming down the stairs, wearing his hat at a jaunty angle and with his old Pan Am satchel slung across one shoulder. Did I say goodbye to Robert already? Is the car service here? He gives me a quick hug, promises to send postcards.

I go back to Los Angeles and a few weeks later discover I'm pregnant.

Endangered Species

Landing in New York City. 2016. I'm disoriented, in between cities, decades, versions of myself.

I see it over and over again. Alex putting on his sunglasses and adjusting his posture. His back, walking in front of me. Our arms almost grazing and then grazing. Nineteen years ago, and my body remembers. I've thought about this, in different ways. Not thought about it, in different ways.

My father's body, not to be replaced. He will die and this rope of tension between us will go slack. I will pull one more time and fall backward.

I think of Xavier's puppets, crashing into each other.

Alex. The bandanna and the wrist cuff, the angle of his shoulders. The consuming passion one can have for another body, the thing they say always fades. Was it better or worse for James, that he never had the real man under his real hands? Is it better or worse for me that I did?

James's body, slight under a blanket on a hospital bed. *At any rate, I live. Sensation.*

I have been angry at Alex too. Not for what happened later but because his telling me he loved me is still the most romantic moment of my life and he will have had others.

I leave the airport, take a cab to my hotel in Midtown. It's too early for check-in but my plan is to divest myself of my bag and walk to the Performing Arts library. I have a stack of *Firebird*-related things waiting for me. It all feels like nonsense now. But it's what I know how to do, I suppose.

I don't know what to do.

I walk. After the sprawling fecundity of Los Angeles, New York City looks to me like a background replica of itself. Unreal, theatrical. "Grimy corner." "Upscale block." No haze, no canyons. All these vertical lines.

I watch a FedEx worker swing himself into his truck. He hops onto the first step with his right foot, grabs at the side bar handle with his left hand, crosses his left leg over to take the second step as his right hip juts forward to slide into the cab, at the same time releasing the handlebar and cocking his head so as not to hit it on the cabin of his truck. Beautifully done. This is his choreography. He didn't start doing this on the first day of work, it developed. Now it's his dance.

All the ordinary gestures of life. Set them to music, make them formal or abstract, lose the FedEx truck, replace it with another body, put it on a stage. Now you have a ballet.

My body, after the flight and the lurching cab, begins to find its measure. This vertical city is good for tall women. It's changed in ways I'm not yet able to track, as have I. But this city wasn't ever *mine*.

Some forty blocks south, in a bedroom, a bed, my father. Waiting for me?

I cut through Central Park, strolling like I do when I'm in a foreign town, shoulders back, eyes tracing the architecture of people and buildings, cataloging. I *don't* know this city, not truly. Two weeks out of the year. One summer. After college, a handful of visits.

What do I want to happen here?

I'm back into crowds on the other side of the park, picking up my pace to match the flow of traffic. Here's Lincoln Center. The School of American Ballet has been completely redone; there are dorms and all kinds of improvements. I remember a small café a few blocks uptown, tucked into the side of a residential building, next to a laundromat. It's still there, and this makes me feel like I'm doing something right; like I have a piece of the city. I order and sit at a table. The feelings of a younger me return on a rush of senses. I take a sip of cappuccino and revisit old wants, set aside now for years: a cigarette, sugar in my coffee, to live here. I look out the window and realize I'm two blocks away from where James will be teaching ballet class in about half an hour. He could pass this window right now. He could stop inside for a coffee. I shrink back, retreat to a corner, then further to the ladies' room. A twinge deep in my pelvis alerts me to my period. A surprise, but I'm starting to become irregular. Premenopausal, I suppose. I need tampons, Advil, a quiet room, a chair, containment.

At the library, half an hour later, I settle myself at a workstation with a collection of materials and open my notebook. I've gotten to the point where I find the score of *Firebird* interesting, but I can't *see* anything happening, have no question in my head for this ballet other than *What is the point?*

I look at the notebook in my lap. All those years of not talking over projects with Robert and James. Every summer I wasn't invited to work on something at Boxhill. Robert has nurtured other talent; he is a great promoter of American choreographers.

Every piece of mine they were never in the audience for.

Is he lying in his bed at Bank Street still waiting for me to tell him *why*?

On the screen in front of me, I scroll through photos of New York City Ballet, circa 1970. What's known as a "costume parade." Balanchine is inspecting the re-created Chagall designs for his latest *Firebird*. The dancers pose casually in a large, windowless rehearsal studio at State Theater. It looks like a fun day, everyone playing around in their newly completed costumes. Here is Balanchine, in discussion with the choreographer Jerome Robbins, his associate artistic director. They've collaborated on this production: Robbins has provided the monster dances. Robbins is bearded and trim; he's holding up a monster headpiece. The men appear to know exactly what they want. I scan through more slides.

Oh. Oh, here's my mother. She's in a group of three dancers, each looking in a different direction. Her Chagall monster costume—more whimsy than terror—is a lumpish bodysuit painted with abstract garden-like vines and flowers. Her hands are covered with large mitts depicting line drawings of hands, her headpiece a pie-shaped face with modernist geometric features and a mop of hair. It sits on top of her head like a hat. Below it, she's smiling, grinning really. So are the two other girls. They dance for Balanchine. They are monsters; they are art. She's the tallest in the group. She looks so happy.

Her name, along with her companions', isn't listed. The caption names them only as "three dancers." I click through the file until I get to images of *Firebird* from 1972. There's no costume parade or rehearsal footage for this year, but I'm able to pick Isabel out—or think I can—from a curtain call photo. I want to believe that's her profile, under the kokoshnik headdress. I'm there too, invisible inside the woman invisible inside the Maiden.

I close the file, close my eyes. Another twinge from the place in my body where babies start or don't start. It's like my uterus pinches me. Sharp little stabs. Will I miss the power of something I never wanted to use? Maybe this is a sign I should lean into the Great Egg of It All, with my *Firebird*. Get rid of the Evil Sorcerer entirely and make Firebird a witch of the forest. She has put her femaleness into an egg and buried it under a tree so she can be a woman free of being female. Replace Prince Ivan with a Princess Vanna, who gets lost in the forest. She sees Firebird and wants to be like her. Firebird teaches her how to bury her femaleness and gives her feathers. They kill monsters together. But then Princess Vanna meets a Lost Prince and falls in love. Firebird shows her how, in order to be with him, she has to dig up her Femaleness Egg and crack it open. The Princess does so and loses her powers and her feathers but gets the guy. Finale shows Triumphant Firebird happy being free, and Triumphant Princess with her Happy Prince and Baby. Red feathers descend on the audience from the ceiling of the theater. Oh my God, it's like *The Little Mermaid* meets *Buffy the Vampire Slayer*. What am I even saying? One is either a Firebird or a Mother? Offensive as well as simplistic.

I do like the image of feathers descending on an audience.

Maybe I've been working in Hollywood too long.

James is teaching class right now. Is Robert alone? James said they have nursing assistants who help with baths, an RN who comes twice a week, a lovely woman from hospice. If things were different, perhaps I'd be there now, Robert's hand in mine.

There aren't so many of them—men of their generation, their circle—who got to die of old age. To say goodbye to their partners after so many years. To call their partners their husbands.

I hesitate a long moment before entering Robert's name into the database. I'm not sure what I can bear to look at, what more I can know.

There are things about Boxhill, but I stumble into a huge cache from LaGrange Ballet. They must have turned over their entire archives; I could spend days hunting through it all. I read LaGrange, speaking about my father to *Look* magazine in 1965:

> Robert Martin came to my class one day, wearing a suit and tie, and asked if he could watch. I told him this was a professional class and if he wanted to watch dance, he could buy a ticket like anyone else. Then he says he's a student and I say, "Well go get changed then. Class is a buck unless I know you." And he leaves and I'm thinking, *There goes a dollar,* but he comes back and takes the class. He worked harder than everyone. I said to myself, *Look at this guy: big legs, big feet, big everything. No lines.* But he danced on the music and he was coordinated and tall. I thought: *This guy, I can make something of this guy.* I love oddballs. He was going to go to law school and ends up a dancer. You want loyalty? Find yourself some oddballs and make them stars.

I press my fist against my sternum. Remember my father standing outside Carnegie Hall, years ago, telling me how he'd taken his first class with professional dancers in a studio there. "I almost didn't do it and just watched from the doorway," he'd said. "It turned out to be the day my life really started. I was invited in. Everything changed that day."

I look at footage from a LaGrange tour to the USSR in '64,

one to South America in '70. I find an audio recording: a radio interview with LaGrange and Robert for WNYC-FM in 1969. The file says they're discussing their vision for American dance. I press my hands against the muffs of the earphones, like a code breaker or a radio operator from a World War II movie my father and I might have watched together. Here is his voice. A baritone from the Midwest with a good education. I haven't heard his voice in so long.

LaGrange has a Jersey accent, higher pitched.

INTERVIEWER: LaGrange Ballet is known for introducing young choreographers, and some, I guess what you might call experimental choreographers to a wider audience.

LAGRANGE: Listen, from the beginning we were teaching our audiences. Our first tours, we did four dances. First, we warmed them up with something free and upbeat, big smiles, the girls in skirts, the boys in pants. Then we challenged them with a solo or a duet—not too long, right—in the modern style. For education. The third ballet was classical: tutus and pointe shoes and boys in tights and Tchaikovsky and all of that. Then we'd leave them on their feet with something patriotic and sunny, lots of kicks and jumps, to Gershwin or Copland. I called it: Reach 'em, teach 'em, preach 'em, and beach 'em.'

MARTIN: From the beginning, LaGrange Ballet has put engaging and promoting important new work at the heart of its programming and vision.

LAGRANGE: Stars of tomorrow! That's what LaGrange is all about. Stars of today and stars of tomorrow! It's like with my dancers. I don't look for the perfect body. Tall, short, long legs, short legs.

I look for the right energy, the right spark. What the kids in my company have in common is energy and dedication and spirit and loyalty. Ya know: Pow! Pow! Pow! That's America! America ain't Europe. In Europe, culture is the cathedral, the museum, the opera house. Culture in America is the baseball diamond, the church picnic, the marching band. We don't have fairies or sylphs in our folktales. We don't have princes and princesses. What are princes to us? Why should those be on our stages, in our ballets? Who cares about yesterday? Yesterday is dead.

MARTIN: We see ourselves as part of the incredible tradition of American dance. Ballet didn't start here, but it's been remade in America's image. We want Americans to feel a national pride in their ballet companies. To look at the work and say, "This is us. This is who we can be."

He's younger than I am now in this interview. He's met Eleanor Turnball, rechristened her Isabel Osmond. In a few years, he'll marry her. Make me.

I love him, in this interview. I can't help it. I see him sitting slightly behind LaGrange, as he was always sitting behind. Believing he could show his country what he loved, make them love it too. Accept it. Accept him.

I scroll though more archives, discover that one of the early stars of LaGrange Ballet wrote a memoir about the '64 tour to what was then Leningrad. I hunt it down, flip through looking for references to Robert. There are many; the author had known my father since the days of touring around middle America with the Shasta trailer christened Le Cochon Vert.

"Robert Martin, our beloved and indefatigable manager . . ." "All of this would have been impossible if Robert hadn't . . ." "As always, tempers were soothed by Robert Martin's quick tact and diplomacy . . ." There's a picture of my father in Leningrad, standing with a group of dancers along a canal, in front of "The Church of the Savior on Spilled Blood." He's holding out his arm for one of the girls striking a pose. He wears a hat and a thick coat and looks wonderful. I search for information about the author of the memoir, who sounds as if he was truly fond of my father. He died in 1984, of AIDS.

I can't. I don't think I can.

I should have asked my mother to come with me.

She's in this database too. I find a performance of *Stars and Stripes* and watch the photograph in my hallway come to life: Isabel Osmond marches on pointe with her sisters in the corps. She pirouettes and salutes. A happy soldier. I think of Robert and James, with their portraits of fathers in military uniforms. *Our fathers never liked to talk about the war.* Well, neither did my mother.

I imagine walking into Bank Street tomorrow and pressing my father's hand and telling him I love him. He asks if I forgive him. I say yes. I ask if he forgives me. He says yes. Against all the sorrow in the world, we should behave with love and forgiveness, even if we don't always feel it.

I do feel it.

In my fashion.

But I'm still on the outside.

I can't, at my age, still be *becoming* a person, can I?

I decide to take a break, walk around the block and clear my head. I get another coffee from a deli and then find myself half-running with it back toward Central Park, abandoning the day of research.

My phone rings. It's Freya.

"Hi."

I'm on a beautiful street I have no associations with. These buildings are probably all occupied by oligarchs and venture capitalists. Friends have reported: nobody real lives in Manhattan anymore. I remember James, speaking of his years in Denmark. *Even now, I find myself thinking,* I'll go back. *As if one could pick up a life left at fourteen. There's no back* left.

"Freya—" My voice is breaking. Here it comes, at last.

"My darling," she says.

I don't *want* to love him. Them.

"I don't want to do *Firebird,*" I say, instead. "It's this wonderful opportunity and just feels like the dumbest fucking thing. You saw that Xavier Larks piece *Assigned Seating,* right? What happened between me and Robert and James is so ridiculous compared to the terrible things in the world."

"If you carry on with that logic," Freya says, "certain *genocides* are not as bad as other genocides."

"This is just one death—"

"I know, I know."

"I can't do a magic bird ballet. I mean, on a certain level, anything any of us are doing right now that *isn't* about climate catastrophe is irresponsible, although making *art* about climate grief is probably even more feckless."

"Okay, I'm not *quite*—"

"*The Endangered Firebird,*" I say. "That's what I'm gonna do."

"Carlisle."

"Firebird enters, snagged in plastic, dripping with oil from a tanker spill, starved from habitat destruction. Flops over on her face. End of ballet. Curtain. Her death is all our deaths."

"Oh my God."

"I can't talk about it," I say, a little frantic. "I can't talk about them. Please talk to me about something else."

"Yes, yes, right." Freya is fast, she can do this. "What about this," she says. "You make the prince a naturalist. He goes hunting in the jungle for rare specimens. He captures Firebird and tries to put her in a box. When he gets in trouble later, he lets her out to help him, but she kills *everyone* in a berserker rage."

"That's very good." I choke on the coffee, laughing, look at the red lipstick imprint on the cardboard cup. I could *almost* throw it across the street, or at one of these doors. Throw it with all my strength and maybe scream. *All this wasted time.* For nothing. For ego. Because nobody could get exactly what they wanted. Because nobody knew how to stop themselves from being themselves.

There's another story. James was ill. Robert was frightened to death. If I had forgiven them first, they might have had space to forgive me. Maybe I can't answer why I did what I did, but *how* did I let it go on?

I didn't need all this wreckage to become—what, exactly?

"Carlisle?"

"Tell me how to live with this mistake," I plead. "I've never known. I didn't know how to live with it while I was *making* it. Then everything just got worse. And my father got to tell me I was a monster and shut the door. He could live his life as the person who'd been horribly hurt by me and I had to live shut out, wearing this monster costume."

"Your father wasn't *forced* to react the way he did," Freya says. "It wasn't some kind of inevitable consequence. And you weren't out to hurt them."

"But I knew it would. A part of me always knew."

"That doesn't disqualify you from being loved."

People are moving around me, inside their own choreography. Here I am. Standing. Unsure.

Set this to music and it's a ballet.

I picture Freya stroking her neck, tucking her fingers under the top of her shirt, a characteristic gesture, one I love.

"Maybe I stayed away all this time," I say, "because I *needed* it to be awful. I think I might be more like my father than I realized. I needed a crime to justify the wounds. The ones I received and the ones I inflicted."

"I think it's time," Freya says, "to lay your burdens down."

I go back to the hotel and take off my Strawberry Thief suit, close the shades against the afternoon sun and get under the covers. I'm just drifting off when James calls.

My pod room is small. I roll off the bed, bump into the chair. The round mirror on the wall is set at the wrong height for me. All I can see is the lower half of my face and my naked chest.

James. It was six days ago when he called to tell me Robert was dying. I'd been so struck with the familiarity of the words, expected, anticipated. Now I hear *him*, the person. It's odd how human he sounds. How simple. A man on the phone.

"My thought was this," James says. "Perhaps you might meet me after my class, and we'll go down to Bank Street together? It'll be lunchtime and that will be an activity, you see. Robert doesn't eat much but he likes the idea that he might. He likes to feel we can still eat together. After, I'll clear up and you can spend a little time together alone."

"Right." I'm reminded this whole meeting with Robert is being managed, even stage-managed. My stomach hurts. I open my duffel and pull out my alternate clothes. I should walk more. I can't stay in this small room, looking at the lower half of my head, and my resentment, and the place where my heart is supposed to be.

"One has to stage-manage it a little," James says. The echo of my thoughts shakes me back to focus. "To make it seem *not* stage-managed. I'm trying to avoid a ceremonial advancing on the deathbed. Does that sound horribly harsh? One gets in a sort of gallows humor place. My class is over by eleven-thirty and I can meet you on the street by eleven forty-five. Or you could come up and watch the end of class if you like."

"I could *take* your class," I say.

Where did that come from?

"Would you want to?" He sounds equally surprised.

What am I doing? I want to prepare for meeting Robert. Be freshly groomed, in my suit, lipstick in place. I had pictured myself walking down their street slowly, calmly. That was my costume and my choreography. Dignity. Control. Containment.

"I think it would be fun," I say. "Full circle. The last class I took in New York was from you."

What am I doing?

"I have some wonderful dancers in class now." James starts naming people. "I was also trying to think if there's anyone we know who can be helpful to you. Or who you might find interesting. In other times, we could have done a dinner. Of course, you don't need us. You're very well established."

Other times? Other times during my two-decade banishment? *Well established?* Between the two of them they know *everyone* who could be helpful to me. Being invited to Boxhill would have been helpful to me.

I'm still on the outside.

"Let's not think about that right now," I say.

"He's asked about you," James says. "I'm telling him tonight that you're really here. It seemed to me you might change your mind. Which I'd understand."

"Well," I say. "I'm not there yet."

"Oh," he says. "No. Of course not."

Silence.

"What do you need?" he asks. "What would be helpful?"

It's a graceful question, a kind one. I ask him to tell me what state Robert's in. I don't want to be shocked or knocked off balance by pity or fear. We discuss Robert, not as a man or an emotion but as a body. James mentions blood pressure and skin pallor. I ask about pain. He talks about coughing and sodium levels.

"His lovely legs are swollen," James says. "His face is a little gaunt. He sometimes needs help with breathing. There's a portable machine, but he finds the mask uncomfortable. And then, you know, there are moments when he looks almost well. The expressions on his face and his gestures. We don't talk in a sort of grand-summing-up way. Quite ordinary things, mostly. He does revisit the past. We laugh. He does—know. That he's dying."

"I've been revisiting the past too," I say to James.

"A foreign country," he quotes, lightly. *"They do things differently there."* Is that a warning in his voice?

We say goodbye and I decide on a walk to a dance store in the East Thirties. New York appears no more realistic than it did earlier in the day. The feeling of being in between cities and selves returns. At the store, I get shoes and things to dance in.

I must think about work. It's what I have to give. As a woman, a person, what do I have? Not much. The best of me is in my work. Not that I'm selfless there. I use my dancers. I use their talent, their devotion, their endless training and ambition, their desire for approval from the mirror and from me. I mine it all and polish the gems. I make them do what I want, and I try to give them something that says, *You are seen. There is only one of you in this world. I have never seen anyone exactly like you. Take this movement, it's yours alone.*

Some people say *Oh, your ballets are your children,* but from what

I've seen of children and parenting, I'd say only your children are your children.

I've used memories of Alex in my work. Muscle memory is so much more valuable than the other kind. Muscle memory, you can deploy. It never did me any good to remember, in the time following Mexico, what Robert *said*, or James. I repackaged the feelings in different ways but never sent them away. Clutter. Pointless monsters under the bed. But I could place two dancers side by side and have their arms just brush each other and Alex's body would return to me.

Alex was like a dream, but the work, the work has been the most real thing in my life.

I don't regret not having the child. But sometimes I wish I was the kind of person who would have kept it.

I could have gone to my father, at any time, and asked for forgiveness. I made choices. My banishment was devastating.

My banishment was the making of me.

Back at the hotel I put on the ballet slippers I just bought. I opted for black.

I need to see this through.

I could cry. I could almost cry.

No Regrets

1997. Robert and James go to France. I go back to Los Angeles. James sends postcards.

The pregnancy seems such cruel luck. Alex and I are children of the eighties; we used condoms. There'd been one night, when we woke up after being asleep for a few hours and had hot, still-drunk, laughing sex and sort of passed out on each other and then I moved to go pee and we fumbled the condom, and it came off inside me. We said, "Oh shit," but didn't worry. What were the odds?

I tell my friend Liesel, who I know has had an abortion. I'm embarrassed, ashamed, a little frightened, but not conflicted. I've only just figured out what I want from my life. "Tell him," says Liesel. "It's not his decision but it's his responsibility too." Alex is sweet on the phone. I can hear he's relieved when I tell him my choice, but he offers to come out, to pay. "I want kids," he says. "But when we're both ready." It's a romantic thing to say but a little alarming. I can't imagine wanting children, not really. Alex sends flowers. Liesel take me to the clinic, where everyone is kind and looks me in the eye. There are no protesters. Nothing is made worse for me.

I buy German language instruction CDs. I start taking class seriously and going to see dance in Los Angeles with some purpose. "Come for Christmas," Alex says. "Stay and we'll go to Germany together." The company there is helping him with housing. He wonders if maybe they can help me with a job. Ushering in the theater, he suggests. I picture myself ushering in a theater where Alex is performing. This is not what it feels like to dance around in a man's shoes. I fantasize about getting involved with some kind of avant-garde dance collective.

James calls me from the studio, where we can "talk more freely."

"I asked Robert if you're coming for Thanksgiving and he said no and the subject of Carlisle is off-limits for the moment. I won't ask you to betray confidences, but of course I'm worried this involves me or what happened."

I'm going to have to tell him I'm going to Germany with Alex. I can't. I'm scared of losing him too. "Nothing to do with you," I say. "At all. An issue between us." He takes my assurances too easily. How can he *possibly* believe them?

He asks me, a little shyly, about Alex. Did we have a good conversation? Did I like him? Did I see him dance?

Is this another trap? Yes, I say. A nice guy. Great dancer. We got along. "I'm surprised he didn't make a pass at you," James says. "Well," I say, and laugh. He laughs too. *Is this the moment?* "It all feels a bit of a nightmare," James says. "But the crisis has passed. Do you know, we all just need a little time. And time is a gift."

I go to Atlanta at Christmas, and watch Alex perform the

Snow King in *The Nutcracker*. I'm the girlfriend waiting at the stage door. It would be sexier, I think, if I was *also* something else. We do fall into each other's arms. Together, everything is made right. "It's always going to be Mexico," Alex says. "Wherever we are together." I might be built for the solo, but it's not my destiny.

I have found the one who will love me best of all.

Alex confesses it's a lot of responsibility, my coming with him to Germany. What if I'm unhappy, what if I can't get work, can't make money or friends. He would feel awful, me giving up everything. He'll need to be super focused at work, the first year is so important. He'll be gone all day, and when performing, all day and all night. I take responsibility after responsibility. I promise not to be a bother, a burden, a source of guilt. I'm good at assuring people I won't need anything from them, and for a while doing so makes me feel pretty great about myself. I enjoy the idea of Alex's perfectly independent and self-sufficient girlfriend as much as he does. We agree I'll come for a visit first, once he gets settled. He will know more about things. I can see if I like it. We can decide what to do from there. There's no self-sufficient way for me to say, *Let me come with you.*

Alex moves to Germany, and for a while, things intensify between us, aided by change, abetted by insecurity. I keep practicing German. This is going to work out. These are the big feelings. There will be love and art.

Alex calls. He says we have to talk. He has just gotten a long letter, from James. In this letter, James alluded to his suicide attempt. "Which you obviously know about," Alex says. "You told me he was fine. You also said he knew about us, which he clearly doesn't." James apologized, in the letter, for the imposition of sending his notebook. "One of those mad gestures," Alex quotes, "you were absolutely right not to indulge."

Now, from Alex, the same questions. *Why, Carlisle? Why?*

I didn't want it to touch us. I didn't want to stop. I didn't want you to choose James over me. I just wanted what I wanted. A question of morals.

I say nothing.

Alex says he doesn't see how he could ever trust me again.

How can I argue with this? I don't. Everything my father said was right. There is no excuse. I even tell Alex I *understand.*

This is the reckoning.

I don't go to Germany.

We stop speaking. I assume at least part of this means he has, or already had, met someone else. I imagine it was a relief for him, to have an excuse. I take the German-language CDs to Goodwill. I want to be allowed to be devastated but don't know how or who will grant me this. Not myself.

He never loved me best. He only loved me *when.* When I was in front of him, when I was easy, when, perhaps, I was a part of James.

There's a big gathering in Ohio for grandmother's seventy-fifth birthday. Isabel and Ben pay for my ticket. "We missed having you here for Christmas." My aunt Pat and uncle Joe are there, along with cousins and their significant others. There's a lot of storytelling and looking at family albums. This makes me uncomfortable, or sad, or something. I can't say exactly what or why. Isabel seems to feel the same. She suggests we take a walk. "This is nice," she says. "But it's all a bit much."

She asks me how I am. I think I must look pretty terrible. I look at the sidewalk and the trees and the pleasant ranch houses and Isabel's exercise sneakers and leggings. I tell her I had an abortion.

We walk in silence for a minute. She asks if I'm okay and I say yes.

"Do you regret it?" she asks.

"No."

I have thought, *If I'd kept the baby, Alex would have had to forgive me.* But that's not what children are for.

"If you don't regret it, then you did the right thing," she says. "I guess it's not my place to say. But I can see how— Well, anyway. I'm glad you told me."

She puts her hand on my back, then takes my arm. We walk like this, in an almost courtly way.

"I'm sorry, Carlisle," she says.

"Do you ever regret having me?" I ask. It's a silly question, she'd have to be a monster to say yes.

"Not *having* you," she says. I wait for the rest. It takes her a block to think through it. "Sometimes I think about how my mother was always so involved and *too* interested in me," she says. "I didn't like it and wanted you to have more space. But you weren't me, so maybe you didn't want space?"

I'm not sure how to answer this.

"I think we did pretty well," I say. "I know it was different for you, with Yuto. I'm not comparing us, it's just—" I wave my hand and so does she, like she's catching my unspoken words in her fist.

"I have one kind of love for Yuto," she says. "I don't know how to say it right. From the moment he was born it was a certain love and it's always been that. With you, it's never been just one feeling. I don't mean it's less but—"

"I know," I say.

"You *don't* know."

No, I don't. I won't.

We walk.

"Not everything was as automatic as everyone said it would be," she says. "I mean, being a mother."

"It doesn't seem automatic to me at all," I offer.

Her fingers grip my arm. Gently.

"I thought I needed to let you go," she says. "But you got farther away from me than I thought you would."

In a little bit, we have to stop walking because we are holding on to each other so tight and our bodies don't line up. We rub each other's backs in circles.

Before we get back to the house, I ask her if she still has the photos I remember from childhood. The one of her dancing with Balanchine and the one from *Stars and Stripes*. "In the attic," she says. She sends Yuto up to get them. He undoes the wrapping, looks, and tells her they're cool. He sees we're having a bit of a moment and—preternaturally diplomatic at thirteen—leaves us to it. Isabel laughs at the *Stars and Stripes* pose. "Thank you for your service to our nation," I say. I'm filled with pride and affection and—it comes to me—gratitude.

"You're very brave," I tell her.

"So are you," she says.

For once, we seem to—if not perfectly understand—*feel* each other. That sensation will fade, but not be forgotten.

I begin performing in my friend Yves's cabaret and make dances in my living room. James and I email, but now we take weeks to answer each other. I write my father a letter. At the time I think it's a very good letter but realize later it was mostly a masterpiece in self-pity. A kind of, *I'm sorry you were upset by the things I did while miserable/Nothing worked out if that's a comfort.* When someone is ready to forgive you, they will accept any form of apology, and when they aren't, you need to hit a bull's-eye or forget it. I have not aimed well.

He replies by email: *Received your letter. Sorry to hear things are hard for you.* In the history of the world, has anyone ever been forgiven because they said, *But I didn't mean to hurt you?*

I get angry and send an angry email. Nobody is perfect, and he is supposed to be my father. Maybe he doesn't understand part of being a parent is loving and forgiveness. I didn't even do such a terrible thing. By not forgiving me, *he's* now the person in the wrong. I receive no reply. Maybe certain parents *need* to love their children no matter what, so they can believe they are good parents, or their children are good people. Maybe some genuinely do. But it's not a given.

I start to teach adult ballet, and an opportunity to choreograph comes from one of my students, who works on a television show. I hustle. I build. I often don't have health insurance, so I don't go to therapy, but most of my friends go and I absorb what I believe to be the concepts. A friend talks to me about self-sabotage, a concept I find intriguing. Perhaps this is what I did? I make a short dance about it.

I exonerate myself a thousand times. I never believe it.

September 11, 2001. When I get through on the phone, my father answers, thanks me for calling, and almost immediately hands the phone over to James. A few months later, my father sends a stiff email, saying he appreciated the call but he's also aware I recently categorized our relationship as "toxic." He is disappointed, he says, to hear I am publicly maligning him to his family and, after all this time, have failed to make an accounting of myself to him other than accusing him of being a terrible father. He signs it *Robert*.

The toxic line is true, is something I said to his niece—my

cousin Michelle—when she stayed with me in LA. Did I say it with the expectation it would get back to him or spread among the family? Maybe. I have, once again, demonstrated my disloyalty.

Los Angeles is more interested in options than in judgments. It offers to bathe me in sound, read my cards, teach me to meditate; purge me, plunge me, float me. I read a book on narcissism like a person anxiously flipping through a yearbook to find pictures of herself. I have something, clearly, but maybe not narcissism. It's more basic. I'm only not *good*. In daily life and interactions, yes, of course. I have friends and occasional lovers and good relationships with colleagues. I get by on the veneer of goodness.

Believing I'm fundamentally not good is, of course, a cop-out. Also, liberation. I'm set free to be just as much of a monster as I need to be. Do I not say, on some level, *Fuck it. If you cast me out of your presence, then I will no longer be in your shadow. At the very least, I will source my own light.*

Freya, when I tell her everything, exonerates me too. But she's hearing only my side.

I stop having imaginary conversations with Robert and James. I go longer periods of time without thinking of either one of them. I'm busy. Life opens up. My career is always, nearly, practically, getting to some kind of next level. Robert sends me a congratulatory note about *My Friend*, and I reply briefly. We now send cards at the holidays, but no more. I have meaningful friendships, less meaningful but fun lovers. Yuto comes to LA for a week, and we have a great time. I feel myself to be a sister at last. I love my work. I love my dancers.

Sometimes I think about my father and touch my chest, as if I might find there the talisman, the dark jewel of my not forgiving, not being forgiven. There are even times when doing so gives me a sense of power or settles me. Is it a curse I'm reluctant to lift?

Who knows if it will be ever like this? Alex had asked me. How did he know? For me, it never was. It just didn't happen.

There was a time when I said to myself: *It wasn't love, between me and Alex. Jealousy, lust, disorientation, sublimation, the sheer heedlessness of youth. Self-sabotage.* The words were meant to make me feel like I hadn't lost something. The body knows differently; it has no sense of time. It remembers and it loves.

There might be undanceable truths.

Contained

New York City. 2016. Now.

I stretch as best I can in my little pod room. I put on my Strawberry Thief suit and take the tags off my new leggings and leotard. I borrow a hotel towel. I run out and get coffee and an egg on a roll at a deli. I take some Advil and put on lipstick. I feel young, not in a good way.

James still teaches at the same studio where I took class from him as a teenager. This section of Broadway has gone more commercial. The city in general. I wonder if all you need is money for this New York, not courage.

The studios have barely changed. The same front desk, a wall of headshots of famous dancers and teachers, wooden benches in the hallways. You can pay for class on an app now, and a downstairs studio has been converted to a café, but otherwise it might be 1988. A class is in session in the smaller studio, the pianist riffing a Broadway show tune. I can tell what kinds of jumps they are doing from the sound of the landings. I'm almost laughing.

James is right in front of me, sitting in the hallway. In all three dimensions, flesh and blood. Himself. All this time and now it's happening too fast.

I have a moment, before he looks up. He's chatting to a dancer next to him on the bench. She's rubbing something into the sole of her foot while talking, describing, perhaps, a pain. James nods, and sculpts a motion with his hands, providing, perhaps, a technical diagnosis.

How funny to think there was a time when looking up to this man was the greatest pleasure of my life.

Now it's him looking up, seeing me, his blue eyes instantly filling.

"It's really you," he says. "My God, it's really you."

It was never our move to hug, but we do it now, not perfectly well. He puts his hands on my shoulders, not my back, and we bump cheeks. We say it's wonderful to see each other. We agree it's good I'm here. We are both surprised about my wanting to take class. Up close, I can chart how he's aged. Less color, more lines. I should get changed, I say. I'm sweating. He hopes I didn't pay for class, of course I must not. We're in public, there are dancers all around us, including the one he was speaking to seconds before, who I now recognize as a principal with American Ballet Theater. We follow each other on Instagram. James notices the twitch of recognition between me and the dancer and says, "Oh you must know each other. This is the choreographer Carlisle Martin."

"I love your work," she says. We chat for a moment and I teeter to the same too-small dressing room, roll up my suit so it won't wrinkle, and put on my new clothes. Why am I here?

By the time I'm out of the dressing room people are filing into the open studio and claiming their places at the barre. James ushers me over to a spot by the piano. He fusses with a window. He's nervous. I'm nervous. I want his class to be impressive, for me to see him as a great teacher. I don't want to be mistaken in everything.

I anticipate I might be too self-conscious and distracted to hear what he's saying, but one should never underestimate ballet. The body, which doesn't understand time, remembers movement. Once class starts, my body falls into positions like batter filling a pan. And James's voice, the way he arranges steps, describes them, lifts his hand to sketch a tempo for the pianist, are like sentences from a beloved book. This window, the view of the buildings opposite, the feel of the barre under my hand, it's all homecoming. And yet I was only ever in this classroom once. *My God*, I think. *Bank Street is going to lay me out.*

I have missed him. Them.

". . . and fifth position," James says.

There are wonderful dancers in class, members of companies I would like to work with. For the first time, I feel a surge of something—inspiration—over this *Firebird*. I will give movement to dancers like these.

I see Alex here, in my mind. I see his neck, his arms, his thighs. Maybe it's why I wanted to come to class, to see him once again. But we were never here together.

". . . And contain," James says. ". . . And contain."

The ninety minutes go quickly. James and I catch each other's eyes and smile and nod, but I let him teach and he lets me take class. I'm grateful for the deep and helpful etiquette of ballet, the attention it requires, the respect and self-respect. I'm proud of the way the dancers listen to James. The gravity and care in his attention. His sweet seriousness with a prodigiously talented adolescent girl, all limbs, who seems to be a favorite. She might be me at fifteen. I watch the professionals. I look at the corded muscles of their backs, their legs, their necks. I see the training, the endless classes, the injuries surmounted, the camaraderie, the loneliness, the frustration, the relief, the fear, the love, the containment. I will work with dancers at this level in England. I will look at them and give them things to dance and when they dance them, they will forget about me and everything else but the movement. I will give them freedom. They are all my Firebirds. And I am theirs.

After class, I shower and redo my makeup and climb back into Strawberry Thief. Another dancer from ABT introduces herself to me in the dressing room, says she loves my work. She saw *My Friend* when she was twelve, has a video of it, taught herself the She solo from the first act. "It's my dream to do it," she says. Her face is sincere, and beautiful. I could weep from the beauty of it. She cannot see the ghosts all around me, my past, the man dying. "Thank you," I say. "Thank you so much."

"You still dance beautifully," James says to me when I join him in the hallway. "But, of course, you're a young person yet."

"Your class is incredible. And hard. My legs are shaking."

Now we're on the street and now we're walking to the subway and now there's no stopping this business of going to Bank Street. James and I are a little manic, talking over each other, bright eyed, not *quite* personal. I can't do this. I can't see this man, these men.

"It's your movement quality," James says. "That doesn't change. It's all I'm trying to teach now. The kids can *do* everything. They can promenade on pointe by themselves. Multiple pirouettes in any position. Everyone can get their leg up around their ear or jump to the rafters. The work is to find something in them that's compelling and not just impressive."

James's own movement quality is a little slower but astoundingly unchanged. He's only the age he pretended to be for years. We push through turnstiles, descend the stairs.

"You know they all have their social media accounts and their brands and their side projects," he says. "They have babies and degrees and therapists and blogs. And I wonder if it's all gotten a bit lost. The mystique, the devotion. The offering one used to make of one's soul to a thing. But they seem happier. Less interesting, on the stage, but happier off it."

"I don't think they're less interesting, on the stage," I say. "I think they've outgrown a lot of the work they're asked to do, and how they're asked to do it. You can't keep asking men to prince the same old princes. You can't keep asking women to die the same old deaths."

"You're right of course," he says.

"You're also right," I say. "We're all turned outward too much. We understand the representation of things more than the thing itself."

Well, that's philosophy settled. The platform is crowded. James looks at his phone. Fumbles with his bag. Takes out reading glasses. He taps out a text like an old person, with his index finger. I feel a rush of the old protectiveness. And it is so strange to be next to his body.

"I'm just checking in," he says. "He was a little rough when I left him this morning."

"Rough how?"

"He gets frustrated." James reads a reply and nods. "He's fine. There are different moods. He might be, a little, afraid."

"Of my coming?"

"Of everything."

He looks at me. I remember that blue pellucid gaze.

"You know in the eighties and nineties, when one of us was dying, everyone gathered." James adjusts his bag. "Unless you couldn't bear it. Which I couldn't, very often. But from that time, all these wonderful groups were created. Our lovely hospice lady is from an LGBTQ place. Oh, did I tell you, Alexei died last year?"

I freeze.

"The sweetest of all our cats," James says. "The last of the Romanovs."

I remember a day in Mexico. Alex, kissing me in a square.

The subway car arrives in a metallic whoosh. We're really going.

"I saw your *Curtain*," James says, as we fit ourselves into the crowded car. "Last year, in Canada. I went up to Toronto."

A company in Canada had included my *Curtain* in their Contemporary Voices Festival the year before. It's my most-performed work, probably because of its length—fourteen quick minutes— and because it's a little bit funny. My original title for it was "The Greatest Ballet in the World," because the conceit of the piece is that the dancers are in performance of a ballet, which we never see. The stage design mimics the stage left wing of a theater, and we see them "exiting" from that unseen stage, and interacting with each other or having private moments before "entering" again. I don't do anything cheesy like have squabbling partners or jealousy or what have you. It's theatrical, though. I was interested in where dancers go inside themselves, before and after dancing. What *that* dance was.

"I was there." My throat is dry. "Opening night."

It was my only ballet to be shown anywhere last year. I went up to rehearse the dancers and stayed for first night. They'd brought me onstage; I'd taken a bow with the company.

"Ahhh, well," James says. "We went the second week."

"We?"

"Robert and I both went. I told him I wanted to see it, and he came too."

I can't speak.

"We *loved* it," James says. "It worked on every level. I also have a video of your *Artemisia* and I managed to get a copy of a rehearsal run of *My Friend*. Oh, Carlisle. I *wept*. But I so wanted to see something of yours in a theater, and I wanted that for Robert too, and it was getting harder for him to travel. After, he said, 'She's the real thing, isn't she?' When we came back to Bank Street, I left the videos out for him. We didn't talk about it, but I know he watched them. Many times. Especially *My Friend*, because there's a moment, at the beginning, where you can be seen. You're talking to one of the dancers. Your face, your gestures. You. We hadn't seen you in so long and there you were. But in command of it all. The person you were meant to be."

I can't speak, I can't speak. I can't speak.

How dare they support me, praise me, love me, *in secret*?

"This morning," James is talking again, "Robert said to me, 'She had to go away to be able to do all that.' He meant your work."

I swear to God I will set a match to Bank Street. I will watch it burn to the ground.

"And what do you have coming up?" James's eyes are clear, but his hands are twisting around each other. His hands show his age more than his face. Dark spots. Thickened knuckles. There's a silver chain now, on his right wrist.

"*Firebird*," I say, tightly.

He throws his head back, grabs my arm, then looks at me with such a complicated mixture of delight and complicit dismay that I bark out laughter like it was lodged in my throat.

"*Oh God*," he says, with feeling. "I mean, *absolutely marvelous* and also—"

"Yes. What does one do with that old thing?"

"Who wants it?"

I name the company in England.

"Oh, Carlisle." Now he shuts his eyes. His hand is still on my arm.

"*How* I want to see what you'll do," he says.

How am I to get through all this? I'm tired. I want to go back to bed.

"Betsy!" James cries. My head snaps up. I'd fallen into silence. "Where?"

"No, no." His eyes crinkle. "I don't think I told you. She married! A first-time bride at seventy-one. Well, this was ten years ago. They're living in Ireland. She's finally going to bring out that book she's been working on for ages. *He's* rather a dear. An actor. They knew each other from her Paris days, but he was married then."

"Jesus Christ, I thought she was on the train."

"She's coming next week."

We stare at each other.

"Not long now," he says.

We've reached our stop.

We climb the stairs and are on the street. I'm having trouble with my legs. And throat.

"The hospital is gone." James points. "There's an AIDS memorial now. Oh, but now there are terrifying amounts of baby carriages and bankers and things."

James prattles. The Village has changed. Hillary might make a good president, the other choice is a joke not even worth discussing, all New Yorkers know him as an oafish crook and not even a competent one. This restaurant is new and popular, but they've not been to it, the music is terrible and too loud. Did I want to see anything while I was in town? The spring seasons hadn't started but there was lots of good theater, had I—

We're here. The famous Belgian-block pavement. Brownstones, Greek Revival townhouses, brick-front houses. There's construction, some scaffolding. I'd somehow never noticed the cars, the air-conditioning units. I recognize everything, and don't, which makes me feel unsteady. But of course my memories are for a particular interior.

I'm afraid.

I can see the house, the front gate, the door, the windows. We're here.

No, it's too soon. I veer to the opposite side of the street, James following. We lean against someone else's railing. I look across, at the windows. The curtains are drawn shut.

"Are you all right?" James asks.

"Yes," I say.

We look at each other. His eyes are pinkening with emotion.

"I missed you," he says.

"Yes." It's the best I can do right now. He turns to look at the windows too, and we stand quietly together, watching, waiting. There are so many possibilities for our bodies right now. To embrace, to fall, to run.

The front door of Bank Street opens, and a woman appears, with a baby strapped to her chest, facing outward.

"New tenants on the fourth floor," James says. "One only hears the baby if one's in the hallway. The husband is a dreadful investment banker somebody but she's *very* nice. French. Robert thinks they'll move though, now the baby is here." His voice catches at the end. Robert will not live to see this happen.

I watch the woman walk down the street, the baby jigging on her chest.

"You're doing such good work," James says.

I have no idea what he's talking about. Oh, my career. I don't want him to tell me how well I've done without their help. I press myself back into the railing and stare at the curtained windows. I tell him I just made a ballet for an animatronic puppet.

"Ah, well, that's what one does, you know," he says. "Balanchine choreographed for Ringling Brothers. He made a ballet for elephants."

"I know."

I wish he would go inside and leave me here to collect myself.

"It all *counts*, you know," he says. "Even obstruction. Even crap. Even silence."

I didn't need to go away, I think, *to become what I am.*

Unless I did. Did it help me make more, to feel loved less?

When I turn to face James there are tears in his eyes.

"Do you forgive us?" he asks.

"I don't know yet," I say.

Bank Street

"Oh, we do this now," James says, taking off his shoes. "But you don't have to, of course."

I will not meet my dying, estranged father in my socks. I take them off. Bare feet have more dignity. And if I run, there's less chance I'll fall.

James offers me a pair of slippers, which I decline.

We move into the front room. There is the piano, and there are the library steps. The glass-fronted cabinet with its iron handles shaped like birds. The gold brocade lampshades. The Strawberry Thief wallpaper. (Not so very much like my suit, not truly.) There's the portrait of Aunt Daphne in her gorgon pearls. The scent of books and old building and must and lemons. It's shabby and splendid. A little shabbier, after all these years. More splendid as well.

Is my father listening to us come in?

The nursing assistant—an eastern European woman with

harshly dyed hair and spectacular false eyelashes—is giving James a précis of the morning events. I stand a respectful distance from this business of Robert's body.

I want to roam among the things, touch them, hold them to my face. Instead I fix my eyes on a stack of mail on the dining table, feeling Bank Street hover around me, waiting.

To have all this.

Maybe I need to use that egg in *Firebird* after all. Maybe the whole ballet is about the Firebird trying to protect her egg.

There is death here. I don't mean Robert, not yet. Older ghosts. The place where I sat and understood my father was a gay man, and James was a gay man, and gay men were dying. Where Robert stood listening to a phone call and looking up at James and saying the name of a young man who was going to die. Where James told me about his father killing himself, and how it was something he understood. The place where Robert ironed a shirt for James, his hands shaking with fear.

I am all the ages I ever visited Bank Street. A greedy and clever child. A greedy and dreamy adolescent. A young woman in her twenties, greedy and sad. And now? *And now?*

The nursing assistant leaves. "Oh, for goodness' sake," says James and moves to the stereo, tuned to classical radio. I hadn't noticed music was playing. I can't think of when that has ever happened in my life. Barber's Adagio for Strings.

"I don't think we need all this just now," he says, and turns it off.

Maybe I didn't notice the music because you hear Adagio for Strings everywhere, on TV and in movies and synthetic versions in car dealership waiting rooms and in elevators. Agony is ordinary.

"Shall we?" *He's afraid too*, I think.

We move down the hallway. The door to Carlisle's Room is pulled almost shut. I'm aware of walking and observing myself walk at the same time. We pass Carlisle's Room, and then James is entering their bedroom and I'm following him and there he is.

Once again, absurdly after all this time, it's too fast. He's just there. And I'm here.

We're here.

The bed faces the door. His eyes are closed. I see an oxygen machine near the bed, but he's not wearing a mask. A soft-looking gray blanket is pulled up to his waist. His hands lie curved in his lap. He appears to be taking up a lot of the bed. I thought he'd be smaller, I don't know why, some idea we all have of dying as a shrinking, buckling, wasting thing. But, no. However gently or not Robert is going into that good night, he is going just as large.

His hair—a full head of it—is neatly brushed. The window is open. On a breeze, Robert's aftershave scents over to me just as he opens his eyes. My hello happens on a sigh.

He squints. Pushes himself more upright from underneath the bedclothes.

James moves past me to Robert's side. This takes maneuvering, as the bedroom, never large, is crowded with the addition of a hospital bedside table, a walker, a commode, another table where the portable oxygen machine rests, and, on the other side of the bed, a new chair, ergonomic and bulky.

I am being looked at. My eyes are in his direction, but I see nothing, only the act of his looking.

James pats Robert's shoulder, almost awkwardly.

"Carlisle is here," he says.

"Doesn't she"—it takes my father another breath to complete it—"look terrific?"

James says something, but I can't hear it. Now I see my father again. The shape of his face. I've become very like him. What's bred in the bone.

"She has your jaw," James says. "I don't know I ever noticed that before."

"Isabel's eyes," Robert says. It's as if I've just been born or discovered.

"We've been looking at photographs," James says. "From the old days. There are some fantastic ones of Isabel. And you, Carlisle. Some of them I hadn't ever seen. I'll get them."

I'm not at all ready for James to leave the room, but he does, squeezing past me and saying something about lunch.

"He likes to do." Robert looks after James's retreating back and takes another breath. "All the things."

I don't want to sit down, though there's something comical about my position at the foot of the bed. The Grim Reaper in a pantsuit. Something comical, something Shakespearean, in this whole setup. My father's face is flushed. *Yet who would have thought the old man to have had so much blood in him.*

There's a book on the bed, an old hardcover with a battered cover. Robert sees my eyes travel toward it, and he taps the book. His hands are large. Like James's, they show his age. He still wears the heavy gold watch.

"Look," he says, and taps the cover again.

To pick up the book, I must move closer to his body. Why is it still so large? Bigger even than mine. The book is next to the mound of his leg under the blanket, next to his large hand. If I take the book, then I won't have to take his hand. I'm afraid of his hand.

I edge around the side of the bed and extract the book delicately, attempt to sit down in the ergonomic chair, which rolls slightly away from me and bumps into the dresser, which rattles. The Awkward Grim Reaper.

The cover of the book is illustrated in a 1950s pulp fiction style I remember from library-borrowed Nancy Drew mysteries. This one shows a man in evening dress about to fall down a flight of stairs. *Death in a Tuxedo.*

"Open," says my father. "First chapter."

The pages are tea brown with age. The first chapter begins with a letter from someone called Lady Foster and Taggert to her niece, Miss Carlisle Fellowes.

My dearest Carlisle,

Have you heard the news? What a palaver, as Nanny used to say. You'll understand why I'm writing when I tell you, darling Carlisle—

I look up. My father is watching me.

"There you are," he says. "Your name. I found it."

He nods to a bookcase against the far wall, tightly packed with mysteries from the Golden Age of crime. "Was there," he says. "Had it—the whole time."

James comes back in, carrying a photo album.

"Oh, the book!" he says. "Isn't that marvelous? We've been playing this game. Did Robert tell you?"

I shake my head.

"Betsy made it up. We collect stacks of books at a time, and we hold each one up and try to remember *one* thing about it. Plots or character names or scenes. We decided it also counts if you remember where you bought it, or what you were doing when you read it, or who gave it to you."

"Cheats." Robert makes a motion with his hand toward James. He's smiling. They're both smiling.

"I took this one out," James says. "Oh, a few months ago. And Robert said—"

"Tour." Robert nods at the book. "1956. We had a van."

"Le Cochon Vert," I say.

They both look at me, startled. Is it possible this is the first thing I've said, other than hello? *The Green Ham?*

"I read something," I say. "About the early years of, of—"

"LaGrange," says Robert, looking pleased. James perches at the foot of the bed and rubs the heap of blankets over Robert's feet.

"We had to wash—our own costumes," Robert says. "Sometimes—not enough time—to dry before—next show. We would hang them—on the windows—of Le Cochon Vert—and drive. Someone would watch to—make sure they didn't—fly out."

"Can you imagine?" James smiles. "Driving on a highway in Idaho in 1956 and seeing tutus and tights coming out of a Shasta?"

"America," Robert says. We both look at him, but he seems to have finished his thought.

The paper cover of the book, with its dying man, tears a little as I turn it over in my hands. "Oh sorry," I say. "This is maybe valuable."

"No." Robert appears to struggle with his breath, his face concentrating. "It's not in good—enough—condition." He pats his chest. "Like me."

"Or me," James says. "But Carlisle is a young person still. You should have seen her in class, Robert. Still that fabulous facility."

"Yes. I can tell."

So, I am going to sit here, and they are going to praise me? And what will I do?

"Le Cochon Vert." Robert rasps a faint chuckle. "Aunt Daphne gave us—the money—for that." He looks at James. "Green box," he says. "Hall." James leaves again. I look at the book, so as to not look at Robert.

"I was reading"—he moves his hand toward the cover—"that book—on tour. We had—such good times. I hadn't thought—in so long. Then I opened it and there—it was. Your name. The mystery—solved. At the end."

James is taking things out of the closet. We listen to the sound of objects being moved: boxes shifting, coats being slid along a pole. I look at the oral syringes in a plastic bag on top of the bedside tray, a timetable chart clipped to the side, a bottle of liquid morphine. A cup with a straw.

"Your mother called." Robert smiles. It's the same smile—complacent, almost smug—he always used when talking about Isabel. "Yesterday. We talked—like—old times."

Is this what we will do? We will be fond and kind? We will pull out old books and see what we can remember of them? Because anything else would be cruel to this large, breathless old man, and to what purpose?

"She's been happy," Robert says. "Good life."

Yes. We have all been happy. We have good lives.

James returns, flushed, carrying a rectangular green leather box. Robert motions to him to open the lid. Programs. Photographs. Maps. A silk ribbon, an ornamental braid, postcards and letters.

"Oh my goodness," James says. He extracts a thick piece of paper, creased into squares, and unfolds it. *LaGrange Ballet, 1956*, it reads. *Graceful Movements Set to Lovely Music!*

"They weren't sure—" Robert's hand traces a figure in the air. "People would know. What ballet was."

This is not awful. This is dying in a nice home with people to care for you, on good drugs. Robert's hand is trembling.

"I had to leave—my family, my—everything." He fixes me for a moment with his eyes.

"I wanted always—to have a home." It's hard to tell if his voice is breaking, or it's the struggle for breath. "I couldn't—" He looks at James, whose eyes, damn him, seem to be filling with tears. "I couldn't be alone. I had to make—"

"We know," James says. Robert looks at me. Am I supposed to say that too? It's easy enough to say. Why not? This dying man.

"Carlisle is working on a new production of *Firebird*," James announces.

This makes me feel like a child. Like a big, goofy, overgrown child, sweating now, into my suit.

"How—marvelous," my father says.

"I don't know," I say, because I don't.

Robert laughs, so deep in his chest it almost sounds like an inward cough. But he's always laughed like that.

"Do you remember"—he leans toward James—"Lincoln telling us about—*Birds of America*?"

James throws his head back. "Oh, Carlisle, *did* we ever tell you?" James laughs for both of them now, Robert watching with pleasure. "Oh, Robert, you must tell Carlisle," James says, but Robert waves at his chest.

"It was an idea Balanchine had, for a three-act ballet," James explains. "He worked on it forever. Commissioned a score, had costume designs, writers working on the scenario. He wanted to do a full evening tribute, to our great land and his adopted home. A story ballet for America, such as has never been done."

It's very strange, in the midst of great emotional turmoil, to have people want to tell you a ballet anecdote.

"*Birds of America* was to open like *Firebird*," James explains. "Only instead of Prince Ivan, you have James Audubon. Yes." He widens his eyes. "Naturalist and writer/illustrator of *Birds of America* James Audubon. He gets lost in an enchanted kingdom, which is Virginia."

"He finds—birds in trees," Robert says, his own eyes bright. "All the birds—of America—they dance. Then American eagle—chases him out."

"Audubon becomes Johnny Appleseed," James says. "And is saved by Pocahontas. He scatters his seeds and all the apples spring up. I'm not making this up! He wanted an apple dance. Well, that's like *Firebird* too. Only instead of princesses dancing with apples, it's the apples themselves dancing." He whoops with laughter. Robert's chest is heaving.

"Brandywine," he gasps. "Delicious. P-Pippin."

"Of course, it was Balanchine, so they wouldn't have looked like the Fruit of the Loom apples," James says, wiping his eyes. "Smart red tutus and apples in a headpiece or something."

"Indian attack," gasps my father.

"Yes! After the apple dances, Johnny Appleseed née Audubon gets attacked by Indians." James thumps the bed. "Princess Thunderbird shows up. A Native American Firebird. And saves the day and marries Johnny Appleseed Audubon and their wedding celebrates all that America has accomplished and is also somehow like Versailles."

They turn to receive my appreciation.

"That's—that sounds crazy," I say, faintly.

"But entirely true," James says. "We heard it from Lincoln himself. Balanchine really wanted to do it. Only it was going to be expensive."

"Even geniuses"—Robert gasps out—"have bad ideas."

"Genius isn't taste," James agrees. "Unless your genius is for having good taste. Which is one of yours, dear." He puts his hand on Robert's shoulder.

"But to dream big—is good." Robert turns his head to me. "LaGrange believed in—himself. He made—big things."

Is there a kind of pleading in his gaze?

"You made them together," James says. Robert nods, still looking at me.

LaGrange is forgiven too.

Reach 'em, teach 'em, preach 'em, and beach 'em.

Robert's left hand shifts toward me.

"You do what—you want," he says. "Don't be—afraid—of it."

James was right. Death is ordinary.

"Carlisle," Robert says. "Bank Street—will be yours."

James moves to the foot of the bed. Robert makes the small gesture with his hand again. His fingernails have a bluish cast.

"I'm glad—I have something—to give you. We both are."

Dance is very good on love, and also forgiveness. The hand outstretched, the hand taken.

I shut my eyes.

"Carlisle."

I look at him.

"Yes," I say. "I understand. Don't worry. Everything will be okay."

"You have—you have to take it."

"I understand."

To take it is to forgive him. Possibly to forgive all three of us.

"It's for you," he says. "I'm so glad—I'm so glad—" Now he is able to lift his hand off the bed. It's still larger than mine. I move closer. His grasp is weak, but he's able to bring our joined hands to his lips. Dry bird pecks. Puts my hand on his chest. After a few minutes it looks as if he's fallen into a doze. I can't actually feel his heart beating, but his breathing—a kind of periodic staccato pant—tells me we're both still alive.

I pet, gently, his heart. My father and I stay like that for a while.

Good person, bad person. Success, failure. Outside, inside. These are danceable truths. To be flesh of his flesh, blood of his blood. That's danceable too. But the work of my life has been to ask undanceable questions and find a way to make ballets out of them. There's nothing to do with this dance but be still.

I become aware that James has left the room and my arm is cramping and my father is sleeping for real. I pull the blanket up over him.

In the hallway, I push open the door to Carlisle's Room.

The smell of roses. No hint of cigarettes. Some of the furniture is different. A filing cabinet, an office chair for the desk. The bed is made up. For a hospice worker? I go to the window, with the shutters I once thought were "like Europe." I want to realize profound things in this room, which in a sense has never been more mine. For the moment, I don't. I still feel my father's hand in mine. It's all I can feel.

The bears are all on the shelf. He would have seen them every time he came in.

I find James in the kitchen, emptying the dishwasher.

"We had the floor redone," he says. I look at my feet. In my time, the kitchen floor had been red and white checkerboard linoleum. Now it's the same honey wood as the rest of the apartment.

"It looks nice." Everything smells different. No cats. I rub my arm, then my jaw. My hamstring, my back. There are a lot of places. James straightens with a handful of flatware and shuts the dishwasher.

"He's happy," he says. "He's so happy. It might go more quickly now. I should call Betsy."

James is crying. Not sobbing or choking, but tears. He puts the forks and spoons down on the counter. I don't want to watch him cry in this lovely way so I don't. I move to a cabinet and take down a glass, go to the sink for water. James scrubs his eyes with a dish towel. I wait for him to contain himself.

"Isabel told me about Bank Street a few days ago," I say, after a minute. "That it comes to me."

"You didn't know?"

His surprise appears genuine.

"I didn't," I say.

"You should—" He takes a breath. "Robert has everything organized. And we have a lawyer, a good one, who will explain everything and help you. If you want. You might have your own?"

"Okay," I say. *Am* I keeping Bank Street? "We can talk about it later. What you want to do with everything. What you—want."

It feels strange to talk like this. These aren't our positions.

"What about you?" I ask.

"We have arrangements. Robert took care of things. Investments. I'll be fine." James waves a hand. "I can also stay with friends in the immediate future."

"James," I say. "I'm not going to throw you out of your home." What I mean is I won't let him make me that person.

"Robert is my home." He says it simply, with no affect. "This was—" He glances out the kitchen door toward the main room. "A part of it all, yes, but I don't want to be here without him. While he's here, I'd like for him to go with everything just as he likes it, but then? To be honest, I never expected—not really— that he would go first. Now so many things don't seem important. Bank Street? Well, why should it matter anymore?" He opens a drawer and begins placing cutlery in the tray. "I think, oh, a new little place, something easy to take care of, a rental where I can just call a superintendent if something goes wrong? Something uptown, near the studio, near friends. Why not?" He catches my eye. "I'm old. One can't just go on, just the same, when you're old. Things begin to happen."

There is a gently dying man, with his happy memories, in the other room. James, here, with his arrangements and his sorrow. I can't figure out where I am.

"I don't want to leave New York," he says. "Except for the days when all I want to do is leave New York. But that's how all New Yorkers feel."

"You used to talk about Denmark."

"Mhmm." His eyes are far away. He dabs his face with the towel again and we turn to the business of lunch. He empties a plastic container of soup into a pot, unwraps a paper bag full of hard rolls. I'm lonely for all my old feelings for James. I don't enjoy feeling detached. There's no satisfaction in it. There's not even power.

I would prefer to love him.

How alike my father and I are.

"Carlisle." James sets his knife down, carefully. "I'm afraid, growing up, you were with us during some difficult years. We didn't treat you like a child. *I* didn't. And you were a child, in certain ways."

In actual ways.

"It was an education," I say, lightly. We listen to its banality for a moment.

"I never wanted children," he says. "For me, it's always been rather a benefit of loving men. But also, I wouldn't want to pass it on. What my father had, what I have. It's hard enough to see oneself reflected in a *mirror*. But I hope—I do hope whatever influence I had on you wasn't entirely destructive."

The feeling returns. The desire to burn Bank Street to the ground.

"It wasn't entirely destructive," I say. This is true. It *wasn't*.

"One of the things about teaching," James says, "is that the relationship is so much more—contained."

"You didn't contain it," I say. "With Alex."

I feel something move off my chest, not a weight but a heat. It blasts James. His face flushes, and the muscles of his neck go rigid. I can see he's gripping the counter behind him, the veins and tendons of his forearms too coming into sharp relief. I have done this. I watch my anger fill the room, with wonder. I'm a smoking stove.

"I wasn't well," he says. "It's not an excuse, it's an explanation. I won't ask you to forgive *me*."

I walk out of the kitchen while he's still talking. I'm not clear on what is happening or where, exactly, I need to go. All these things, at Bank Street. Beautiful things, old things. Things real and unreal. What belongs to me now? The rug has gotten so thin. I'm aware of the bones of my feet on the floor. What's bred in the bone.

The library steps are still by the window. I sit at the piano.

James follows me, stands at the window. He won't sit on the library steps. This isn't a farce.

"I was a coward, Carlisle," he says, in a low, quick voice, half-facing the curtains. "I sent you to Mexico on a mad errand, made you my confessor and messenger and all the rest of it. Sent you to make excuses and apologies to a young man who must have been perfectly bewildered by it all. It must have seemed so ridiculous to you. It *was* ridiculous. I was never in love with Alex or anything like that. The whole mess was only the sort of embodiment of my unhappiness. And then I asked you not to tell Robert I was alone. Of course, you were not responsible for me, good heavens. Neither was Robert. But I could see, I could imagine, how in his anger and shame and all the rest, he would have blamed you. Sometimes I imagined you said terrible things about me, and that's what caused the rift. I wanted to believe that, I suppose, because I knew I deserved them. But I should have fought, to make him see it wasn't your fault. I should have fought for *you*. For all of us."

He turns to look at me, even opens his shoulders and arms slightly, as if ready to receive a blow.

So. My father was wrong. James didn't try to kill himself because I stole his muse, his love, and betrayed him utterly. James didn't know. Has never known.

He could be lying, of course. I remember the notebook he gave me. What looked like poems. Alex's name. The word *love*. He could be trying to spare me some measure of remorse. Or himself a dram of dignity.

I should have fought for all of us too.

We are all of us monsters. Even the failures.

James looks out the window. I try to see his soul in his shoulder blades, but that's not an accurate system. I see only a man, my teacher. A first love, in a way.

"Do you ever talk to Alex?" I ask.

James gives a little start, turns back to me.

"I wrote to him a few months after I had my—come apart. I was embarrassed, of course. I never heard back, which I expected." There's a pause, and then he continues. "Maybe seven or eight years after that, he showed up in class. The company was here on tour. He introduced me to his wife—she was in the company too; they'd just gotten married—and the three of us had a very nice lunch. Since then, I get the occasional nice email. And you?"

The dance world is not large. I've been aware of Alex's career, though not his personal life. We've not found each other on social media. I've not looked for him. I've made a point of not looking for him.

"I haven't been in touch with him," I say.

"Do you want to be?" James asks. "He knows about your work; he's mentioned it several times. I can give you his email. He's also on Facebook."

This maybe *is* a farce.

I ask if Alex is still dancing.

"He retired two years ago. He had quite a good career, you know."

"Yes, I heard his name mentioned from time to time," I say. "Saw the *Dance Magazine* cover and stuff like that."

We are looking at each other now, and I see relief on his face. After nineteen years, and all this guilt and shame and separation, it turns out the easiest thing to talk about is Alex.

"A kid from Florida, dancing on the great stages of Europe," James says. "The new American dream. To escape the new country for the old, where one might have a better life. And health care. One does like to think of it."

Yes, I suppose one might.

"He and his wife are in Spain," James says. "Where she's from. He's directing a company there. She teaches at the school, I believe. Two children."

Dancing on the great stages of Europe. A wife and two children. A company in Spain. I'm still smiling as a lava rush of self-pity rises and threatens to rain down on my head. Here I am, nineteen years later, and still the person no one loves best. I sit very still, let the molten rocks find me.

It's not so bad, really. Not even hot. I watch the wave of self-pity ooze past. Can I move my feet? I can. I'm not stuck.

I look at the music on top of the piano.

"Poulenc and Scriabin still," I say.

"Oh, Poulenc and Scriabin always," James says. "Though I don't think I need a piano so much now. I'm happy to listen. Also, there's quite a lot of good TV on."

I can't help laughing. So does he. We laugh because we are exhausted and afraid and sad and because there really is quite a lot of good TV on.

I stand. I find I'm able to stand.

"It was always my dream to live at Bank Street," I say. "And then it wasn't. But now I'm not sure I can let it go. It's very weird. How you can not want something, and also not let go of it. Like being sad about a dream you no longer have."

"I understand," James says. I'm sure he does.

"But it does make me so happy," he says. "To know it's yours. You can do whatever you want with it. Sell it. Sell it and go be free."

I do see he wants this for me, that it releases something in him. It occurs to me maybe my father was able to feel better about the separation because he *knew* this gift was always here. In the end he would do what a father does—or is afraid to do—and pass something on.

James was right about one thing. It all counts, even silence. These nineteen years apart have not been empty. Different.

We go back to the kitchen. We set out the lunch on trays and carry them back to the bedroom. I think, *This won't be as overwhelming, I've already seen him.*

But now I see, more clearly. He's dying.

Robert stirs and opens his eyes, reaches out his hand again.

"Oh, James, doesn't Carlisle—look terrific?"

"She does."

"Are we having—lunch?"

"Unless you want to sleep, sweetheart. If you can eat a little first, we'll sit and talk. I got those rosemary crackers you like so much."

Robert puts out his hand for James to take. This is their private choreography. I won't forget it.

"Carlisle, I showed you the book?" Robert turns his eyes to me. "With—your name?"

"You did," I say. "It's from a mystery novel, like you thought."

"We—solved it," he says.

Did we?

I want to hear his voice more. It would be nice to talk and have lunch, not as if nothing ever happened between us, but as if we both no longer care about those things.

"So, who is Carlisle?" I ask. "In the book? Is she a villain?"

"No, no."

"The victim?"

"No, no." His eyes close as he smiles. "She's the girl—the—" He searches not for breath but for the right word.

"The heroine?" James suggests.

"The witness?" I try.

"She's just—a character," my father says. "The one I remembered. I liked—her name." He opens his eyes and looks at me. "You're the—real one."

Firebird

I don't cry when I leave Bank Street that afternoon. I walk with a sort of helpless rhythmic energy. I feel crispy, burnt, dry. Stray embers of sensation glow red, spark into flame. I might be leaving smoke trails.

I'm not fleeing the scene, exactly, because I'm going back for dinner. James has asked if I want to stay a few days longer in New York, stay at Bank Street, in Carlisle's Room.

With my father there have been no accusations, no deep coming to terms, or understanding, or Jesus, or whatever it is people come to in these circumstances. My father is, I think, at peace with me but he's also on drugs. And I'm—

I'm walking fast. I could be anywhere. No really, I *could* be anywhere. I will have choices, soon, that I've never had before. My father's gift to me.

I keep walking until I'm back at the hotel. I take a nice long shower because there's no drought in this city and I have all these flames. Is this what it feels like to forgive and be forgiven? Is that what just happened?

The thing I've burned to the ground is me. It's not a terrible sensation.

I pack my little bag, take the subway downtown. Back on the street, I need music and also to walk more slowly because with class and the hourlong march uptown and not sleeping, I've burned out my legs.

Maki Namekawa and her husband recorded a four-handed piano arrangement for *Firebird*. I decide to listen to that. It's instructive because without all the orchestration one can hear—

Oh. I've had an idea.

I need to sit down. There's a lovely, tiny park at hand, and a bench occupied by two chatting women, a little older than I am. We smile at each other the way women do when we're signaling our gratitude that the stranger invading our space is a woman rather than a man.

A breeze blows through the trees. The leaves make a wonderful papery sound. Like when you can hear musicians turning the pages of their scores from the orchestra pit. I love that sound, its churchly focus. Devotion.

A question of morals.

I look down at my free hand. My fingers are splayed. *Carlisle walks with her fingers splayed when she's thinking,* James had written, all those years ago, in his notebook. *Like she's blind, like she's wading through invisible tall grass.*

I always loved the way he saw me.

My phone rings. Isabel.

"Hey, Mom."

The women at the other end of the bench hear this and turn. They are maybe mothers themselves. Perhaps they have said goodbye to mothers. Anyway, to be able to *Hey, Mom,* in the way I just did is not a small thing. I might be imagining it, but I feel an acknowledgment of this pass between us all.

I move away from the bench. Isabel wants to know how I am, and I tell her. I say I feel not flooded with emotion but crisped with emotion. That I think Robert will not live long, but his pain is being managed, he is home, he seems at peace. I tell her my father and I have held each other's hands and he has said he is so glad. That I didn't say I was so glad, but I'm going to be able to tell him that I love him. He will not die without hearing me say it. I say I think James is doing the best he can and sometimes the best James can do is not great for other people but this time it is.

I tell her I'm grateful she went to Bank Street all those years ago and reunited with my father and let him and James be a part of my life, and me a part of theirs.

It gave me so much, I say.

I ask if I can talk to her about something else.

"I think I do want to make a fairy-tale ballet," I say. "I just want to make a different fairy tale. I'm wondering if you can help me."

"Of course," she says, quickly. Then, "What do you need?"

"I want to get into a studio and start working on some things. I mean, London won't be for months—if it all happens—but I want to start workshopping some things right away. I *need* to do that."

I wait for her to say "Right."

"I understand," she says.

I am blood of her blood.

"Can you come work with me?" I ask.

"Work?"

"Dance."

"I can't dance anymore. I haven't danced in a hundred years."

"I don't need you jumping or throwing your legs around," I

say. "You still understand movement. You understand Stravinsky better than I do. Don't tell me there isn't dance left in your body."

"Are you making me the Evil Sorcerer?" I can hear her smile.

"Not evil," I say. "Definitely powerful. I'm reimagining the role. I think mothers and daughters are an underrealized theme in ballet."

"Mr. B said there were no mothers in ballet."

"Mothers-*in-law*, he said. He also apparently wanted to make a ballet about Johnny Appleseed. My point is we all get to make our own messes."

"That's true enough."

I imagine her chin coming up, her spine straightening. The way she used to turn it all on, just a little, when she came to pick me up from ballet class.

"I have this idea for a *Firebird* that's about power and freedom, the gaining of it, the loss of it, the trades you make for it," I tell her. "Instead of Maiden, Mother, Crone, we have Princess, Firebird, Sorcerer. Monsters too, of course. *Maybe* a prince, but maybe not. I know this sounds strange. I need to think through it more. But most of all I need to start working. Whether the people in London hate my idea or not, I need to make it. So, will you come to me? Maybe in Los Angeles, or here, or London? I'm not sure exactly where I'm going next. But will you come help me?"

"It seems like you have enough going on with—"

"I will," I say. "I will be here for what is happening with Robert. But then—"

I held my father's hand today. He held mine.

That's another dance.

"Just say yes," I tell her. "Tell me you'll come help me."

"Of course, I'll come," she says. "Of course."

I leave the little park then and walk to Bank Street. Here are the windows, the curtains drawn, one of them open. I put my hand on the gate and look up. James is playing the piano. Poulenc. A good composer for restless souls, he called him once. I know the piece, can picture the title of this section on the sheet music. *Le Coeur sur la main*. The heart on the hand. The music stops. Starts again. No longer Poulenc. James is picking out a theme from *Firebird*. First the berceuse, the lullaby. Then the finale. "Collapse of Kaschei's Palace and Dissolution of All Enchantments." It is a magical thing, this lifting of all magic.

I'll be in the room when my father dies, six days later.

Betsy and her husband will have arrived, and James and I will go to the store to shop and give Betsy and Robert time together. We'll come back and cook and eat and Betsy—quick-witted as ever, though slower-moving—will get a little drunk and fall asleep on the daybed. Her husband, who *is* charming, will take the sofa. James and I go to sit with Robert.

I'll be in the chair by the side of his bed, dozing, when he dies. I'll wake up not because of a sound but because some sound has been removed. James will be sitting on the bed, with his hand on my father's chest.

We will follow my father's instructions for his death, which are simple. The *Times* will run an obituary with a photo of Robert at Boxhill, and also the one of him in his youth, dancing with LaGrange Ballet. The obituaries will mean a great deal to James. "So many of us didn't survive," he'll tell me. "To remember him. This makes me think history will." Boxhill Festival will dedicate their following season to my father and rename their second stage after him.

I will tell James to take all the time he needs and go back to Los Angeles. I'll talk to their lawyer and think about selling Bank

Street. James, who has been left the contents of the apartment, along with enough money to make staying in Manhattan doable, will move from wanting every object to find a worthy and loving home, to hiring someone to cart things away en masse. He'll beg me to choose things for myself and I will ask for the library steps and the portrait of Aunt Daphne. We all need gorgons.

James will send me my father's watch, which I hadn't asked for, but will be so grateful to have.

My mother will come to Los Angeles and spend two weeks with me and my assistant, Ian, in the studio. The first day she'll be intensely shy and insist on doing nothing more than running the music. On the third day, Ian and I will mostly sit on the floor, rapt, while she tells us stories about dancing for Balanchine. By the end of the week, I'll have to remind her to take breaks.

I will not be able to describe to anyone in this world or the next what it feels like to dance with my mother.

I'll do the film in the summer, and then go to London—oh yes, I do get the commission—to meet with my creative team and have a look at the dancers. When Freya and I see each other we will do sort of a reenactment of the scene from *My Friend*, with the two women running into each other's arms. She will be my dramaturge on *Firebird*, and we'll know from the start this is a creative partnership that will continue.

Back at Bank Street, the upstairs tenants in the building—the French woman with the jigging baby and the terrible investment banker husband—will ask about renting the apartment for six months, for the French woman's parents, who want to make a long visit. James finds an apartment and I agree about the rental. James leaves behind some basic furniture and appliances for the French people, plus the piano, the library steps, and Aunt Daphne. The walls are repainted, but the Strawberry Thief wallpaper remains.

My *Firebird* has its premiere. Isabel and Ben will come for it. As will Yuto and his fiancée. So will James. And Freya and her husband, of course. I will say to a stage manager, "My whole family is here."

I'll touch the wrist that carries my father's watch. Every ballet is about time.

I can't quite tell if my *Firebird* is good, because I'll love it so much while I'm working on it, including times when I'm convinced it's pretty bad. When I see it onstage, in performance, I will think mostly of the dancers, and dance itself, and be grateful. A few times I will think, *Oh, I need to change that*, and a few more times, *Oh, that's actually pretty great.* My agent, Annika, will forward me reviews with *YES YES YES* in the subject line. The company will commission an original work for the following season. It will seem like this maybe is the breakthrough thing.

I'll start to imagine how my green vases would look on my little table, in front of the Strawberry Thief wallpaper. I'll find new renters for Bank Street in the interim, as my work schedule is too packed to make decisions. I'll discover it's difficult to sell a piano. I'll visit New York and take the library steps and the portrait of Aunt Daphne up to James in his new apartment on the Upper West Side. He will have agreed to take care of them until such time as I return to Bank Street.

"You're wearing the watch," James will say, pleased.

We'll sit on his couch side by side and talk and talk.

All of that will happen, but for now—

Feel what I feel, see what I see, imagine what I imagine, remember what I remember.

I'm standing outside Bank Street. I have just seen my father for the first time in nineteen years. I've held his hand. I don't know what's going to happen next.

James is playing the piano. The berceuse from *The Firebird*. A lullaby and a dissolution of all enchantments. I put my hand on the gate and look up, listening. I think, *I'll make something of all that*. And also, *I can love*.

James stops playing.

Listen to this silence, where all movement is contained.

Watch this dance, even if it's still.

Here it comes. Here it is.

A rising, an exaltation.

All this wreckage. All this gorgeous, unrepeatable wreckage. Life.

Acknowledgments

Thank you to writers Sarah Tomlinson, Sarah Langan, Chris L. Terry, J. Ryan Stradal, Peter Nichols, Lacy Crawford, David Francis, and Gian Sardar for generous readings of drafts-in-progress. Thank you, Keith Kuhl, for sharing knowledge on the working lives of choreographers, and to Amy Taylor, RN, CHPN, for insight on hospice care. Thank you to Jay Huguley for listening and inspiring. Thank you to Lauren Lovett for a room in the desert and general emergency services. Thank you to my parents for their support and my brother for support and good gin. Thank you, Jen West, for that letter. Thank you to Justin Messina for talking Stravinsky and restoring my heartbeat. Thank you, Sarah Tomlinson and Kirby Kim, for the introduction to Emma Parry.

Thank you, Emma Parry, agent of my dreams in all senses. I'm the luckiest writer in all the land. Thank you to Ben Izzo at A3 for championing Carlisle and company. And thank you to my wonderful editor, Cara Reilly, for your confidence and for lending this book your insight and acuity. (Repeat: luckiest writer in all the land.) Thank you to everyone at Doubleday, for the belief and the home. Thank you to Emma Herdman and Bloomsbury UK for a home across the sea.

Thank you to the doctors, nurses, advocates, and activists who faced the world's fear, contempt, and indifference in the darkest days of the AIDS pandemic. Your courage and your love, like the lives of those we lost, will not be forgotten.

Thank you, dancers.

ABOUT THE AUTHOR

Meg Howrey is a former professional ballet dancer and actress. She is the author of the novels *The Wanderers*, *The Cranes Dance*, and *Blind Sight*, and a coauthor of the bestselling novel *City of Dark Magic* and of *City of Lost Dreams*, published under the pen name Magnus Flyte. Her nonfiction has appeared in *Vogue* and the *Los Angeles Review of Books*. She currently lives in Los Angeles.